PLEASE DON'T LEAVE ME HERE

Tania Chandler is a Melbourne-based writer and editor. She studied professional writing and editing at RMIT University, and her work was awarded a special commendation in the 2013 Writers Victoria Crime Writing competition. *Please Don't Leave Me Here* is her first novel, and she is currently working on a sequel.

For Reece, Paige, Jaime, and Greg

And to the memory of Kurt Cobain

PLEASE DON'T
LEAVE ME HERE

TANIA CHANDLER

SCRIBE
Melbourne • London

Scribe Publications
18–20 Edward St, Brunswick, Victoria 3056, Australia
2 John St, Clerkenwell, London, WC1N 2ES, United Kingdom

First published by Scribe 2015

Typeset in 12.75 / 16.5 pt Dante MT by the publishers
Printed and bound in the UK by CPI Group (UK) Ltd, Croydon CR0 4YY

National Library of Australia
Cataloguing-in-Publication data

Chandler, Tania, author.

Please Don't Leave Me Here / Tania Chandler.

9781925106770 (Australian paperback)
9781925228250 (UK paperback)
9781925307030 (e-book)

1. Detective and mystery stories.

A823.4

A CIP record for this title is available from the British Library

scribepublications.com.au
scribepublications.co.uk

CONTENTS

PART I
2008: Come as You Are
1

PART II
1994: About a Girl
123

PART III
2008: Come as You Are (cont)
279

PART I

2008: Come as You Are

1

It's another slow-news day by the look of *The Age* online: *Acting Prime Minister Julia Gillard condemns the binge drinking of a football player; Celebrity chef Nigella Lawson hires a personal trainer to help keep her famous figure in shape.* Brigitte sips her coffee, yawns, and scrolls down further. *Victorian cold-case detectives to reopen 1994 investigation of slain concert promoter, Eric Tucker.* Her heart stops. The missed beat catches up and hammers on top of the next one. She glances over her shoulder, shuts down the computer, and stares at the blank screen while Kitty figure-eights around her ankles. The blast of a train's horn down at Clifton Hill station makes her jump and spill her coffee.

Phoebe's up first — looking like a zombie-child, eyes half-closed, arms outstretched for a cuddle. Brigitte lifts her up, winces at the stab of pain in her back, and pushes the fine blonde hair off Phoebe's face. Underneath is a little turned-up nose, a pouty mouth, and the biggest, bluest eyes: a Manga cartoon face. Then Finn runs out demanding his good-morning cuddle and kiss. Brigitte smiles as if nothing is wrong, and makes cups of warm milk for the twins. The cartoons bubble away on TV.

Sam surfaces half an hour later to the sound of the smoke alarm going off for burnt toast.

'Is Mummy trying to cook again?'

'Morning, Sam.'

'Morning, Ralph. Sleep OK?'

'Coffee?' She pours him a mug — black, no sugar.

His mobile rings in his bathrobe pocket, and he takes it into the study.

Bad butterflies flutter up to her oesophagus.

'Mum.' Finn pulls at her dressing gown.

'Shh.' She's trying to listen through the wall to what Sam's saying.

'Mum, Mum, Mum …'

'What!'

'Love you.' He runs off, and her shoulders slump.

'OK. Send a car for me in ten.' Sam hangs up and comes back into the kitchen.

'What?'

'Nothing.'

'Tell me, Sam.'

'Stop it, Brig.'

'What then?'

'Nothing! Just an incident in Preston.'

She's standing in his way and he pushes her aside, too roughly. Her hip knocks against the cupboard. 'Sorry. Have to get ready for work.'

He makes calls while he gets his clothes — a charcoal suit and a white shirt.

He takes a three-minute shower and comes out of the bathroom smelling of sport deodorant, his cropped blond hair smooth with product.

'I see they're reopening the Eric Tucker case,' she says as she taps her fingers on the sink and looks out the window. The strip of grass between the house and bungalow is knee-high.

'And?'

She turns, opens her mouth to speak, then shuts it and wraps her arms around him.

'Don't worry about it. It's busy work. Not enough new murders to go round.'

She doesn't believe him.

He untangles himself from her arms and kisses the twins

on the way out. He leaves without breakfast — he'll pick up something on the way, as usual.

Finn runs to see his friends in the three-year-olds' room at kinder. Phoebe clings to Brigitte's leg, crocodile tears in her eyes.

'Hello, Phoebe.' Yasmine smiles. She's wearing a paisley shirt and a silver stud in her nose. 'We're going to have lots of fun today. Would you like to do a puzzle, or help me sort out the art smocks?'

Phoebe's not talking to the kinder assistant.

'Is everything OK, Brigitte?' Yasmine places a tub of crayons on the table.

Brigitte nods and smiles as she peels Phoebe off her leg. She goes outside to find Finn for a kiss goodbye. He's kicking a ball around the play equipment.

'Mum, watch this!' He kicks the ball and scatters the crispy brown and yellow leaves under the big elm tree. She claps, and he runs over to her.

'Daddy shoots people.'

'No sweetie, that's not true.' She crouches to do up the buttons on his jacket.

'He's got a gun.'

'All police people carry guns. It's part of their job.'

'To catch the bad guys and keep the good people safe?'

'Yes.' She pulls a tissue from her sleeve and wipes his runny nose.

'Bye, Mum.'

'Bye, sweetie.' She kisses him before he wriggles away.

Something in the sand pit has caught his eye, and he takes aim at it with his index finger. 'Bang!' He pulls the trigger with his thumb.

2

The heating's on the blink, and Brigitte shivers as her towel drops to the floor. She looks in the bathroom mirror and traces a finger along the pink caesarean cut — the most recent but least prominent of her scars. If her mother could see, she'd focus more on the extra few kilos: told you you'd turn into a cow after having kids.

When Brigitte was a child, Joan spent hours in front of the mirror at the old pink house in Brunswick, cigarette balanced on the edge of the basin: applying make-up, doing her hair, looking at herself. Smoke mingled with the smells of green apple shampoo, blow-dryer burnt hair, and Chanel No. 5. When Brigitte stood on tippy-toes, she could see dozens of little make-up pots lined up in the cabinet. Joan gained so little weight, she liked to tell Brigitte, that nobody could even tell she was pregnant. And she regained her figure within weeks of giving birth, although it was a bit harder the second time. No stretch marks, thank God. *Unfortunately, you and your brother are built more like your father. You have child-bearing hips*, she told Brigitte, just as the straight lines of her lean little body were starting to soften into curves. There was nothing worse than child-bearing hips.

Brigitte sucks in her stomach and shuts out her mother's voice.

She should have realised how revealing the white Marilyn Monroe costume would be, should have tried it on at the fancy-dress place. Stupid. She never wears anything so low-cut. Too late now. She camouflages the scars under her collarbone with Dermacolor make-up.

She hears Sam complaining in the kitchen while the twins

giggle and stuff pillows into his Elvis suit. 'Put them back in the bedrooms. I'm not going out like this.' He loses the scowl, and whistles when Brigitte comes out in her Marilyn dress.

The doorbell rings: it's their neighbour Kerry reporting for babysitting duty. Brigitte takes the black wig from Phoebe, places it over Sam's hair, and goes to answer the door.

Manny's dead-celebrities party is at one of those hidden cocktail bars in the city, 15 storeys up — the kind you don't know about when your life revolves around children. Sam groans about the Pink song playing as they enter, and Brigitte elbows him in the ribs.

Manny has a lot of friends. Brigitte doesn't know any of them. Manny is Sam's mate, but Sam rarely sees him since he quit the force to become a filmmaker. Manny looks like a pirate with a red bandana around his head. He can't be Johnny Depp. Keith Richards? Sam holds out his hand to shake. Manny hugs him and kisses Brigitte.

'Keith Richards isn't dead,' she says.

'Close enough.' Manny laughs. They wish him a happy thirtieth, and he rushes off towards Bon Scott and Jim Morrison.

'How about some champagne?' Brigitte says.

'Thought you weren't drinking.'

'It's a special occasion.'

'Why?'

'Long time since we've been out without the kids.'

He goes to the bar, and she takes a table in a corner. He comes back with a glass of champagne and a lemonade.

'You on-call?'

He nods and places his mobile on the table.

She scans the plush art-deco bar. It looks like a 1920s Manhattan speakeasy: wood panelling, brown-leather couches, velvet curtains, and bell-shaped lampshades. 'Wanna dance?'

He shakes his head.

'Did you see the painting Phoebe did at kinder?'

'How come whenever we go out, we always end up talking about the kids?'

'Let's talk about you then. Thought any more about teaching?'

He looks into his drink. No, of course not. 'I'm not sure I'd be happy doing that, Brig.'

Does he think she's happy worrying about him getting killed at work every day? She looks at her unkempt fingernails — not very glamorous for Marilyn. She should have got some fake red ones.

'Maybe you should start thinking about getting a job,' Sam says.

'I have a job.'

'One article a month for a parenting magazine is not really a —'

'I was talking about looking after the twins.' She looks away. Manny takes a seat at the piano and plays 'Sympathy for the Devil'.

Sam reaches across the table and holds her hands.

She pulls a hand away and finishes her drink. 'There's no new evidence?'

Sam frowns.

'For that old case.'

'Nope.' He shakes his head. 'Waste of resources.'

His mobile rings, and he takes the call out on the balcony. She looks down into her empty glass.

Sam comes back inside, pulling off the wig. 'Sorry, babe. A situation in a building on Collins Street.' He steps out of the costume, revealing slacks and a pale-grey shirt underneath — always prepared, just in case. She almost laughs at the super-hero nature of what he's doing. He dumps the costume and wig on the table. 'Go hang out with Manny. I'll try to come back, but if it takes too long, catch a cab home.' He gives her a fifty-dollar note from his wallet and a hasty kiss on the cheek.

'Be careful.' He doesn't hear her over the music.

She frowns and folds her arms across her chest. Everybody else is laughing and dancing. She looks around for Manny. He's busy with a frothy pink cocktail in one hand and Heath Ledger in the other. She may as well just go home, but one more drink first. She tightens the halter ties of her dress, pulls her breasts up higher, and goes to the bar for another glass of champagne.

After a third glass and not enough finger food, she heads to the balcony for some fresh air.

The cigarette smoke outside nauseates her. She leans against the rail; the lights of the cityscape swirl like a kaleidoscope. Kurt Cobain is talking to Princess Diana in the corner. Brigitte sits — falls — on a bench seat. When Diana goes inside, Kurt removes his white sunglasses, smiles, and walks towards Brigitte. *Oh, God.*

'Hey, Marilyn. Great party, huh?' A tall guy in black jeans and a flannelette shirt unbuttoned over a T-shirt — not even dressed up — pushes in front of Kurt. Kurt turns and decides to follow Diana.

'You OK?' the guy in the flannelette shirt says. His voice is deep, soothing.

'I'm not feeling so good. Would you mind getting me some water?'

'Sure.' He puts his beer down next to her on the seat and goes inside.

She swallows, and has breathed away the nausea by the time the flannelette-shirt guy comes back.

'You look like you've seen a ghost.' He must have been thinking of that line while he was getting her glass of water. But she finds it funny — stupid, but funny — and, even though she feels like crap, she can't help laughing.

'How do you know Manny?' He has a crooked smile, one side higher than the other. She can't decide if it makes him look clever or smug.

'He's a friend of my husband.'

'Where's your husband?'

She sips her water. 'He left.'

He sits next to her.

'How about you?' The skyline has stopped spinning.

'Same. Separated. Nearly a year now.'

She should clear up his misunderstanding about her marital status, but she doesn't.

'Any kids?'

'No.'

'You're lucky.' She finishes her water. 'I mean lucky because of the separation, not …'

'It's OK. What's your name?'

'Brigitte.'

'I'm Aidan.'

'How come you're not dressed up?'

'I am. I'm Jeff Buckley.'

She turns to look at him, and realises he's wearing a wig. He quickly lifts his gaze from her chest, city lights in his dark eyes. Did he notice her scars?

'Smoke?' He holds out a pack.

She shakes her head.

'Me neither. Given up.' He puts the pack back in his pocket.

'It's a bit cold out here, Aidan — I mean Jeff. And I'm feeling better, so I think I'll go back inside.'

All the tables are taken, so she sits at the long, polished-timber bar. Aidan follows her, takes the next bar stool. Down-lighting glints diamond shapes on the hundreds of bottles lined up on the shelf behind the bartender, who's making a show of mixing a drink in a cocktail shaker.

'Feel like a cocktail, Marilyn?' Aidan says.

'Sure, Jeff. Maybe a Margarita.'

'How about a Slow Comfortable Screw Against the Wall?'

She narrows her eyes at him.

'What? It's a drink.' He laughs as she snatches the cocktail menu from his hands. His high, squeaky laugh doesn't suit him.

The bartender winks and places two orange-coloured drinks in front of them.

They both drink quickly and order a second cocktail.

'Take off your wig, Aidan.' She reaches for it, he ducks, and she laughs.

'Why? Not a Jeff fan?'

'Go on, take it off.' Perhaps he's bald under there.

'I'll take it off if you'll dance with me.'

'Deal.' She sips her drink.

His dark-brown hair has been flattened against his head. It's the same as the wig, just shorter.

'Come on.' He runs a hand through his hair and fixes it.

'What?'

'Dance.'

'Changed my mind.'

'You can't, we had a deal.' He takes her hand and drags her, giggling, to the dance floor. Manny has stopped bashing out his dreadful renditions of Rolling Stones numbers. A Nick Cave and Kylie Minogue song wails through the sound system: 'Where the Wild Roses Grow'.

'I love Nick Cave!' she says.

'Me, too.' He stoops to drape his arms around her shoulders.

Most people have left the floor because the song is too slow to dance to. Brigitte and Aidan don't mind — slow-dancing, not even dancing, just holding each other up and moving slowly, out of time to the music. She sings the words, and he pretends to know them. On the shiny timber wall, a lean figure towers over a Tinkerbell shape: their silhouettes reflected by the dance-floor lights.

Has she let this go too far? How's she going to get out of it? Maybe she doesn't want to get out of it. They're not doing anything wrong — just dancing — until he pulls her closer and bends down to kiss her. She turns her face away, and he whispers into her ear, 'Come back to my place?'

She can't, can she? Of course not. 'No.'

'Just as well. I don't really have a place anymore. Can we go to yours?'

'Be quiet and dance.' She rests her face against his flannelette shirt. It's so soft, and the faint scent of citrus — perhaps bergamot — cologne takes her back to another time. She closes her eyes, and loses herself for a while.

3

'Sorry I'm late. Phoebe was being difficult at kinder — just for something different.'

Ryan's at a window table, his coffee finished. The café is full of retirees with expensive shoes and fluffy little dogs, and forty-year-old mothers with babies in designer grow-suits.

'God, Little Sis, you look how I feel.'

'Take it that's not a compliment?' Brigitte orders a flat white, scrapes out a chair, and sits opposite him. 'How are things with you and Rosie?'

He shakes his head. 'Don't ask. She's vegan now.'

'And training for the marathon?'

'Uh-huh. Looks like a stick insect. She's gone all weird, had her hair cut really short. Something about turning 40.'

'Well, you always had a thing for older women, so— '

'And what's with the no-sex-ever thing?'

'Too much information, Ryan.'

'You're a woman. Thought you could help me figure this stuff out.'

She shrugs and yawns.

'How come you look like shit?'

'Late night.' She's bubbling to tell him all about it — like a silly teenager. Ryan probably knows Aidan; the Melbourne film industry is a small community. The waiter brings her coffee. She stirs in some sugar and sucks the spoon.

A woman pushes a baby in a jogger pram along the street. Ryan looks over at the cakes on the counter. 'You and Sam still having sex?'

'Ryan!'

'What? Don't be such a prude, Brigi.' He turns his empty cup around on its saucer. 'Well, are you?'

She twists her mouth.

'How often?'

She shrugs and sips her coffee. 'So what *is* going on with you and Rosie?'

He leans back and crosses his arms. 'Rosie says I have to get a *real* job. I've just picked up this series of insurance TV commercials that's going to pay heaps. Not good enough for her. Says it's too hard paying off the mortgage with just her income.'

'Well— '

'Like I don't contribute, which is total bullshit.'

'You agreed to the McMansion, so— '

'I was happier when we were renting the house in Groom Street and I had that role in *Neighbours*.' He looks out the window. A man in lycra cycles past on a state-of-the-art bike.

'That house was shit. It was falling down and— '

'At least we had a bit of money left over at the end of the fortnight — for a pizza or bottle of wine, something.'

'Sam's on at me to get a job, too. Not sure what he expects me to do with the twins. He has no idea what childcare costs.'

'Maybe Maggie and Doug could babysit.'

She laughs at the idea of her parents-in-law doing anything to help her. 'Want another coffee?'

'I want a beer. Let's go to the pub.'

They walk past the fish-and-chip shop, the hair salon where a woman's having a blow wave, and across the road to The Royal. The bar is empty. Ryan goes up to order drinks, and Brigitte takes a table by the window.

She sips her orange juice slowly. Ryan drinks his beer quickly and gets another.

'You and Rosie are really having problems, aren't you?' she says.

'Think it's pretty serious this time.'

She reaches across and squeezes his shoulder.

'Sure you don't want a beer?'

She shakes her head. 'You know I'm not drinking. And it'll be time to pick up the kids soon.'

'Come on — one won't hurt.'

'No.'

'Come on.'

'No.'

'You sure?'

'OK, just one.'

The beer tastes good.

'Ever wonder if you're with the right person, Brigi?'

'What, like a soul mate?'

'Suppose so.'

'No such thing. What's the probability of finding the one right person out of all the billions of people on the planet?'

'Thought women were supposed to believe in that shit.'

She shrugs, sips her beer, and looks up at the specials board, pretends to read it, doesn't want to talk about this anymore.

'Brigi! You're not having an affair, are you?'

'Don't be stupid, Ryan. Where would I find time for that?' She laughs, and finishes her drink. 'Another one?'

She goes up to the bar, and spills beer down the front of her shirt on the way back.

'You know, it's really fucking hard being married to a cop.' She puts the beers on the table, and sits down.

'Try being an actor married to a project manager.'

'Always thinking that today might be the day he won't come home, waiting for the call.'

'That would be pretty fucked.'

'Like when we were little — waiting for Dad to come home. Joan carrying on about her *bad feelings*, telling us all those horror truck-crash stories. That's where all the anxiety about being left alone comes from.' She shifts in her chair, but can't get comfortable.

He nods. 'Mum had depression, you know.'

'No shit.'

'You ever feel depressed?'

'No.' A lie. 'You?'

'Not really.'

She sighs. 'Whatever happened to fun, Ryan?'

'Don't ask me.'

'Cheers.' She clinks her glass to his, and they drink.

'Your back sore?'

She shakes her head.

'Should go back to the quack.'

'I'm fine.'

They drink up and order one more.

'Brigitte Campbell, has anybody ever told you that you drink like a man?'

'You know, I think somebody did tell me that once.' She laughs and looks out the window at the deserted street. 'A long time ago.'

Ryan takes a big drink, and his round, lineless face clouds over. He swallows and clears his throat. 'I saw the police are reopening that old case.' He weaves his fingers together on the table, and clenches them. 'Sam say anything about it?'

'Says it's a waste of time. No new evidence.' She scrapes back her chair and goes to the bathroom.

The pub's very up-market these days: organic handwash, polished stones in a bowl, a jar of fragrance sticks. Her cheeks are red, so she splashes cold water on her face. There's a reflection in the corner of the mirror. She turns. Nobody there. *Shit*. She's starting to lose it — she shouldn't be drinking. She dries her hands quickly on a paper towel, afraid to look back in the mirror.

She trips up the step. Deep breaths. *OK. OK.*

'You OK?' Ryan says as she sits back at their table.

'Yep.'

They're too drunk to drive, so they leave their cars in Clifton Hill and catch a taxi to pick up the kids — just in time.

'Ryan Weaver, you are a bad influence.'

'You are.'

They rush into kinder — Brigitte to the three-year-olds' room, and Ryan to his daughter, Georgia, in the room for four-year-olds — sucking on Tic Tacs in a lame attempt to cover up their beer breaths.

4

Brigitte yawns as she parks on the side street in the shadow of the brown-brick building. The twins are nodding off in their child restraints.

'Come on, sleepy heads.' She unbuckles them, lifts them out of the station wagon, and reaches for the box of fruit on the passenger seat.

'Can we go home? Papa smells,' Phoebe says.

Brigitte tells her to stop it; she's not in the mood.

The cigarette-smoking man with one leg — Brigitte can't remember his name — waves at them from the bench seat on the porch. He's always out the front of the home, cigarette drooping in the corner of his mouth, whether it's 40 degrees or hailing. Brigitte balances the box of fruit on her hip and opens the childproof gate at the front. Oranges fall off the top, and roll down the street and onto the road. The twins squeal with laughter as a van juices one under its tyres.

'Good morning,' she says cheerfully, through gritted teeth, to the cigarette-smoking man. She keys in the security code, and the sliding-glass doors open.

She signs the visitors' book in the foyer. The manager's office door is open, so she sticks her head in to enquire about Papa's health.

'He's doing really well.' Petula swivels her chair around, away from the computer screen. 'But you look tired, Brigitte. Those cheeky twins keeping you awake?' She smiles at them. Phoebe scowls, and Finn hides behind Brigitte's leg.

'It gets better,' Petula says.

Brigitte forces a smile. Tiger, the resident cat, wanders past, and the twins rush over to pat him.

They take the lift to level two, where it's always overheated, and the smells of stale urine, vomit, and cleaning products sting Brigitte's nose. She sneezes. The twins run down the corridor towards their great-grandfather's room. They stop and wait outside his door, never brave enough to go in by themselves.

Papa's sitting in his old Chesterfield chair — its worn arms mended with gaffer tape — watching TV with the sound blaring. He's wearing his favourite dressing gown, brown and threadbare, and slippers from Dimmeys. Ten years drops off his face when he sees them. He hoists himself out of his chair to kiss Brigitte and run a hand over her hair. Phoebe's right: he could do with a shower.

Brigitte empties the box of fruit into a bowl on his little wooden table. She removes her jacket, turns off the TV, and sits by the window on a green-vinyl chair. Papa finds some Freddo Frogs in a drawer for the twins.

'Brigi?'

She looks into Papa's faded blue eyes.

'Saw an old blue Camry on Bridge Road yesterday.'

Here we go again. He pulls a small, no-brand notepad out of his dressing-gown pocket.

'Got the rego number.' His hand shakes as he tears off a page and passes it to her. 'For Sam to check out.'

She puts it in her handbag — to go into the recycling bin with all the other rego numbers Sam never checks out. Papa has a bigger, leather-bound book with hundreds of old blue Camry registration numbers recorded in his scratchy hand.

'One of these days they'll catch the bastard.' He looks out the window. Construction workers are building another high-rise complex across the road. A tram rattles along Church Street.

The twins jump on the single bed. Brigitte tells them off, and straightens the bedspread. They play with Papa's service medals, and turn the hands around on the old mantel clock. They're fascinated by his egg-shaped paperweight on the bedside table — how the blue-and-green swirls got inside the glass. They fight over it; Phoebe drops it on her foot and bawls.

'Here.' Papa produces a pink bag of salt-and-vinegar chips from down beside his chair.

Brigitte shakes her head.

'Just potata chips, Brigi.' He hands the bag to the twins. Brigitte frowns, but it keeps them quiet. Papa talks about the war, and Fitzroy in the old days.

Brigitte makes listening faces, but she's distracted — as hard as she tries to stop it, her mind keeps drifting back to Manny's party. The softness of Aidan's flannelette shirt … a cold, empty fireplace, cinnamon and bergamot, sailing ships — *no!* That was somewhere else. Somewhere never to be thought about … His crooked smile. The citrus cologne mustn't have been synthetic — it didn't make her sneeze.

'I'm all right here. They're good to me.' Papa coughs. 'You tired?'

She was far away: *Where the wild roses grow.*

'Not sleepin'?'

She shakes her head.

'Want some of me sleepin' pills?'

'No, thanks.'

Phoebe pushes the buttons on Papa's cassette player, and Finn pulls her hair. Brigitte wrangles them to the kitchenette at the end of the corridor for some biscuits and milk. She flicks on the kettle, and washes a spoon and a cup from the shelf — doesn't trust the dishwashing of old people. There's only instant coffee, so she makes a cup of tea and takes it back to Papa's room. Papa never wants anything; he always says he's just finished a cuppa.

The twins are good for another ten minutes or so, and then

it's time to go. Papa puts his tobacco pouch and papers into his dressing-gown pocket and comes downstairs to see them out.

'Thanks for comin', Brigi.' He kisses her at the front gate.

'Love you.' She holds his bony, brown-spotted hands. They're cool, and feel like paper-tree bark. 'We'll see you soon.'

The twins run off towards the car. The cigarette-smoking man waves as Brigitte rushes after them.

Were his eyes dark brown or light brown? He had full lips ... She jumps when her phone rings.

It's Sam. The knife blade of guilt twists between her ribs. Nothing happened: just a dance. Not even a kiss. Not really. Thoughts don't count. Sam says he's coming home early — for a change — and asks her to put on some pasta; he'll make the sauce. And he's bringing a workmate home for dinner. Good — a distraction. It's been hard to look into his eyes since ...

She opens a bottle of red wine — for Sam to use in the pasta sauce. Maybe she'll have one small glass while she's waiting for the water to boil.

She's on to her second small glass when she hears Sam's keys rattle. She meets him at the front door. The smell of cold rushes in.

'Hey.' He laughs, surprised by the passion in her kiss. His face is freezing, his breath steamy. He wipes his feet on the doormat. He's holding a new heater in a box. Behind him, she can see that his workmate has a slab of beer cans under his arm. He steps out of the shadows — tall, long limbs — into the porch light, and follows Sam in.

'Brig, this is Aidan Serra.'

No fucking way.

'He used to work with Manny.'

He's from the police! Not one of Manny's filmmaker friends? You've got to be joking. Panic raises every hair on her skin.

21

'Brigitte.' He reaches out and shakes her hand. 'I think we met at Manny's party.'

She pulls her hand away. 'Sorry, I don't remember.' Can Sam hear the quaver in her voice?

'Really? I was dressed up as Jeff Buckley.'

Fuck, fuck, fuck. Her face burns.

He brushes past her in the hallway, smirking. The floor seems to tip sideways beneath her feet.

Sam unpacks and plugs in the heater in the living room. Brigitte glares at Aidan as he takes out two beers and puts the rest in the fridge. *Make yourself at home, why don't you?* She pours herself another glass of wine — a big one — with her back to him, and spills some on the Laminex benchtop.

'Serra needs somewhere to crash while he's looking for a new place.' Sam takes some garlic and an onion from the cupboard under the sink. 'I told him he could stay in the bungalow. If it's OK with you.'

She chokes on her wine, frowns, and tilts her head at the bathroom. Sam follows her and closes the door behind them. 'Don't worry. He's OK. Won't stay long.'

'Doesn't he have family to stay with? Or a girlfriend?'

'Give him a break. He's had a pretty rough time with his wife.'

'Is he in your squad?'

'No. The Cold Case Unit.'

'The Cold Case Unit! But— '

'Keep your voice down.'

She turns on the tap and washes her hands. Kitty — a ginger flash of fur — jumps in through the window.

'He shouldn't be out this late.' Sam winds the window shut and locks it. 'I've put in for some leave.'

Brigitte looks up as she continues to lather her hands with soap.

'Don't look so shocked,' Sam says. 'We need a holiday.'

'You said we couldn't afford a holiday.'

'Just down to Raymond Island. Why don't you ask Ryan to come?'

She nods, and dries her hands on a towel. He leans closer to her. She takes a step back. 'You stink. You've been smoking again.' With *him*.

In the living room, Aidan is sitting at the table, admiring one of Phoebe's drawings, while Finn drives a car across the back of his chair and Kitty rubs against his calf.

'Go wash your hands, guys. Dinner won't be long.' Brigitte stands in the doorway.

'Aidan's going to read us a story,' Phoebe says.

'No, he's not.' Brigitte puts her hands on her hips.

'Yes.' Phoebe copies her mother's gesture.

'Bathroom. Now.'

Aidan shrugs, and smiles his one-sided smile.

'Sam tells me you're a writer,' Aidan says over dinner.

'He tells me you're in the Cold Case Unit.' Brigitte doesn't lift her gaze from her bowl.

Sam returns from the kitchen with a pepper mill and two beers.

'Thanks.' Brigitte holds up her empty wine glass.

'What do you write?' Aidan says as he grinds pepper onto his pasta. 'Murder mysteries?'

Sam laughs.

'Because you'd have a bit of an insight into how the criminal-justice system—'

'Parenting articles.'

Aidan smiles at the twins, and cracks open his beer. 'Thanks for letting me stay.'

Brigitte pushes her bowl aside; she's had enough.

Phoebe asks Aidan to pass the pepper.

Aidan reaches for the mill.

'You don't need pepper,' Brigitte says.

Aidan takes his hand off it.

'Yes.' Phoebe leans across the table and knocks over her glass of water.

'Jesus, Phoebe!' Sam stands up and pushes back his chair with so much force it topples over.

Phoebe starts crying. Brigitte glares at Sam, and he goes to find a cloth.

'Don't worry, it was an accident,' Aidan says.

★★★

In a dream, he's on top of her, moving slowly, rhythmically. He's wearing a brown sweater; it comes off easily over his head. His body feels warm, hard. She claws, with long fingernails, at the serpent tattoo on his back. Desperate wanting, needing. Just about to come. Aidan? No, not Aidan. His hair hides his face. A flash of blue. Almost. Almost. But it's gone …

She opens her eyes. It's Sam moving over her in the ashen lamplight. He squeezes her nipples too hard, pushes her legs back too far.

'That hurts.'

He doesn't stop.

'Stop, Sam. You're hurting my back, my knee.'

He still doesn't stop.

'I said *stop*.'

He stops, and she rolls from underneath him, curls up at the edge of the bed.

'Sorry. I thought you wanted …' He touches her shoulder. 'You were scratching my back really hard.'

She doesn't respond, and he turns his back. When his breathing becomes slow, sleep-regular, she rolls over and sees the scratch marks, and some blood. She flicks off the lamp and waits for sleep.

It doesn't come, and that desperate dream-feeling of wanting, needing, continues to ache inside her. She gets up, walks to the kitchen, and looks out the window at the bungalow while she drinks a glass of water over the sink.

She takes the heater to the lounge room, sits on the couch with a blanket and her laptop on her knees, and starts writing her monthly article for *Parenting Today*. Toddler-taming featured in the last issue, so maybe she should focus on craft this month. Papier-maché balloons? She sighs, unable to concentrate, puts the laptop aside, closes her eyes, and slides a hand down under the blanket.

5

'What's been the best part of your birthday so far?' Ryan asks the twins as Brigitte clears the table of food.

'Red bums,' Phoebe says.

'What?' Ryan chokes on his wine.

'Red-bum monkeys,' Finn says. 'At the zoo.'

'Oh, the baboons.'

'Can we have cake now?' Georgia crawls over Ryan's legs and under the table.

'Good idea. It's nearly time for all four-year-olds to go to bed. And Mummy will be wondering where we are.'

'No she won't.'

'Probably right, Georgi.' Ryan drains his glass. 'Bet she's still at the gym.'

'Can we wait a few more minutes for Sam? He should be home by now.' Brigitte chews her little fingernail. She's about to call him again when her mobile rings. It's Sam — she nods to Ryan. 'You far away?'

He says he's stuck there. Another all-nighter. She hears a background conversation: it sounds like something about a body upstairs. She shivers.

'But it's—'

'Sorry, babe.'

'Sam—'

'Won't be a sec,' he says to somebody at the crime scene. 'I've really gotta go, Brig.'

'I love you.' Too late — he's hung up. She puts the phone into her skirt pocket, and curses Sam under her breath. She looks at the ceiling; there's an abandoned spider web collecting dust in the corner.

'OK. Who wants cake?' She smiles at the kids.

'Me! Me! Me!'

She finishes her glass of wine on the way to the kitchen. Ryan follows, and puts his arm around her shoulders. 'It's OK. He'd be here if he could.'

'He forgot about their party.' She sniffs.

'You know he loves you and the twins.' He hands her a box of tissues; she takes a couple and blows her nose.

'Maybe.' She throws the tissues at the bin, misses, picks them up, and karate-kicks the swing-top lid off. Her outburst is paid back with a bolt of pain through her body. She apologises, replaces the lid, and washes her hands at the sink.

'How about opening another bottle of wine?' She follows Ryan back to the living room with the *Palace of Dreams* party cake that Kerry baked for them.

The kids say 'Ooh' as she places it on the table. It's a deep-purple castle, surrounded by marshmallow toadstools. A lolly-encrusted staircase leads to sherbet cone towers tiled with chocolate and hundreds and thousands.

Brigitte lights the candles, and Ryan takes photos while they sing 'Happy birthday'.

The kids scoff the cake, and Brigitte pours more wine.

'What happened to not drinking?' Ryan says.

'Changed my mind.'

'Fair enough. I can't imagine having to listen sober to Rosie complain.'

'And worrying about Sam not coming home.'

'No fun at all.' He goes to the stereo on the bookshelf, and walks his fingers across the tops of the CDs. 'Nick Cave still your favourite?'

The padlock clicks; the side gate squeaks. Ryan frowns at Brigitte.

'Aidan! Aidan!' the twins squeal.

'Just the guy who's staying in the bungalow.' She dismisses it with a shrug.

'Oh, that's right. Your tenant. How's that going?'

She rolls her eyes, and hopes Ryan doesn't notice she's blushing.

Five minutes later, there's a gentle knock on the kitchen door at the back of the house. She groans and gets up to answer it, muttering, 'What does he want now?'

He apologises for interrupting, says the light's blown in the bungalow, and asks if she has any spare globes. His shirt is un-tucked. He smells sweaty and looks tired, dark shadows etched under his eyes. He sees Ryan over her shoulder, and frowns.

She scrounges through the junk drawer in the kitchen cabinet. 'Is it a bayonet?'

'No.' He locks eyes with her — they're cocoa-coloured — and says, 'It's a screw-in.'

'Sorry, don't have any of those.' She looks away and bangs the drawer shut, her heart rocketing.

'That's OK. I've got a torch.'

Phoebe walks into the kitchen, purple icing and hundreds and thousands all over her face. 'Aidan, it's my birthday.'

'Really? Happy birthday.'

'And Finn's birthday, too. You want some cake?'

He looks at Brigitte, and gets the message. 'Sorry, sweetie, I have to go.'

'Aww.' Phoebe sticks out her bottom lip.

He walks towards the back door — an affected swagger. He must think she's watching. She looks at her hands, searching for something clever to say. She fiddles with her wedding band, and asks if he's eaten.

He turns and says he hasn't.

'We've got plenty of leftover party pies and fairy bread. If you want to stay.'

'And cake,' Phoebe says.

He stays.

Brigitte introduces him to Ryan and Georgia in the living room. Ryan stands, and they shake hands.

'Busy day, mate?' Ryan pours him a glass of wine.

'Thanks.' He takes the wine. 'Yeah, very busy at the moment.'

Ryan's mobile rings. 'On our way ... Yes, yes, I know ... All right. Won't be long.' He hangs up. 'Sorry, guys. It's past our bedtime, and we're in trouble.'

Aidan smiles his crooked smile and nods, like he empathises.

'Finn and Phoebe must be very tired, too,' Brigitte says. 'And they're going to do their hands and face and teeth nicely in the bathroom, like good big four-year-olds, as a thank you for a lovely day at the zoo with Uncle Ryan and Georgia. Aren't you?'

As she walks Ryan and Georgia to the front door, she hears Aidan asking the twins to show him what kind of toothbrushes they have.

'Will you be OK if I go?' Ryan leans a shoulder against the doorframe.

'Of course.' She folds her arms across her chest.

'Don't do anything silly, Brigi.' His voice is low, serious.

'What are you talking about?'

'I can see what's going on.'

She blinks up at him, eyes wide, innocent.

'You and him.'

'You're drunk. Go home to Rosie.'

'Don't you—'

'Go.' She kisses him, and pushes him out the door.

When she comes back, the twins are all clean and brushed. She puts them to bed; it's way past their bedtime, and they fall asleep before she tiptoes out their door.

In the living room, Aidan is looking at the framed photographs on the bookshelf, his head leaning to one side. He hears her come in, but doesn't turn around.

'You look like a teenager in this one.' He picks up the photo of her and Sam sitting on the front fence not long after they bought the house. Sam has an arm wrapped tightly around her shoulders; her hair is in a ponytail, and she's not looking directly at the camera. They're both smiling. The house hasn't changed, except for the front door. She stripped and sanded the weathered brown, and painted it cherry-red.

'Not quite.' She takes it from him, their fingers brush, and the heat lingers on her hand. She should have told Ryan to stay.

'How long have you and Campbell been together, anyway?'

'Got married in '97.'

'God. Cops don't usually stay married that long.'

'Maybe that's just you.' She places the photo back on the shelf. Nick Cave's finished, so she presses *Play*, and the CD starts again. When she turns, Aidan's sitting at the table.

'I was thinking about you and the twins today.'

'Really?' She frowns.

'Do you know much about the investigation Sam's working on?'

She shakes her head. Only what's been in the news: all of them women alone, with young children. Sam doesn't talk about work.

'You need to be careful.'

'Think we'll be right, with two cops around.'

She walks to the table thinking that *Murder Ballads* was not a good choice of CD.

'You must get to work on some interesting cases.' She sits down, and moves her chair a bit further away from him.

'Occasionally. Tough one at the moment — not what it seems.'

'What is it?' They both reach for the bottle, and their hands touch again. She pulls away quickly, with the bottle, and pours more wine.

'You know it's against protocol to discuss cases.' He changes the subject. 'How did you and Campbell meet?'

'I got hit by a car when I was young. Almost died. I was in hospital for a long time.' She sips her wine. 'Sam came in to question me about a homicide investigation.' She laughs at how ridiculous that sounds. 'Some bizarre thing happened with evidence getting mixed up, or something.'

'That's unusual. Campbell's always so ...' he strokes an index finger down the stem of his glass, '... thorough.'

'And then he kept coming back to visit me.' She blinks a slow blink.

'Uh-huh.' He nods. 'Where was the accident?'

'East Melbourne.'

'Did you live there?'

'No, I lived with my grandparents in North Fitzroy.'

He continues to question her. 'Why were you in East Melbourne?'

'Don't know.' She's not as drunk as he must think. 'I lost my memory of what happened before—'

'Sorry.' He tops up their glasses with the last of the wine.

'It's OK.' She reaches for her glass, winces at a flash of pain, shifts her weight in the chair.

'Are you always in pain?' He rests his chin on his hand.

'No.'

'Must be hard taking care of the twins on your own?'

'I'm not on my own.'

'I know what kind of hours Sam works.'

'It's not always like this.' She stands, and leans across the table to clear away the cake. She is aware of his gaze on her back; it prickles through her T-shirt like heat.

'Here, let me help.' He reaches for the empty wine bottle, too close, his breath on her neck. The arm that was reaching for the bottle brushes against her. She should push it away, but she doesn't. She leaves the cake, leans back, and lets her body melt into his as his arm snakes around her waist. She closes her eyes, inhales his smell of sweat and citrus. He lifts his hands to her shoulders — instant warmth — and they relax as he rubs them. Nick and Kylie start singing 'Where the Wild Roses Grow'.

'This must be our song,' he whispers in her ear as his hands roam down her body. She knocks her glass, spilling the remaining wine, as she turns to face him. His lips are soft, but his end-of-day stubble scratches her face. She sucks his top lip, he tangles his fingers in her hair, they kiss more, deeper, their tongues circling each other. Her skirt rides up as she slides onto the table and wraps her legs around his hips. She pulls her T-shirt down when he pushes it up, trying to hide her scars. He doesn't seem to mind, and shoves it back up and kisses them. She feels self-conscious about how hard her nipples are, how wet she is. At the same time she needs his skin against hers, and undoes his shirt buttons, too urgently — a button pops off and rolls onto the floor somewhere under the table. She'll have to find that before morning. Before Sam gets home.

'Should we stop?' he says.

Her breathing is fast and shallow against his chest as she unbuckles his belt.

Oh God. She stifles a cry against his shoulder as he moves inside her. Sex has not felt this good for as long as she cares to remember.

She pushes as hard as she can against him, pulls him in deeper.

He grips her hips, moves her faster with him.

Yes. Yes. She curls up her toes, tenses her muscles. *Yes,* 'Oh, fuck.'

He groans at the same time, slumps forward, and pushes her back into the leftover *Palace of Dreams* she was saving for Sam.

'Are you OK?' he whispers.

She can't speak.

The doorbell rings. *Fuck*. She opens her eyes, pushes Aidan away, brushes off cake, and straightens herself up. She pads quietly down the hallway, and takes a few deep breaths before opening the door.

'Kerry.' Brigitte's voice is croaky; she clears her throat.

Kerry's brown hair is pulled into a ponytail, with a few greys peeking up along the part. Her face is bare. She never leaves the house without make-up, so something's up.

'It's Kitty,' she says. 'He's been hit by a car. Got him at my house.'

Fuck, fuck.

'He's still alive.'

'OK. I'll just get my jacket and tell ...' Her face is burning as she looks at her feet. '... I'll tell Sam, and come straight over.'

She closes the door, turns, and bumps into Aidan in the hallway. She asks if he can stay with the twins. He nods and hands her her jacket.

Kitty's wrapped in a blanket on Kerry's front porch. Brigitte trips up the step. She wasn't expecting to see blood. But he'll be OK, she tells herself.

When she was five, her father had carried their old blue heeler back to the parking bay from the place where he'd been run over on the highway. Digger's tongue was hanging out, his collar missing, blood all around his mouth. While they'd slept, he'd chewed through his lead that had been tied to the truck. Dan had wrapped him in a blanket, trying to hide the damage, but Brigitte saw his guts hanging out, dripping. Ryan started crying. She asked Dan if Digger would be OK. He didn't answer. She felt like she couldn't breathe, and vomit was rising in her throat. It was the first time she'd seen anything dead. Joan just sat there, smoking, in the red-and-white Kenworth cabin, and watched as Brigitte and Ryan helped Dan dig a hole for Digger just beyond the parking bay.

'Come and say goodbye to Digger,' Ryan called out.

'No.' Joan screwed up her face. 'I can't stand endings. I only like beginnings.' She flicked her cigarette butt onto the gravel and pulled the door of the Kenworth shut, *Dan Weaver* painted in swirly writing along its side. She said the same thing when she refused to go to Dan's gravesite at his funeral.

'Kitty needs to go to the vet *now*,' Kerry says.

'Yes.'

'I'll drive you?'

Brigitte nods and hears herself swallow. Kerry picks Kitty up carefully and passes him to Brigitte. Brigitte's hands shake; she's afraid of holding him in case she hurts him more.

Kitty pants fast, watery little breaths on Brigitte's lap — as if his lungs are filled with blood. She winces at his gurgled meows when they hit speed humps.

Kerry parks in front of a grey double-fronted house. A rusted sign hangs from a post: *V — ary Surgeon*.

Brigitte follows Kerry down the dark sideway to the surgery at the back. Moonlight illuminates the little white flowers pushing up through cracks in the concrete. Brigitte always takes Kitty for his check-ups and needles to the shiny, new clinic in North Fitzroy, but it's not open after hours.

The vet asks Brigitte if it's her cat.

She nods.

He runs his big hands over Kitty. 'It's got significant head and spinal injuries. Needs to be euthanased.'

Kitty squirms around on the stainless-steel table. Blood covers most of his head, and Brigitte sees that one of his eyes is missing. She wants to stroke him or hold him, but the vet tells her to keep back. The sterile, disinfectant smells — hospital smells — make her dizzy. *Please, please, just do it quickly.*

'Shouldn't have been out at night,' the vet says.

Brigitte leans her back against the cold wall, and tears fill her eyes.

The vet asks her to pay first. *Prick*. She searches for her credit card in her purse, but can't find it. Her legs feel like jelly, and the clinic spins. Kerry organises payment while Brigitte sits shaking in the waiting area. Had she been a cat the day of the accident, they would have put her to sleep, too.

Kerry gets a clean blanket from her car. A yellow one.

'Do you have any other colour blankets?' Brigitte says.

Kerry frowns.

'Sorry. It's fine. Thanks.'

'You have something in your hair.'

Brigitte brushes her fingers through it.

Kerry helps her wrap up Kitty, and drives her home.

Brigitte walks through the quiet house, carrying a cold, heavier Kitty wrapped in the blanket. Aidan has cleaned up the cake, but left the spilt wine on the table — it's the same colour as the big round stain on the road where Kitty used up his ninth life. She frowns at the cigarette butts in a saucer on the kitchen bench.

He's in the backyard wearing a black trench coat. The shovel leans against the plastic cubby house. Brigitte kneels, and places Kitty in the hole he's dug in the garden.

Aidan waits a couple of minutes before clearing his throat. He reaches out a hand to help her, but she pulls herself up on the cubby house. He dumps a shovel-full of dirt onto Kitty's grave and smoothes it over with the blade. Brigitte shivers and pulls her jacket tighter around her shoulders. She looks up, and can only see one star in the sky.

'Will you get another kitten for the kids? Or wait a while?' Aidan says, leaning on the shovel.

'Don't know.' She wipes the tears from her cheeks. 'Maybe a female wouldn't wander as much. We could make it an inside cat.

I'd like another ginger one.'

'Thought ginger cats could only be males.' His breath is a swirl of steam in the air.

'That's an old wives' tale. Females have two X chromosomes, so they need two copies of the ginger variant, instead of one like males. Less common, but you can still get them.'

'Not just a pretty face.' Aidan stands the shovel against the fence. 'You've got cake in your hair,' he says, with the hint of a smirk on one side of his lips. He brushes it off and tries to kiss her, but she turns her face away and tells him to please go.

He goes to the bungalow.

Inside the house, she locks the back door and has to lean against it as her knees buckle.

No, no, no. She shakes her head. *What have I done?* She covers her mouth with her hands. She'll never be able to look Sam in the eyes again.

She makes it to the bathroom, turns on the taps, kneels, and vomits red wine and purple cake in the shower. When the last of her stomach contents gurgles down the plug hole, she washes her body thoroughly — inside and out. She brushes her teeth, shampoos her hair, and scrubs frantically with the bristle brush every centimetre of skin until it is red and sore.

Through the window she can see torchlight in the bungalow. Is he doing the same? Washing away every trace of evidence?

She catches her naked, dripping reflection in the mirror as she dries herself. *We all have our reasons, our circumstances*: Joan's voice in her head.

She winds Kitty's window shut and locks it.

In the bedroom, little sobs rise from her abdomen and shake her whole body as she pulls on her least-sexy night shirt (the black one with the sleepy cow) and a pair of old track pants. She balls herself into a tight knot of pain at the edge of the bed, and waits for sleep, which takes a long time. Sirens scream up and down

Hoddle Street, trains blast and rattle through the station, cars slow for the speed hump in front of the house — some don't decelerate and hit it at 60. A cat meows like a crying baby, and rain starts dripping.

The serpent tattoo on his back breathes as he breathes; blue-and-green scales rise and fall with every inhalation and exhalation. She reaches out to touch it, but it slithers away as he rolls over and curls into a foetal position. Soft light, a silver mist on his dirty-blond hair. Sam? It's not Sam. But somebody familiar. It's … Kurt Cobain.

A dream within a dream. She wakes and dozes, and he's gone. A curtain flaps across an open window. Shoes? Where are her shoes? Not on the floor. Not under the bed. She hurtles barefoot — staggers, falls, twists her knee — down a long, airless corridor. She has to find him.

He's standing at the top of the stairs, wearing the brown sweater. She climbs towards him. In one hand he holds a red dog collar, and in the other, something metal — dark, heavy, shaped like an iron.

Then she's running — clutching a yellow bunny rug — down the stairs, out the door. She slips in a pool of blood on the road. A siren howls. Somebody screams — until she is wrenched from sleep by the image of the button on the floor under the table.

6

'Kitty's not dead, Mummy,' Phoebe says.

'Yes, sweetie, he is.' Brigitte presses down the dirt around Kitty's plant with her fingers. It's a little bush the twins chose at the nursery for its orange flowers — the same colour as Kitty — and heart-shaped leaves that mean they loved him.

'No, him sleeping.'

'Well, dead is kind of like sleeping,' Kerry says. 'But you don't wake up.'

'Him sleeping on my bed last night,' Phoebe says.

'No. He's sleeping under the ground now.' Brigitte stands and straightens her back, feeling a twist of pain.

'Yes, him *was* on my bed last night.'

'No, he wasn't.'

'Yes, Mummy.'

'Stop it, Phoebe.'

'You stop it, Mummy.' Phoebe runs inside and slams the door behind her.

'Can we get a puppy now?' Finn asks.

Brigitte and Kerry sit on the old love seat on the back porch. It was a wedding gift from Sam's parents. Now the blue paint on the arms is faded, and the floral cushions are torn; it's ready to go out in the next hard-rubbish collection.

Kerry opens the cheese and crackers and the bottle of wine she brought for the wake. She pours the wine, and they raise their glasses to Kitty.

'How was the cake?' Kerry asks.

'Good. Thanks.' Brigitte nods while her stomach churns.

'What's with all the furniture against the fence?'

'It's out of the bungalow. Somebody's renting it.'

'Who?' Kerry squints at the sun.

'Dunno. Just some guy Sam knows — a cop.' Brigitte takes a cracker, and slices some cheese.

'What's he like?'

Brigitte shrugs, pretending to concentrate on her cracker and cheese.

'Young?' Kerry balances her glass between her knees while she rolls a joint.

'No. About my age.'

'That's young. Cute?'

'Haven't taken that much notice.' She takes a big sip of wine, and feels like vomiting again.

'You have! You're blushing, Brigitte.'

'Am not. It's just the wine.'

'Oh my God.' Kerry laughs, blows smoke through her nose, and passes the joint to Brigitte.

'Don't be stupid.'

'You know that's why Tony and I broke up?'

'Why?'

'The boarder.'

'You didn't?'

Kerry nods, mock-sadly, and pours more wine.

7

A pistol-grey sky threatens rain most of the way along the Eastern Freeway. It holds off until they turn onto the Gippsland Highway. Then it pours. Sam turns the wipers on full. The station wagon's windows fog up, and it's hard to see the road. The twins eat rice cakes, chatter, and fall asleep in their child restraints. Brigitte feigns sleep to avoid talking to Sam.

The rain stops as they drive into Paynesville. They queue for the chain ferry at the water's edge. It's the only way to access Raymond Island, in the middle of a saltwater-lake system that feeds from Bass Strait. Moored fishing boats, cruisers — all different shapes and sizes — bob on the olive-green water. The ferry operator waves them on and collects the fare.

The vehicle section is half-full with seven other cars on board. A local, with curly grey hair, wheels her tricycle on, with an I HEART THE R.I FERRY bumper sticker decorating the basket. Two more seniors shuffle into the pedestrian shelter, clutching string bags of groceries from the Paynesville supermarket. A couple read a tourist brochure — *koala sanctuary* printed on the cover — while their child pushes his nose against the glass and makes faces at the twins.

The hydraulic ramps at either end groan as they're raised. Brigitte catches a whiff of diesel as the submerged chains engage and start to haul the ferry across the 150-metre strait. Sam checks his phone messages; something's up, but he doesn't say what. Finn and Phoebe unbuckle their seatbelts, and squeal and jump around in the back of the car. Sam yells at them to sit back down in their seats. The ferry wobbles as it juts and aligns with the concrete slip on the island.

They drive past the park and community centre, and turn left into Sixth Avenue. A Blue-tongue Lizard slinks across the road. Sam beeps the horn and shouts at it to hurry up. Brigitte glares at him. 'We're not in a hurry.'

'Sorry.' He drums his fingers on the steering wheel while he waits for it to cross.

'Remember the first time you and I came down here?' It was their first dirty weekend. Not that it was that dirty — she hadn't been out of hospital long, and was still fragile, almost a year after the accident. Sam doted on her then: cooked for her, brought her breakfast in bed, massaged her back and legs when she was in pain. She did really love Sam once. Still loves him, she reassures herself. Nothing has changed. She puts a hand on his thigh.

He's distracted.

'And remember when the twins were little?' She smiles. 'They used to kick around on their mat on the porch.' Finn rolled over for the first time, and Phoebe started crawling there.

He's still not listening as the tyres crunch to a stop on the gravel driveway beside the white fibro house. The last time he was here, Ryan painted green over the faded sky-blue window frames and doorframes. He missed a few patches.

The twins bounce out of the car. Brigitte slides out slowly. It takes a while to straighten up, for the stiffness to leave her body after sitting for three-and-a-half hours. She inhales a deep breath of eucalyptus-scented air as she takes a bag from the back of the car. A mother koala cuddles her baby in the gum tree next to the house.

Inside, the house smells of stale air, dust, fish, and mould. She opens all the windows and doors, Sam turns on the power at the main switch, and they start unpacking. There's a shoebox on the breakfast bar. Brigitte lifts off the lid. It's full of dusty shells. She picks one up and turns it over in her hand. Did the twins collect this? Or did she and Ryan when they were little? Or did somebody else?

'What are you doing?' Sam stands at the screen door, loaded with bags and soft toys. 'How about helping?'

She returns the shell, closes the lid, and walks across to open the door for him.

The kids pull out the boxes of toys and pencils in the sunroom, and then abandon them for the little bikes with training wheels in the shed.

Sam takes one of the adult bikes for a long ride around the island. Brigitte takes the twins for a short walk along the boardwalk, to the playground, and then for a ride on the ferry across to Paynesville and back.

That night, the smells of wood fire and mosquito coils fill the air. Brigitte and Sam sleep in her Nana and Papa's old bed in the middle bedroom. When Sam reaches out to touch her, she pretends to be asleep. The twins sleep together in the bottom bunk bed on the opposite side of the room — for a while anyway, before they climb in with their mum and dad.

Brigitte lies awake. The pillow feels hot, and hair tickles her face. She kicks Sam — *go into the twins' bed, give me some room* — but he doesn't move.

Pain curls its fingers around her lower back, spreads into her pelvis and down her legs, cramps her toes. She twists, and tries to shift the pressure to different nerves. Breathing away the pain — good air in through her nose, bad air out through her mouth, filling the pain zones with pure, healing white light — doesn't help.

Guilt competes with physical pain. It worms its way under her skin, stirs the juices in her stomach, and wraps darkness around her throat, making it hard to swallow. Something casts a moving shadow on the wall; it looks like the curtains, but there's no breeze to stir them. She starts at the guttural, unearthly noise — not quite grunting, not quite screeching — of koalas mating. Maybe she should just tell Sam, and get it over with.

★★★

On the second day the weather warms up, and they walk to their favourite swimming spot at the back of the island. Brigitte stares at her feet and concentrates on the crunchy, rhythmic sound her sneakers make on the dirt road.

Brigitte and Sam sit on a beach towel in the shade of the gnarled tea-tree, watching Finn and Phoebe roll in the sand and splash at the lake's edge. A big black swan leaves its bevy and waddles out of the water towards the twins. They scream, giggle, bump into each other, and fall over. Brigitte laughs, and Sam shoos away the swan. The sky reflects blue on the water, and sunlit-silver wavelets shimmer in the distance. Brigitte fears the water, hates to swim, never goes in.

'Sleep better down here?' Sam says.

'Yes,' she lies, and looks at a passing boat. 'A bit.'

He scoops up a handful of sand and lets it sift through his fingers.

Sam takes the twins fishing at dusk. Brigitte stays at the house; she tries to watch TV, or read a book, but she can't concentrate, can't sit still. She walks through the rooms. Her grandparents and great grandparents look down at her from old portrait photographs on the walls.

'What am I going to do, Papa?' she asks the black-and-white shot of a young, handsome Papa fishing on the lake.

He smiles at her from his old tin boat. *He never caught the bastard in the blue Camry; he won't catch you either.* She runs her hands through her hair and looks away — straight into the big, gilt-framed mirror above the couch. She averts her eyes quickly.

When they were kids, Ryan used to tell her that if they looked into that mirror they would see ghosts. She tells herself to stop being silly. There's no such thing as ghosts. In the kitchen, the clock ticks loudly on the wall above the sink. She takes a bottle of white wine from the fridge and pours herself a glass.

Footsteps pound across the porch, and the screen door slams. Fishing didn't last long. Sam's just behind the twins; he wipes his feet on the doormat. The house comes alive again.

'We catched a big crab, Mummy,' Finn says.

'Yes, but it jumped off the line and back into the water, didn't it, Finny?' Sam picks up the twins' abandoned fishing rods from the floor and stands them in the rack at the corner of the kitchen.

'Seaweed, too,' Phoebe says.

'Yes, lots of seaweed.'

'And did Daddy catch a fish?' Brigitte asks.

'No,' the twins say in unison.

'It was a bit noisy. Fish like quiet.' Sam gets a beer from the fridge and puts it in his I *HEART* THE R.I FERRY stubby holder. The twins giggle and run off to play with the toys in the sunroom.

'Would you like a little glass of wine?' Sam takes the bottle from the fridge door. 'God, Brig, you've drunk half the bottle!'

'I'm on holiday.' She holds out her glass for a refill. 'So what are we going to have for dinner now? I was planning to cook the fish you caught.'

Sam laughs.

'Yuck, you smell fishy.' His whiskers scratch her face as he kisses her. 'And you need to shave.' She pushes him away.

'Fishermen don't shave.' He rubs the stubble on his chin.

'Go have a shower.'

'Coming with me?'

'Maybe.' She doesn't meet his eyes.

'Whack on a DVD for them, and come on.'

She doesn't go, pretending that the twins need her for something.

'Somebody lost in this house,' Phoebe says, in between screaming about having her hair washed in the bath.

'Pardon?' Brigitte combs the conditioner through Phoebe's hair.

'Somebody else here. Lost.'

'No. It's only us here.'

'Didn't come with us.'

'What are you talking about?'

'Somebody lost in this house. Forever. A kid. A baby.'

Brigitte shivers. 'Don't be silly.'

'Risotto's nearly ready,' Sam calls from the kitchen.

'Phoebe, I love you, but sometimes you really creep me out.'

'What that means, Mummy?'

'Nothing.' Brigitte rinses the conditioner, and Phoebe starts screaming again.

Brigitte lies awake in bed again, with Aidan gnawing at her thoughts like a rat at electrical cords. A mosquito buzzes around her ears. Old dreams are trapped here; family secrets push down on her and mingle with her own dreams and secrets. Maybe there are ghosts. *Somebody lost in this house. Forever.* Sleep. Don't sleep — heart palpitations drag her up just as she falls into the dark dream-place. She sucks in her breath, but can't get enough air into her lungs.

She gets up and walks through the house, pulse racing. Tick, tick, tick: the clock above the sink in the kitchen. She drinks a glass of water and goes outside. A lot of stars twinkle in the sky. She lights a mosquito coil with shaking hands, and flops in the old black-leather couch on the porch. *Breathe. Breathe.* When her pulse finally relaxes, she closes her eyes.

It's cold in her dream, so she goes into the kitchen.

'Told you it was a good race horse, knew it'd win the Melbourne Cup.' Nana is sitting with Kurt Cobain at the table.

'I thought it was Dune — like the David Lynch film, with Sting.' Kurt holds a shell in his hand; he looks at it, and tosses it into a bowl on the table.

'No, Kurt, it's pronounced Ju-ane. It's French.'

Nana holds a tiny baby swaddled in a yellow bunny rug. To hold that baby would be better than anything in the world. Kurt unties the white ribbon on a little blue box and, from the box, produces the red dog collar and a key attached to a glittery, silver letter-J key ring. 'Put these somewhere safe. Don't lose them.' He hands them to Brigitte.

Nana holds out the baby, and the rug unravels. There's no baby inside — just a metal iron. Nana passes the iron and says to run. Brigitte holds the dog collar and the key, but the iron is too heavy and slippery. She looks down; it's dripping with blood, and she drops it. What happened to the baby?

'Hurry. The tram's nearly here,' Kurt says. 'Run faster this time.'

She wakes on the porch couch, head pounding. It's freezing, silver frost icing the grass; a few birds start to twitter. She goes inside. It's nearly four, according to the clock above the sink. She pulls on a pair of socks, and squashes into bed between Sam and the twins.

★★★

Ryan, Rosie, and Georgia come down on the third day. They unpack their things in the back bedroom. The house feels happy now: it needs lots of people.

Sam and Ryan take the kids across to Paynesville for ice-creams. Brigitte makes herbal tea, and puts out a plate of biscuits on the breakfast bar.

'Wow, you've lost a lot of weight, Rosie.'

Rosie pushes the biscuits away. 'Thanks. I'm taking good care of myself these days.'

The short haircut, cropped around her face, accentuates her huge brown eyes. Ryan was right: she does look like a stick insect. 'It's important to be healthy as we get older.' Rosie's eyes flick down and up Brigitte's body. Assessing her?

'Yes. Apparently all sorts of things start to change when you get to forty.' Brigitte takes a biscuit. 'So I've heard.'

'I wish Ryan would do something healthy. He's really packing on the weight.'

'He walks a lot. He's OK.' *And quite a bit younger than you.*

Rosie raises her eyebrows. There's an awkward silence.

'How's Georgia going at kinder this year?'

'Well, you know — Georgia's always going to be difficult. Ryan lets her get away with too much.' She waves a hand dismissively. 'I seriously don't know how you can stand staying home looking after kids all day, Brigitte.'

'I work, too.'

Rosie ignores her; writing is not a real job to Rosie. 'In some ways, it's lucky Ryan's unemployed — so he can do it.'

'He's not unemployed,' Brigitte says. 'He's got some work on. And auditions.'

Rosie laughs — a fake laugh — and pretends to choke on her tea. She leaves her half-empty cup on the breakfast bar, and goes to her room. Brigitte has another biscuit, and loads the dishwasher.

Rosie comes out in her lycra gear and trainers, ready for a run around the island. 'You should come, Brigitte.' She fills a water bottle at the sink.

'No, thanks.'

'Sorry, I forgot you can't …' she says, with a look that's not quite pity.

Rosie jogs off, and Brigitte takes a book out to read on the porch couch — the book Rosie gave her last Christmas: *Alias Grace* by Margaret Atwood. She can't concentrate, and keeps reading the same page. She thinks about opening the wine in the fridge.

Where are the boys and the kids? Rosie gets back before they do. She showers, and stays in her room with the door shut.

Sam and Ryan come back with alcohol on their breath; the kids have ice-cream all over their faces and T-shirts. Ryan holds a slab of beer under his arm. Brigitte closes her book and follows them inside.

'What's for dinner, Little Sis?' Ryan jokes, putting the slab on the breakfast bar and an arm around her shoulder.

'Go away. You've been at the pub. You stink of beer. Both of you.'

'Just kidding. Sam and I'll go back across and get fish and chips.' He hiccups. 'Where's Rosie?'

'In your room.'

He goes to her. Sam puts the beers in the fridge. 'Want one?'

'OK.'

They take their drinks outside. The kids are riding bikes around the yard. Sam kisses Brigitte against a pole on the porch, his hand up under her T-shirt. She turns her face, and looks around his shoulder.

'What's wrong?'

'Ryan,' she whispers. He's standing in the doorway, clearing his throat. Brigitte pushes Sam away and straightens her T-shirt.

'Everything OK?' she says.

'Yep. Rosie's resting.' He takes the plastic cover off the pool table, and plugs in the ancient yellow-and-aqua CD player that nobody can remember bringing here. Every time they come down, they speculate about where it came from. Ryan reckons Nana and Papa left it as a gift for the 'young people'. Brigitte knows where it came from, but says Joan must have brought a boyfriend down for a dirty weekend and left it here.

Rosie comes out an hour or so later, and screws up her nose at the fish and chips on the porch, the grease soaking into the paper. Sam and Ryan are playing pool, and Brigitte's watching the kids dance with glow sticks on the grass.

'Hey, Rosie, want a beer?' Ryan says.

'You know I don't drink beer, Ryan.'

'There's a bottle of vegan wine in the fridge,' Brigitte says.

'I'll have a glass when the kids go to bed.' Rosie puts her hands on her hips and shakes her head when she sees Georgia's dirty face. 'Georgia — bedtime.'

'I'm not tired, Mummy,' Georgia says, pouting.

'Let her go a bit longer, Rosie,' Ryan says.

'It's nearly eight o'clock, Ryan.'

'We're on holiday.'

'Georgia. Come now, please.' Rosie glances at Brigitte. 'You can do what you like with your kids, Brigitte, but Georgia has to go to bed now. Or she'll be very grumpy in the morning, won't you?' She frowns at Georgia, grabs her hand, and drags her inside.

'Suppose I'd better put the twins to bed, too.' Brigitte sighs.

When the kids are asleep Rosie helps herself to a glass of wine, and Brigitte gets another beer.

'Wanna play doubles? Girls versus men,' Ryan says as they come back outside.

'No, thanks. And we're not girls, Ryan.'

'Sorry, Rosie. *Women.*' He ejects Paul Kelly and looks through the pile of CDs on the shelf next to the barbeque. 'What do you want to listen to?'

'Foo Fighters,' Sam says.

'Haven't got it. Tom Waits, The White Stripes ... Nick Cave —

for Brigi.' He puts on the CD, takes her hand, and they dance. Sam sits back on the couch, laughing, his feet up on the table.

Rosie glares at Brigitte. 'Why don't you get up on the pool table? Just like the old days, Brigitte.'

Brigitte freezes.

'Shut up, Rosie.' Brigitte's never heard Ryan speak like that to her before. They stop dancing. Sam stops laughing, and takes his feet off the table.

'Oh, that's right. You don't remember, do you?' Rosie says.

'What's she talking about, Ryan?' Brigitte looks at him; he's walking towards Rosie.

'Just don't get on the wrong side of her when she's angry, hey, Sam?'

Brigitte looks at Sam, then back to Ryan.

'It's amazing what some people can get away with.'

'I said shut up, Rosie.' Ryan's angry. He never gets angry.

Rosie slams her glass on the table — the stem snaps — and she monsters off down the driveway.

'What was that about?' Brigitte says, her heart pounding. What has Ryan told her?

Ryan shrugs. 'Rosie shouldn't drink.'

'Want me to go after her?' Sam says.

'No, let her go.'

Brigitte and Sam clean up the broken glass without speaking, and Ryan turns up Nick Cave.

***

Brigitte's sitting on the porch couch in the morning sun — a cushion in the small of her back, her laptop on her knees, writing an article — when Sam comes out with his mobile in hand. She knows what he's going to say before he says it.

'Sorry, babe. I have to go back.'

She doesn't look at him.

'We fucked up big time — arrested the wrong bloke.'

So Finn and Phoebe will have another holiday without their dad. She's learned a trick: if you tickle the roof of your mouth with your tongue, it stops the tears from reaching your eyes. A three-year-old at the twins' kinder taught her that — how to be brave when something hurts.

'Sorry. You stay. And Ryan. No reason to ruin your holiday as well.'

She keeps her eyes focused on the keyboard as Sam takes the twins' child restraints out of the station wagon and fits them into Ryan's car. He reluctantly agrees to give Rosie a lift back to Melbourne, kisses his family, and throws his bag on the back seat.

Ryan's on the couch, kids bouncing all over him, as Sam and Rosie drive off. 'Don't be too pissed off, Brigi.'

She goes inside, and slams the screen door behind her.

***

A drunk woman upends a white plastic table as she falls over in the beer garden at The Old Pub. A bowl-full of cigarette butts scatters across the ground.

Brigitte and Ryan try the bar instead. A big plastic fish hangs on the wall above bottles mirrored on dusty shelves. *Happy hour 5–7* is scrawled in yellow chalk on a blackboard. Young Shannon greets Ryan like an old friend. 'Where's your mate?'

'Sam?'

'Yeah, the copper.'

'How'd you know that?'

'Always can tell, mate.'

'Had to go home this morning. Those murders in Melbourne.'

'Dreadful business.' Shannon shakes his head and clicks his tongue. 'This ya missus?'

'No, my sister, Brigitte.'

Shannon kisses her hand, then goes back to talking to old Jim about his ancestors who own castles in Ireland. One of them was the first aviator to circumnavigate the world, according to Shannon. Jim tells them he's lived here for forty years, fishing. He buys them beers, and gives the kids coins to play with the machine-gun video game in the corner.

When Shannon's and Jim's conversation turns to boar hunting, Brigitte and Ryan rack up a game of pool.

'Anything happen the other night?' Ryan pockets one of the smalls on the break. She feels her cheeks redden.

'After the twins' birthday?'

She looks at him with wide eyes, innocently — she has no idea what he's talking about.

'Watch yourself, Brigi.'

She nods, and chalks her cue. He leans across the table to take another shot.

'Only allowed one shot on the break,' she says.

'Bullshit.'

Brigitte takes her shot, and the ball just misses the pocket. 'Do you know what Rosie was talking about last night?'

'No. She totally lost it, didn't she?' Ryan pots three balls in a row. 'She's jealous of you.'

She sips her beer and laughs. 'Why on earth would Rosie be jealous of me?'

'Because you're cute and funny, and everybody loves you.'

'Rosie doesn't.' She flukes two balls in one shot.

'No, but I reckon Aidan does.'

She miscues, and pots one of Ryan's balls. 'Stop it, Ryan.'

'And those local blokes do. Not one of them hasn't had his eye on you since we walked in.'

'Don't be stupid.' She looks over her shoulder. Shannon waves and points at the drink he's bought for her. Ryan shrugs — *Told you so.*

'Rosie thinks I spend more time with you than I do with her.'

'You do.'

He cleans up the table, and pots the black.

The ferry is at the landing when they leave the pub. Ryan throws Finn up onto his shoulders and takes Georgia's hand. Brigitte drags Phoebe along as they hurry across the road.

Finn's sneakers slap on the steel floor of the pedestrian shelter as Ryan, out of breath, lifts him down.

'Look — water lights.' Phoebe sticks her head between the bottom rails and points at the shimmer of red, blue, and silver: the café's neon sign reflecting on the inky water. 'Pretty.'

'Maybe I could move down here, buy a boat.' Ryan leans against the top rail and inhales a deep breath of salty air.

'You're drunk.'

'Am not. You are. I could be a fisherman, grow a beard ...' He strokes his smooth chin.

'And what would Rosie do?'

'Dunno. Be a fish wife.' He hiccups.

They laugh, and Ryan sings 'Don't Pay the Ferryman'.

'What the hell are you singing?' Brigitte grips the rail so tightly that her knuckles whiten. The ferry groans and starts to chug across the strait.

'Don't you remember that song? What was the guy's name who sang it? Christopher somebody? Chris—'

'Oh my God, where's Finn?' Brigitte looks around, and then rushes to the front of the ferry. He's not there. Ryan scoops up Phoebe, grabs Georgia's hand, checks the back.

'Is he there?' Brigitte yells.

Ryan shakes his head. She calls Finn's name.

There's only one car on board, so the view of the vehicle section is clear, and he's not there. And he's not playing on the rails or the steel stairs leading to the ferry operator's compartment.

There's nowhere else he could be hiding. *He's not here. This can't be happening.* Brigitte turns around and around. Everything rushes past and blurs, but slows down at the same time — the glow of the public phone box on the island, the lights of Paynesville on the other side, moonlight on the water. She remembers doing something like this before, and quickly pushes away the memory.

'It's OK, love, your boy's here.' An old man with a red face is holding Finn's hand. 'He was sittin' right up the front.'

How could she have not seen him there? She snatches him from the man, lifts him, and hugs him as tightly as she can. Her back twists. Ryan takes Finn as Brigitte collapses onto the wooden bench seat.

'Please don't tell Sam about this.' She puts her head between her knees and takes short, shallow breaths.

'Nothing happened.'

'Yes, it did.'

Ryan bends to rub her back and Finn says, 'Sorry, Mummy. Sorry, Mummy …'

'It's OK,' Ryan says.

'No, it's not.' She leans towards Ryan and lowers her voice so Finn can't hear. 'I slept with him — Aidan.'

8

The cigarette-smoking man waves and coughs as Brigitte keys in the security code.

Papa's sitting in the Chesterfield, stroking Tiger and arguing with the talkback host on his transistor radio.

'Brigi.' He grins — brown teeth, several missing — when he sees her in the doorway. 'Ya look bloody awful.' He pushes the cat off his lap and turns down the radio. 'You all right?'

'Just tired.' She smiles thinly, kisses him, and takes a chair by the window.

'Where's the twins?'

'Kinder.'

'They go to school now?'

'No.' She speaks louder, 'Kindergarten.'

They sit in silence for a while.

Papa clears his throat. 'Detective bloke was in here a coupla days ago.'

'What?' She looks at him and frowns.

He looks at his hands, clenches them together, his bony knuckles and ropey veins popping out. 'Tall — some eyetalian name.'

'Not Serra?'

'Yeah.'

Her back hurts, but she sits up straighter and leans forward.

'Didn't look real eyetie. Askin' questions bout some low-life music bloke got killed same time you had ...' he looks up and swallows, his Adams apple stretching the thin, wrinkly skin across his throat, '... the accident. Don't remember that, do ya?'

She shakes her head slowly.

'Was in the papers, on telly. You were home with me and Nana when it happened. She had to go to hospital with her heart attack, remember?'

He knows she doesn't remember.

'Bloody bastard got what he deserved anyway.' Papa's getting agitated, tapping his fingertips together. Maybe he hasn't been taking his pills. 'Detective said some other bloke reckons you were with him that night. But he's lyin', right? Cause you were with me and Nana, right?'

'Right.' Brigitte nods and looks out the window at the Pelaco sign.

Petula pokes her head in the doorway. 'Coming on the bus trip this afternoon, Eddie?'

'No thanks, love.' He dismisses her with a wave of his hand and looks at Brigitte. 'What'd she say?'

'Are you going on the bus trip?'

'Won't bloody leave me alone. Bus trips, tai chi, bloody aromatherapy.'

'Aromatherapy is good.'

He scoffs.

'Might go make a cuppa. Want one?' Brigitte says.

'Nah, just had one thanks, love.'

At the kitchenette she slams down a cup and drums her fingertips on the sink while she waits for the kettle to boil. Wait till she sees Aidan!

She drinks her cup of tea quickly back in Papa's room.

'Anyway.' He yawns. 'Did ya see those fat people, Brigi, on — what do ya call it — *Big Loser?*'

'No.'

'Can't understand how people can get that fat.' He sucks his teeth, sounding like the suction device at the dentist. Brigitte grinds hers.

'OK, Papa, It's time for me to go.' She picks up her bag and stands.

'So soon?'

***

Brigitte sits on the love seat watching, from behind dark sunglasses, Finn and Phoebe playing on the newly mown grass.

She starts at the scrape of the bungalow door opening, and her eyes are drawn to his bare feet, faded jeans, and white T-shirt with *Captain America* emblazoned across the front in blue lettering. It's warm in the sun, but she shivers. A black tattoo peeks from under his left sleeve: some sort of foreign script, maybe Gaelic.

'Hi.' He smiles his crooked smile, squints, and shades his eyes with his hand. So fucking smug. He goes back inside for a minute and comes back with a pair of sunglasses.

'What are you doing here?' she says without looking at him.

'I live here, remember?'

'Why aren't you at work?'

'On night shift.'

'Sam'll be home soon.' She glances at the back door.

He walks over and sits next to her — too close. The love seat creaks as he stretches out his long legs. So it is true, what they say about big feet.

'Nice day,' he says.

'What happened to the grass?'

'Mowed it.'

'Nobody asked you to.'

'Don't mind.'

'Why the hell were you talking to my grandfather?' She feels the blood rush to her face.

'Funny coincidence, huh?' He laughs. 'Eddie's a nice bloke.'

'Just answer the question.'

'His old house was in the vicinity of an unsolved murder.

Might have remembered hearing something.'

'His memory's not so good.'

'Oh, he remembered.' He turns his body and looks at her. His knee brushes hers. 'It was the same time your grandmother had her heart attack.'

'I lived there, too. Why haven't you questioned me?'

'What would be the point of that? I know you don't remember.'

Good point. 'So this has nothing to do with me?'

'Not everything's about you.'

She doesn't want to talk to him anymore, and wishes he would just go away — crawl into a hole somewhere and never come back. And that his leg touching hers wasn't causing such a warm, prickly sensation. She should move over, but doesn't.

'Are the scars from the car accident?'

She pulls a section of hair across the one on her forehead and doesn't answer.

'And your knee?'

She stares straight ahead and crosses her legs, ignoring a primal urge to part them.

'What's wrong?' he says.

She pushes her sunglasses higher up on her nose.

'Thought you liked me.'

'Not much of a detective. No wonder you're on the cold cases.'

He clears his throat. 'You wanted it as much as I did.'

'Wrong again.'

'Why did you tell me you were separated from your husband?'

'I did not say that.' She sits up straight and glowers.

'Yes you did, at Manny's party.'

She chews a fingernail.

'That's what you wanted me to think.'

'I was drunk, OK. And upset — if you really have to know.'
The skin around her fingernail starts to bleed; she hides her hand under her leg.

'And that makes it OK?'

'I don't want to talk about it.'

'I do,' he says. They turn and look directly at each other, but she can't see his eyes hidden behind the shades.

'If you don't stop, I'll tell Sam I want you to move out.' Why doesn't she move over?

'Sam wants to keep me closer.'

'What does that mean?'

'Friends, enemies.'

'I'll tell him you're harassing me.' She springs up, a flood of pain ripping through her body. 'Finn, Phoebe inside now.'

'No,' Phoebe says. 'We want to play with Aidan.'

Aidan shrugs.

'Fine. Whatever.' She slams the door behind her so hard that one of the pot plants falls off the windowsill and smashes on the ground.

9

The bouquet of flowers droops on the console. 'Thirty-seven degrees in the city,' the radio announcer says. 'Unusual for November —' Sam cuts him off with a Foo Fighters CD. They're stuck in traffic on Sydney Road, with the air conditioner not working. Sam drums his fingers on the steering wheel; the lights change, but the car in front doesn't move.

'Come on.' He beeps the horn. The car in front moves, and the driver gives him the finger. 'Fuck you, too,' he says under his breath.

It's been nearly six months since they've been to visit Sam's parents in Coburg; he couldn't put it off any longer. Brigitte feels sweat trickling down between her breasts, soaking her dress. The twins are red-faced, quiet, zonked out from the heat. She passes water bottles to them.

While she's turning: *Pop!* Brigitte screams, the twins scream. Sam slams on the brakes, and Brigitte's bad knee smashes into the dashboard.

'Brigitte!' Sam yells at her. 'What the fuck?' Cars behind start beeping.

The tube of hand cream on the dashboard has expanded and exploded because of the heat. The inside of the windscreen is coated with a white film. Brigitte and Sam are spattered — especially Sam.

Sam instinctively turns on the windscreen wipers. Stupid. He wipes it out of his eyes and off the windscreen with the back of his hand, and pulls over. The twins are crying.

'All I wanted to do was visit my fucking parents. Why does

everything have to turn into a fucking disaster with you?'

'What? I didn't do anything.'

'Why was that fucking cream even in the car?'

'Stop it Sam, you're upsetting the twins.'

'Why can't you do anything right? Can't even lock the fucking cat's window?'

She opens her mouth, but can't speak.

'And I heard what you did at Manny's party.'

It's forty-plus degrees in the car, but she freezes.

'Got drunk, embarrassed yourself? Manny had to help you out in the lift?' His face is red, a vein pulsing in his temple. 'Now half the force knows my wife's an alcoholic. You're just like your fucking mother.'

'And you're just like your father.'

He slaps her face. She holds a hand to her cheek — it stings, and tears prickle her eyes. She tickles the roof of her mouth with her tongue, but it doesn't work this time.

Sam keeps yelling at her: 'You were a fucking mess when I met you and still are now ...'

She dissociates — focuses on Dave Grohl singing 'Long Road to Ruin' — and calmly lets Sam's words roll over her for a while. Her silence makes him angrier.

Enough. She shakes her head. Enough years should have passed for her not to need him anymore. She takes a deep breath, unlocks her door, gets out, and walks along the street, rubbing hand cream into her arms.

Sam opens the driver's side door, steps out, and leans against the roof. 'Get back in the vehicle.' It's his policeman's voice, his stupid bully's voice. He still has cream on his face. The twins are hysterical. Brigitte's a few shop-fronts away, so he yells, 'I told you to get back in the fucking vehicle.'

'No!' She keeps walking. Then she looks over her shoulder at the twins, and stops.

Sam slams his door shut, strides after her, and tries to drag her back by an arm, but she fights him. He picks her up like a child, carries her and shoves her into the passenger seat, pushes her arms and legs in, hurts her. Drivers are slowing down for a look, but no cars stop; nobody wants to get involved in such things.

The car rocks as he hurls himself into the driver's seat. He clenches and unclenches his fists, and takes some deep breaths. She leans into the back seat and strokes the twins' legs until they're calm. Then she turns to Sam and says very quietly, controlling her voice, 'I'm not a mess, Sam. I'm not an alcoholic. I'm not like my mother.' And, even quieter, 'And don't you *ever* do that to me again.'

She reaches across and stops the CD. God, she hates the Foo Fighters. They sit quietly — just the twins whimpering — for a long time.

'Anything to get out of visiting Maggie and Doug.' He runs a finger through the cream on the windscreen.

It doesn't get a smile.

'I'm sorry, Brig.' He leans across, takes her face in his hands, and kisses her. 'Sorry. I didn't mean it.' He's greasy, and smells of lavender. She pulls away, and hands him some tissues from the glove box.

'Sorry. Lot of pressure at work at the moment.' He wipes his face and rests it against her chest.

She instinctively lifts a hand to stroke his hair, but stops herself.

'And I don't know why you don't want to sleep with me anymore,' he says.

10

Brigitte finds one of Kitty's old toys squashed under the doormat while she's sweeping the back porch. She picks it up and puts it in her pocket. Maybe it's time to get a new kitten. She leans the broom against the side of the house, walks across, and knocks on the bungalow door. A pair of new-looking running shoes is lined up side by side on the step.

Aidan lets her in, buttoning his shirt. He's listening to ABC radio — the same station she has on in the kitchen. Aromas of wet hair, citrus cologne, toast, and coffee fill the room. She looks around. A cup and plate are drying on the draining rack next to the sink, and the single bed has been neatly made. He has arranged some framed photos on the dressing table: a black-and-white of a pretty woman with fair skin and a turned-up nose, her arms wrapped around a young-Robert De Niro lookalike; a tall, gangly boy, about fifteen, in swimming shorts standing between two older girls with long dark hair in front of a pool; and one of the girls, grown up, holding a baby.

Aidan turns down the radio and asks what's wrong.

'Can I borrow some bread?'

He tilts his head at the chest freezer, and she walks towards it. The bookshelves are filled with books — she didn't pick him as a reader — and as far as she can see, none with shiny titles embossed on the spines. She opens the freezer and leans in, aware of him watching her.

'I was wondering when you'd come to visit,' he says. 'Want a coffee?'

'No.'

'Go on, just stay for a coffee.'

'OK.' She closes the freezer lid, turns, and he's right in front of her. He puts his arms around her, and she pushes him away. What did she expect: a civil conversation, a mutual agreement to leave each other alone? Stupid.

When he tries again, she steps back and swings the loaf of frozen bread at his head, and hits him.

Shocked by the force of it, he lifts a hand to his cheek — it's going to leave a decent bruise. She thinks about what Sam did to her and sucks in her breath: sorry, really sorry, she shouldn't have done that. She ignores her immediate reaction to want to touch her hand to his face.

He takes a few steps backwards. Angry or hurt? 'I know what you did, Brigitte.' A drop of water from his hair rolls down the side of his face, onto his collar. 'I know where you worked. I know what you were.'

She steps towards the doorway, but he stands in her way, blocking it. A pair of boxing gloves hangs on the hook next to the window. He puts his arms on either side of the door frame, trapping her. 'I know everything about you.'

He's making it up; he's going to do something to her, hurt her. She sidesteps, looks around him to the safety of the house, but Sam's already left for work.

'I know what Sam did.' He leans down, close to her face, 'And I know who Matt Elery is.'

She fiddles with the cuff of her shirt. 'I don't know anybody called Matt ...'

'Elery. Apparently, he's a crime-thriller writer.'

'Sure you don't mean James Ellroy?' *Too smart, not funny.*

'He remembers you.'

She looks away — at his book on the bedside table, *In Cold Blood* — and then back, directly into his eyes. 'I have no idea what you're talking about.'

'How many other men have you fucked over, Brigitte? How about Eric Tucker? Does that name ring something?'

She forces her face to stay blank, but he might as well have tipped a bucket of ice over her head.

'Oh, that's right, you don't remember. Just like you didn't remember me from Manny's party.'

She shrugs, and twists her mouth.

'You're so fucking self-centred.' His voice goes up a few decibels.

She frowns.

'Did you really think my interest in you was non-work related?'

'What?' Another ice bucket.

'Yeah.' He nods. 'I've been investigating you the whole time.' His eyes are shining — they've turned almost black, inky. 'An easy fuck on the side was just a bonus.'

She goes to hit him again, but he's too quick this time, catching her wrist before she can strike him.

'So Elery *was* telling the truth. About your violent streak.'

Her heart beats so hard it's going to explode, but she doesn't flinch.

'Don't *you* touch me again.' He pushes her hand away. 'Or I'll charge you with assault.' He snatches his phone and keys from the tri-fold table, his jacket from the back of the chair, and turns and strides out across the yard.

She stands in the doorway, hugging her upper arms against her chest. 'Aidan!' No response. 'AIDAN!' He's gone down the sideway. She drops the bread and sits on the step with her head in her hands.

11

It's after midnight when Sam gets home, but she's still awake. He places his watch and keys quietly on the bedside table. His clothes rustle as he undresses in the dark; the bed creaks when he sits on the edge to pull off his shoes and socks.

'Aidan's working on the case you were working when we met.' The sound of her voice seems to hang in the darkness. 'He thinks I did something. He says you did something, too.'

'No,' Sam says, 'he's just got things mixed up.'

'I don't know, Sam. He sounded pretty serious. Scared me.'

'Is he out the back?' He reaches for his clothes.

'No, he hasn't come home.'

He drops his shirt, and takes her hand. 'I'll sort it out tomorrow. And he can move out if he's upsetting you.' He slides into bed, and she snuggles up against him — warm, strong, a hint of sport deodorant and dried sweat. She needs him more than ever now.

'Don't worry.' He strokes her hair. 'Did Serra say anything about what he thinks happened that morning?'

'Morning?'

'Night.'

'Not really.'

'Have you remembered something?'

She fiddles with the corner of the pillow case. 'No.'

'Brig, there's something I have to tell you about my father.'

'Doug?'

'No, my real father.'

She should be a good partner and listen, but she's drained.

'Can it wait till tomorrow?'

They lie awake for a long time without speaking.

'Sam, I want to have another baby,' she whispers. The twins brought them closer together. New life makes everything better.

Next door's air conditioner whirs, a dog barks, and street-light creeps under the blind.

'Let's talk about that tomorrow, too.'

***

The smell of rain fills her nose before she opens her eyes. Thunder growls, and lightning illuminates the room. She reaches out for Sam. He's gone. It's dark, but the clock radio glows 10.05 a.m. Shit — how could she have slept so late? She reaches for her slippers under the bed, pulls on one of Sam's T-shirts, and stumbles down the hallway, rubbing her eyes. The twins are still in their pyjamas, watching TV and licking icy poles. She's about to yell, but instead kneels and wraps her arms around them.

'We was hungry. Daddy went to work and you was sleeping,' Phoebe says.

'It's OK.' She hugs them tighter. Another crack of thunder, closer.

'Is somebody shooting?' Finn says.

'No, silly, it's just a storm. Come and I'll make you some proper breakfast.'

There are three text messages from Sam on her phone:

Morning Ralph. Sorted things with Serra.

Been thinking about what u said last night. Think I want it 2. Talk when I get home.

Also been thinking about teaching course again.

She texts back: *Morning Sam. I luv u.* He doesn't reply.

The twins have left a chair up against the fridge, with the freezer door open; food is defrosting, melting down the front. Brigitte cleans up the mess, and makes toast and coffee.

The kinder session is nearly over by the time they get there. She goes home and tries to clean the house in the 45 minutes left before pick-up time.

She starts dusting the blinds, stops, goes into the study, and does what she has always avoided doing — what she was lying awake thinking about all night: she googles Eric Tucker. Click.

COLD-CASE DETECTIVES INVESTIGATE UNSOLVED MURDER OF CONCERT PROMOTER, ERIC TUCKER (2008)

VICTORIAN COLD-CASE DETECTIVES TO RE-OPEN 1994 INVESTIGATION OF SLAIN CONCERT PROMOTER, ERIC TUCKER (2008)

TUCKER CASE REMAINS UNSOLVED (1997)

DETECTIVE SAM CAMPBELL CLEARED OF EVIDENCE-TAMPERING ALLEGATION (1995)

POLICE LOST EVIDENCE IN TUCKER CASE (1995)

POLICE SEEK YOUNG WOMAN SEEN LEAVING TUCKER APARTMENT (1994)

CONCERT PROMOTER FOUND DEAD (1994)

She glances over her shoulder, scrolls up to the first search result, and reads the article:

Victorian detectives have reopened the cold case of Eric Tucker, who was bludgeoned to death in 1994.

The body of Eric Tucker, 45, was discovered in his luxury Carlton apartment by the now deceased caretaker, Sean McMahon, on 23 December 1994.

In the coroner's inquest report, Dr Simon Marks, forensic pathologist at the Victorian Institute of Forensic Medicine, attributed Mr Tucker's cause of death to head injury from multiple blows inflicted by a person or persons with a heavy, blunt object.

Despite an exhaustive investigation by detectives, no arrest was ever made over the incident.

Detective Sergeant Aidan Serra confirmed they have recommenced inquiries into the violent assault, and are appealing for public assistance.

Cold-case investigations can be extremely challenging, but in this case they did have a person of interest.

'There was physical evidence that linked this person to Mr Tucker,' said Detective Serra. 'Unfortunately, most of the evidence from the original investigation is no longer available. However, advances in technology mean that the few remaining DNA samples taken from the scene can now be forensically examined.'

Anybody with information about Eric Tucker should contact police or Crime Stoppers.

Oh God. Her stomach turns over; vomit rises in her throat, and she swallows it. The doorbell rings. She jumps, almost screams, and shuts down the computer.

It's Aidan — at the front, for a change. She unlocks the security door reluctantly. He stands there, silently. *Must be enjoying this: a cat with a mouse. He should rub some arnica cream into the bread bruise on his cheek.* Kerry waves as she walks past with her dog and a pink, polka-dot umbrella.

Brigitte waits until Kerry is out of earshot, then says, 'Come on then. Aren't you going to cuff me?' She holds out her hands, angry now. *Wait till Sam finds out about this.*

'Not now.'

'What do you want then?' She looks up. His eyes are serious, remorseful. He has long eyelashes. His Adam's apple moves up and down as he seems to struggle to swallow. She looks away — a snail is crushed on the wet path — and then looks back. The paint is starting to blister and peel on the cherry-red door she painted when they first moved in; but you can't tell, unless you look closely. She frowns, and her legs start to shake. *No.*

'No.' Her voice is a whisper, and she shakes her head slowly.

'Can I come in?'

The call. Expected, but never prepared for. In her imagination, it was always a phone call. *How stupid — this kind of news would never be delivered that way. And why is it coming from Aidan? Shouldn't he be busy trying to ruin her life?* He sits with her on their couch, her and Sam's couch, and tells her that Sam is dead. Another stupid thought occurs to her, and she feels guilty for it: *at least now she won't have to worry about getting the call anymore.*

She wants to know what happened, the details, but it's too soon — he speaks slowly and clearly, but all she hears is: quick, a knife, Chapel Street ... And the blood swooshing around inside her ears. *Would the police band play something by the Foo Fighters at Sam's funeral?* Where are these stupid thoughts coming from? Maybe this is somehow her fault: for not loving Sam enough, for not trying harder, for screwing Aidan. Maybe Sam was suspicious, distracted, more reckless than usual, and let his guard down. He can't be dead; they're going to have another baby. The ground sways, the world shifts, she lets Aidan hold her in his arms. More guilt froths to the surface. She has a flash of the first time here: citrus scent, the warmth, the softness of his flannelette shirt against her face at Manny's party. Today it's a business shirt, rain-damp, and the buttons scratch her face.

'The twins at kinder?'

She nods against his chest.

'I'll ring Ryan,' he says.

'Wait a minute, please.' She grips his arms.

'I'm so sorry, Brigitte.'

When Ryan arrives, he rushes to Brigitte on the couch, and Aidan disappears with the kids. Ryan wraps an arm around her shoulders, and they sit quietly for a long time. She hears his watch ticking, traffic rumbling past on the street, a vacuum cleaner buzzing next door.

'Want a cup of tea?' Ryan finally breaks the silence.

She shakes her head.

'Glass of water?'

She nods, and he goes to get her one. She hears him and Aidan having a whispered conversation in the kitchen, but she can't make out what they're saying. Ryan returns with her water.

'You need to rest.' He hands her a tablet.

She swallows it and lies on the couch. He kneels next to her, cradling her head and shoulders in his arms. She's not sure if the tears on her face are hers or his as she slides into sleep.

In a dream, she's naked in a crowd, at a club. Kurt Cobain is pushing his way towards her, wearing the brown sweater. He drapes a black, hooded robe over her shoulders.

A trail of white flowers with fresh-blood-coloured centres is strewn across the floor. She follows the trail outside to Sam lying in a children's inflatable swimming pool. He's holding Kitty in his hands. It's not water that fills the pool: it's blood. It spills over the sides and turns into an ocean. A puppy wearing the red collar runs along the shore, barking at the waves. Kurt Cobain walks along the jetty, jumps into the ocean, and calls her to swim out with him, but she's too scared. Pearly moonlight shimmers on the surface. He dives under, and doesn't come up. Then everything — the sand, the sea, the sky — turns black.

'You said you wouldn't leave me!' she screams at the ocean.

No answer. Only blackness.

The sound from next-door's radio drifts in: Paul Kelly, singing 'How to Make Gravy'. Is it morning or afternoon? Brigitte drags herself off the couch and staggers to the kitchen, groggy from Ryan's sleeping tablet. Aidan and the twins don't notice her standing in the doorway. They're too absorbed in making a gingerbread house — gluing the walls and roof together with thick white icing and decorating it with an obscene number of lollies. Finn's standing on a step, and Phoebe's sitting on the bench.

'Another lolly, please.'

'Shh, we don't want to wake your mum.' Aidan pops a jellybean into Phoebe's mouth.

'And me.' Finn opens his mouth like a baby bird.

God, they'll be up all night with that much sugar in them. Where's Sam? Then she remembers, and her legs turn to jelly. She holds onto the doorframe. The flouro light is too bright; it's flickering. She feels hot and then cold. Her vision blurs. Her ears are closed to sound. She's falling, fainting. Aidan catches her.

12

Brigitte stares at the traffic light on Bridge Road, waiting for it to change, even though it's green, and the cars behind are beeping. She goes through on the red. She glances over her shoulder at the empty child restraints. After a heartbeat of panic she remembers that the twins are at kinder. She's barely slept — two hours a night, max — since Sam died. Almost a week now. The dreams, the guilt, the physical pain — it's all worse.

The cigarette-smoking man isn't out the front of the home. The doors won't open. She's keyed in the wrong code. She tries again. She can't remember the numbers today. She leans a hand against the glass, tries to take a deep breath, but can't get enough air into her lungs. A carer opens the door from the inside. Brigitte tries to smile as if nothing is wrong, and forgets to sign the visitors' book.

Two carers are clearing out a room upstairs. One fills a cardboard box with personal belongings. The other removes the name card from the door: John Lilly. The cigarette-smoking man's name was John Lilly.

Papa's sitting in his chair, staring out the window at the Pelaco sign, with Tiger on his lap and a Bing Crosby cassette playing.

'Oh, Brigi,' he says when he looks up and sees her in the doorway. She rushes in, drops her bag on the floor, and slumps in the vinyl chair opposite him. Papa pushes Tiger off and reaches for her hands. She lowers her head — can't hold it up any longer. Tears flow down her face, her arms, and onto Papa's papery hands. She squeezes his hands tighter, slides off the chair, and kneels on the floor. She rests her head in his lap, ignoring the yeast-and-brine smell. He strokes her hair the way he strokes the cat. They sit like this for a long time, maybe an hour.

When she looks up, sunlight catches the blue-and-green swirls trapped inside the glass paperweight. She stares until her eyes lose focus, and her vision distorts the swirls — twists and slithers them like a snake. It's the serpent tattoo from her dreams. She blinks hard and looks away.

Papa has fallen asleep.

Brigitte can't breathe; the stale air, the body, and the hospital-like smells smother her. If she doesn't get out she's going to suffocate.

It's worse in the lift. She grasps the rail, and presses her cheek against the cold metal.

On the street, she gulps air and walks down the hill without noticing where she's going. The pub, Bridge Road, the hairdresser, McDonalds, the police station all blur past.

She stops at the playground and watches a man chase two giggling children around the black-and-yellow play equipment. It's not fair that Finn and Phoebe have to grow up without a father. She scuffs the tan bark with the toe of her shoe. An old Asian man in a blue tracksuit does chin-ups on the monkey bars; dogs run without leads on the oval, which is enclosed by a black mesh fence. Brigitte looks towards St Ignatius's church: the building is obscured, but the spire is visible above the roof of the police station. *Not fair, Sam. Not fucking fair.*

She pulls off her jacket, ties it around her waist, and marches around the oval. The burnt-biscuit smell of factory smoke catches at the back of her throat as she breathes too quickly in through her nose and out through her mouth. Halfway around, the four goal posts blur into eight, and then back to four. She stops and leans against the fence until the dizziness subsides. When she straightens up, something in her spine crunches, slips, and doesn't go back into place. She sees spots, squeezes her eyes closed, and grips the fence. An old memory surfaces to block out the pain: her childhood safe place, the sleeper compartment of Dan's semitrailer. She remembers the warmth, the rocking of the motor; the smell of Kitten car polish; and the sound of Johnny Cash on the eight-track tape player singing about love lost and loneliness.

After they started primary school, Brigitte and Ryan didn't go away with Dan much anymore; only occasionally in the holidays. The flash of headlights across the curtains, and then the hiss of the Kenworth's air brakes would disturb the sleeping suburb and signal Dan's return home after a week or so on the road. He'd be up the next morning, with dark bags — more like suitcases — under his eyes, whistling while he made pancakes for them. One time he added a little red food dye to the mixture. The pink pancakes became a fabled childhood memory: so special, so exotic.

Joan didn't love Dan. Brigitte doesn't begrudge her that; everybody has their reasons, their circumstances. Who knows what Joan's reasons or circumstances were, or what Joan imagined them to be. Depression-related or just melodrama? Joan cried about everything, but she didn't cry when Dan died.

Brigitte has no tears left. She opens her eyes. A weak guttural moan escapes from her mouth. Maybe the number of tears is not indicative of the amount of love. But she did love Sam. Not at the start. And maybe not enough at the end. But somewhere in between, she loved him — especially after the twins were born. She must have; she just can't remember the feeling right now. He inherited his bad temper from his father, but he never hurt her. Not really. And he was never rough with the kids, never smacked them. It was a pity that work was more important than his family.

Dan's friends were always around when Dan was away. 'Uncle Len', the mechanic, serviced the car. 'Uncle Keith', the local driver, painted the house and did odd jobs. Some uncle always responded quickly to her call when Joan got scared at night on her own with the kids.

Brigitte leans over the fence to vomit, but her stomach is empty — she forgot to put food in there today. She dry-retches and spits on the grass.

Joan wrote a eulogy for Dan's funeral. She practised it over and over in front of the mirror, as though it was a Logie acceptance speech. But on the day she got so drunk she couldn't do it. Uncle Keith had to hold her up on the way out of the chapel. One of her black stiletto heels snapped when she tripped and twisted her ankle.

Brigitte limps around the rest of the oval circumference. Pigeons bob their iridescent heads, picking at something in the grass. A fire truck screams past. She braces for the searing nerve pain as she lowers herself onto a park bench.

She's struggling with her deep breathing, trying to flood the pain zones with pure, white healing light, when two wasted teenagers sit down next to her. They scratch at sores on their arms, and discuss some doctor in Lennox Street.

★★★

Brigitte waits on the red couch under the 'complications of smoking' poster, chewing her little fingernail. Classical music is playing. A chart of melanomas hangs above a plastic palm tree; she has a mole on her back that looks a bit like one of them. She tenses and un-tenses the muscles in her legs, and keeps chewing her little fingertip until she tastes blood. She's been waiting for 15 minutes. She shouldn't be here, wasting the doctor's time. She's not sick. If he doesn't call her within one minute, she's leaving. Sixty cat and dog, fifty-nine cat and dog, fifty-eight cat and dog …

She starts when she hears her name, and follows the doctor into his consulting room. A painting of a waterfall hangs on the wall: *so relaxing*.

'I'm Doctor Rhys Michaels.' He shakes her cold, sweaty hand. Dodgy Doctor Rhys, the teenagers at the park called him. *Getcha whatever you want. Doesn't ask questions.* 'I don't think I've met you before.'

'No, I usually see Doctor Walpole in Clifton Hill. But I couldn't get an appointment today.' It's a lie.

'What can I help you with, Brigitte?' He sits down, and gestures for her to take the patient's chair next to his desk.

'Do you mind if I stand?'

'Back pain?'

'A bit. And some trouble sleeping. My husband …' The knot in her throat is suddenly too big for her voice to get around. She clears her throat. *Come on, say it.* 'Died.'

'I'm sorry to hear that.' His voice is modulated, comforting, practised. He reaches out and pats her hand. His skin feels smooth, cool — manicured and exfoliated.

She looks at the shelves of faded medical textbooks, disposable gloves, and tubs of specimen jars.

'Do you have any children?'

'Twins — a boy and a girl.' On the bottom shelf, stacks of medication sample packets are lined up next to snow globes, prescription pads, drink bottles with medical logos, and a Nike shoebox.

She looks up as he touches the blood-pressure machine on his desk and tries to straighten her back as though she is a person who has nothing wrong with her, a person who doesn't need her blood pressure checked.

'How old?' he asks.

'Four.'

'A lovely age. Do you have enough support?' Sincere concern, eye contact, a furrowing of his brow — all practised.

She nods, and struggles to take a shallow breath.

Dodgy Doctor Rhys types and prints a prescription for Stilnox.

Doctor Walpole would never prescribe sleeping tablets for her. He'd recommend chamomile tea and relaxation exercises, or something. *Breathe pure, white light into the pain zones, Brigitte.* The last time she saw him he suggested that her memory loss was caused by repression rather than head trauma, and recommended hypnotherapy. He's full of shit.

'I know it's hard,' Dodgy Doctor Rhys says, 'but you need to try to relax. Be kind to yourself, and organise some time out from the kids.'

'I feel like I can't breathe.'

'That's just anxiety. I'm going to give you a prescription for some Valium as well — just to help you get through this time.'

Doctor Walpole would bang on about the time she couldn't stop taking the Valium her previous doctor had prescribed as a muscle relaxant ... her addictive personality type ... and the hallucinations.

'Anxiety is a normal reaction to grief.'

Yes, having your husband stabbed to death because he got in between two junkies having a domestic dispute will do that to you. Especially if it was your fault, because he was distracted by having found out you were screwing his workmate. *Uncle Aidan.* Sam must have known. And now he can't protect you anymore, and his workmate is going to send you to jail. Who wouldn't feel anxious?

He types something in her file. 'Is there anything else I can help you with today?'

She looks at the Di-Gesic logo on his pen, and thinks of the almost-happy, hazy days of wine and painkillers after her second useless back operation. Would it be pushing it to ask for something for the pain as well? She decides against it, and shakes her head, remembering how hard the medication withdrawal was. And the hallucinations.

'Take care then.' He stands.

She changes her mind. 'Actually, I'm waiting to have an operation on my back.' The lies come easily. 'The pain's been really bad lately. Nurofen doesn't help much. Do you think I could get something stronger for the pain?'

He frowns, types, and reads something on the screen. Uh-oh, has he found a link to her medical records?

'You don't have a history of alcoholism or substance abuse?'

She shakes her head.

'No mental illness in the family?'

'No.'

He types another prescription, this time for Di-Gesic. He tells her to take two tablets every four hours for pain, and to follow the directions carefully. And he stresses the importance of not mixing it with alcohol.

'Of course not.' She makes a serious face, furrows her brow a bit, mimicking his body language — practised.

'Would you like another appointment to talk to somebody? A counsellor?' More sincere eye-contact.

She smiles politely, but shakes her head.

'All right, but please come back if you need to. And good luck with the back operation.'

She thanks him and takes the prescriptions. Just having them in her hands makes her feel stronger as she heads home to write a eulogy.

13

Sam's funeral is big, of course. Too big. A sea of dark blue; solemn glances, respectful nods, sweaty armpits, too much supermarket deodorant, TV cameras. Heat radiates from the footpath out the front. It would have been a nice day for the beach or the zoo. Brigitte hasn't attended many funerals, but they've all been on cold, bleak days — appropriate weather. Sam was an atheist, but Maggie and Doug Campbell have insisted on a religious service. They forbade the police band from playing anything by the Foo Fighters, but reluctantly agreed to 'Into my Arms' by the organist at the church.

Brigitte looks towards the domed wooden ceiling, and wishes she could collapse from the heat, be taken away in an ambulance so it would all be over. Maybe she should have started on Doctor Rhys's meds to help her through this. Or at least had a drink. No, she's not like her mother. She stands, sober, at the altar when it's her turn, and pays tribute to 'Detective Senior Sergeant Sam Campbell, my kind, generous husband who was the best father there could be for Finn and Phoebe.'

A few coughs, sniffles, and scuffs of mourners' shoes.

'He loved his job and gave it everything he could offer, and I believe this is why he was so successful in his chosen profession.' She glances at the coffin draped with the Australian flag, and at Sam's bravery medals — useless now — displayed on a small table, bathed in golden, stained-glass light.

'He was courageous,' she says, 'deeply respected by the community, a good bloke who devoted his life to — as our son Finn would say — keeping the good people safe.' She looks out at Finn, who's sitting on Ryan's lap in the front pew; she struggles to smile, takes a breath, and clears her throat. 'He died protecting the community, and this shows the dangers our brave police officers confront every day. Sam's death is a reminder of how precious and fragile life is.' Her eyes fall on Aidan, and she averts them quickly. 'Sam, we love you; you will always be in our hearts.'

After the service, the police band plays, and officers form a guard of honour along the street. A police helicopter does a fly-over as the mourners walk to the cars.

Tears have left streaks on Phoebe's face, and Finn has dried snot smeared across his cheek. Aidan finds some bottled water and tissues in their car; he wipes Phoebe's tears and cleans Finn's face. Joan, in her bright-red suit — the colour for mourning in South Africa, apparently — smokes a cigarette on the footpath.

'Can you be our daddy now?' Finn says to Aidan.

Joan coughs on her smoke, and Brigitte grips the car seat. Aidan explains to the twins that their daddy will always be their daddy.

A police escort leads the mourning cars, through a heat-haze shimmer, to the cemetery.

At the gravesite, Aidan flashes intense, concerned looks at Brigitte over the coffin. She ignores him. A carer pushes Papa up next to her in a wheelchair. Joan pats her arm and asks if she's all right. Phoebe keeps asking how Daddy is going to get out of the coughing box. Ryan shoulders Joan out of the way, and Brigitte squeezes his hand — too hard. She must be hurting him, her fingernails in his flesh, but he doesn't flinch.

After the final goodbyes, Brigitte and the twins lead the mourners in scattering rose petals over the coffin. What would their next child have looked like? Would it have been a boy or a girl? Surely not another set of twins? Ryan coaxes her away with an arm encircling her waist. 'You were very brave at the church,' he whispers.

The private wake is at Maggie and Doug's house. Brigitte sits in a corner, hoping her brown suit will help her blend into the brown-leather chair and brown-brick feature wall. It doesn't work. She nods politely at all the words of sympathy and the offers of help, but she doesn't really hear. It's as if she's watching herself from far away. Her head feels heavy, drowsy, as if she could nod off in the chair. Aidan brings her a plate of sandwiches and a glass of whisky. She takes the whisky.

Joan has taken off her jacket to reveal a see-through blouse. She swishes the amber liquid around in her glass. It's probably brandy, without lime or soda — she gave up mixers long ago. She's perched on a stool at Doug's leather-and-timber bar, her legs crossed, circling a skinny ankle around and around, slipping a heel in and out of a red stiletto — flirting with Doug.

Brigitte feels nauseated. She puts her drink on a table and rushes to the toilet.

She sucks in a few short, shallow breaths in her parents-in-law's cool, peaceful bathroom, with its gold taps, floral feature-tiles, fluffy purple toilet-seat cover, and lavender air-freshener. She lies on the floor, her head resting on the bath mat — it smells of talcum powder and mould. She bends her knees to relieve her lower-back pain, and stares at the ceiling. In the corner, a small grey spider traps a fly, paralysed by lethal venom, in its web. Sunlight glints on the silvery net as the spider wraps its prey in sticky threads of silk. Does the fly feel comfort now? Warm, anesthetised, swaddled, the end near? Brigitte marvels at the intricacy and sardonic beauty as she closes her eyes.

Joan bursts in. 'What are you doing? Get up, silly girl.'

'I feel sick.'

Joan pulls her up by an arm. 'It's just stress.' She turns on a gold tap. 'Splash some cold water on your face.'

Brigitte looks at her white face in the mirror: dark circles under her eyes, make-up smudged, hair frizzy from the humidity and escaping from its chignon.

Joan fishes around in her knock-off Louis Vuitton handbag. She hands her a tablet.

'What is it?'

'Xanax. Now pull yourself together and get back out there.'

It's time to leave when Maggie starts confiding in Brigitte about what a violent bastard Sam's biological father had been.

Brigitte finds Aidan talking to Sam's sister, and asks him to take her and the twins home. She doesn't say goodbye to anybody, not even to Ryan.

That night, Kerry brings over a bottle of Johnnie Walker.

Some sorrows have floated and some have been drowned in half the bottle when Aidan comes into the living room and asks if Brigitte's all right.

'What do you reckon, mate?' Kerry says, slurring.

'I wasn't asking you.'

Brigitte stares at the striding man in top hat and tails on the Johnnie Walker label, as though he's an old friend.

'Where're the twins?'

She shrugs. She's not capable of putting them to bed, so Aidan does. When he comes back, she's nodding off, holding the glass in both hands as if warming herself over a hot drink. She shivers.

'That's probably enough for tonight.' He takes away the bottle.

'Hey!' Her eyes snap open. 'I buried my husband today. You can't tell me what I can and can't do.' There's too much of Joan in her voice.

She stands, sways, lifts her face to him, thinks about kissing him, is angry at herself for the thought, angry at him for even being here, angry at Sam for leaving her and the twins. She balls her hands into fists, and beats his chest. Kerry sneaks out. He lets her take out her anger on him for a while, then holds her hands, lowers them to her sides, and lets her fall against him — again.

'It's OK, Brigitte. You'll be all right.'

'No, I won't.'

'You're stronger than you think you are.'

'Because of Eric Tucker?' She pulls away from him, suddenly sounding sober.

'Let's talk about this later.'

'You think I had something to do with killing him, don't you?'

'I was wrong to discuss that investigation with you.'

'Will I go to jail?'

'Stop it.'

'I can't go to jail. I have two babies to look after.'

'Then be strong for them.'

She takes a step back, steadies herself against the table, and walks away towards the twins' bedroom.

14

'Good kick, Finny!' Aidan kicks a soccer ball back to Finn down the sideway.

Brigitte goes outside and watches for a minute with hands on hips, tapping a foot. 'Time for kinder, Finn.'

He complains, wanting to keep playing.

'I have to go to work, too, mate,' Aidan says. 'But we can play again this afternoon.'

'Inside, Finn, and get your bag.' She turns to Aidan. 'What do you think you're doing?'

'Huh?'

'You're not their father.'

'And your point is?'

She doesn't have a point. She folds her arms across her chest. 'When are you going to talk to me about Eric Tucker?'

Aidan glances at Finn dawdling in through the back door. 'Not now.' He picks up the soccer ball and bounces it. 'I have some good news for you, though.'

She twists her mouth and raises her eyebrows.

'My wife's been talking to me — looks like she might take me back after all.' He turns the ball over in his hands. 'I shouldn't be here for much longer.'

She should feel pleased, relieved.

'Look, I know you don't like me, Brigitte, but why don't you just let me help out a bit? With the twins. While I'm still around. While you're sorting stuff out.'

She's about to tell him to fuck off, but a thick, heavy tiredness blankets her, and any help would be appreciated — even his. She looks at a crack in the concrete, and says softly, 'OK.'

He bounces the ball again and throws it to her. She misses.

'See you tonight then,' he says.

How about a kiss goodbye? Have a good day, honey? Happy families. When he leaves, she leans against the fence and allows herself to indulge in self-pity for a minute or two — to imagine the bleak days ahead, a flat line of loneliness and pain. No leaving the porch light on at the end of the day; no partner to help, to break the monotony. Her limbs feel heavy, as if they're filled with cement. What if it's always going to be like this? What if it never gets any better?

'Let's go to kinder, Mummy!' Finn calls.

Aidan's right: she has to be strong, keep going for the twins. Sam never helped anyway. Wallowing time is over. She sighs and, with a huge effort, pushes herself off the fence.

★★★

She takes sharp, panicky breaths, and sweat beads on her skin as she paces the living room, grasping the Di-Gesic packet. She turns it over and over in her hands. Her back pain has gone up a degree: it's hard to sit; she can only stand or lie flat. If she sticks to the recommended dose, she'll be OK. It has to be better than the pain, better than going back to the hospital. Fear floods her body at the thought of it. Stupid tears fill her eyes, and she rubs them away. Anything is better than the hospital. Finally, she opens the packet — breaks the seal — pops two painkillers from the blister pack inside, and washes them down with a glass of water.

She sits on the couch with her laptop ready to work on an article but, instead, googles Kurt Cobain. His eyes were very blue. He committed suicide in 1994 — the year Eric Tucker was murdered, the year of the accident.

She has a memory from the start of that year: furniture

removalists carrying the last of Joan's furniture out of the old pink house in Brunswick. They'd left Ratsak, mice droppings, crumbs of rotten food, and a dried-out mouse in the square stain where the fridge had stood. 'Don't look so sad,' Joan said. 'This is a new beginning, not an ending.' Joan's car was packed to the roof. She drove Brigitte to Jennifer's share house in Fitzroy. Jennifer was a high school dropout — not even a real friend, just somebody whose father Joan knew. 'I need to see the stars again, Brigitte,' Joan said as she dropped her off with a cold kiss on the cheek. Jennifer's house smelled of bong water, dirty laundry, and spaghetti Bolognese. Brigitte had sat on the worn, flesh-coloured couch, and looked through *The Age* for job ads and flats to rent.

A memory from the end of that year (or is it from the start of the next?) bubbles up: in hospital, Sam had a partner with him, and was asking questions that made no sense, at first. Their words ran together, exhausting her. Her brain seemed to wobble inside her head. And Papa was there, telling them to bugger off and look for the bloody bastard in the blue Camry that had run her over. She slept and woke, and Sam was still there, or there again.

She follows a link to a conspiracy-theory website dedicated to how Kurt Cobain was murdered. It speculates that Courtney Love was involved. Among other inconsistencies in the Cobain case, it says that Kurt had injected far too much heroin to have been capable of pulling the trigger. His fingerprints weren't on the shotgun. And his suicide note was really a letter written to Courtney announcing he was leaving her.

What is she doing? She doesn't have time for dead rock stars. She closes the webpage and opens a Word document, but she's too tired to work. Her head is fuzzy; she needs to rest. She puts her laptop aside and lies on the floor, calves up on the couch to take pressure off her back. She closes her eyes — just for a minute.

In a dream, Papa and Ryan are fixing up the room at the back of Nana and Papa's old house. It's as big as a flat. A safe room — nobody will ever look for her here. A painting hangs on the wall: two sad, ghost-like figures embrace on a finger-painted canvas. The male figure holds a bouquet of white flowers with fresh-blood-coloured centres.

Nana steps in front of the painting. 'It's under the carpet,' she says.

Brigitte kneels and rips it up, pulls up the floorboards, digs under the room. Her fingers bleed, her nails black with dirt. It's wrapped in the yellow bunny rug: the little blue box tied with white ribbon. A shadow falls across it.

'Don't open it,' a gravelly voice says.

Too late. It's open. A bright-blue butterfly flutters out. Inside is a letter from Kurt Cobain, the red dog collar and the key attached to the letter J.

A siren rings.

The phone's ringing. *Sam? What's happened?* She gets up from the floor, rushes to the phone in the hallway, stumbles, trips — her lower limbs have fallen asleep, and she's got pins and needles.

She fumbles with the receiver, drops it, and picks it up. 'Hello.' Her voice is hoarse. She rubs her calves with her free hand.

'Brigitte?'

'Yes.'

'It's Yasmine from kinder.'

'What's wrong? Are Finn and Phoebe OK?'

'Yes. We've been trying to ring you — it's twenty past four. They're waiting for you.'

Shit. Twenty minutes late. She rubs her eyes. 'I'm so sorry. I got held up. I'll be there in five minutes.'

The car keys? The car keys! She up-ends her hand bag: receipts, water bottles, pens, Tic Tacs, toy cars, pills, and other assorted crap spill out. And keys. She grabs them (and the pills), and leaves everything else in a pile on the fake Persian rug.

Kinder is deserted. Brigitte flies through the door. It smells of pine; they've decorated the Christmas tree in the foyer. 'Morningtown Ride' rocks and rolls and rides from the CD player. She shivers — God she hates this song. She bursts into the three-year-olds' room. Phoebe is crying, and Finn is pushing a car backwards and forwards on the rug. She crouches, and opens her arms for her babies. 'I'm sorry,' she says to Yasmine. 'I had some work that took a bit longer than expected.'

Yasmine is cheerful and polite as always. 'It's OK. We knew something important must have come up.' She's taken out her nose ring; the piercing is infected.

Brigitte clicks Finn and Phoebe into their child restraints in the car, and finds lollypops for them in the glove box. 'Sorry, guys.' She seatbelts herself in, and looks at them in the rear-view mirror, sucking away happily: they have her nose, her mouth, Sam's eyes.

'When is Daddy coming back?' Phoebe asks.

15

It's 7.00pm. Bedtime. Here we go again. Brigitte lacks the energy for the night-time ritual and drama. She's begrudgingly grateful that Aidan is here to help.

From the bathroom, she calls the twins to come and get ready for bed. Finn comes immediately and stands on the step stool at the basin. She helps him put toothpaste on his Bob the Builder toothbrush. Brigitte calls Phoebe again.

Finn brushes and rinses and spits all by himself.

'Good boy, Finny.' He lets her help wash his hands and face. She does up the top button of his Spider Man pyjamas, and he runs off. She can hear Phoebe arguing with Aidan in the lounge room.

Please just hurry up and go to bed. Brigitte looks at herself in the mirror. She's lost weight. She should pluck her eyebrows while she's waiting, but she can't be bothered.

'Not tired, Aidan!'

'If you weren't tired you wouldn't be speaking in that voice.'

'Not going to bed.'

Please, just for once, make it easy. Brigitte grinds her teeth and leans against the wall.

'Then you won't get a story or a cuddle.'

'Don't care!' Bang. Something hits the wall.

'Phoebe!'

The sound of naughty little footsteps patters through the kitchen.

'What's going on out there, Phoebe?' Brigitte says.

'Aidan angry.'

'Really? What did you do to Aidan?'

'Nothing.'

'It didn't sound like nothing.'

Phoebe sticks out her bottom lip. 'Not tired.'

'OK. Let's just get you clean anyway.'

Phoebe protests and squirms while Brigitte brushes her teeth and rubs a face washer over her face.

Brigitte drags her by the arm to bed — past a hole in the plasterboard wall that's the same shape as her plastic toy tiger.

Aidan is sitting on Finn's bed, reading him a story. He pauses, looks at Brigitte over the top of the book, and then keeps reading. He's wearing the shirt with the missing button. She feels a flutter in her chest: a side-effect of Doctor Rhys's medication?

Phoebe chooses Dr. Seuss's *Green Eggs and Ham*. Again. Brigitte tucks her in and lies next to her. 'That Sam-I-am! That Sam-I-am! I do not like that Sam-I-am.'

'Sam is Daddy.'

'Yes.' Brigitte turns the page.

'Daddy is sleeping with Kitty under the ground now.'

Brigitte puts *Green Eggs and Ham* aside, and cuddles Phoebe. She smells of sandalwood and rose. She rests her face in the crook of her little neck, kisses her, and strokes her fairy-floss hair until she falls asleep. Finn and Aidan have fallen asleep, too. She kisses Finn's lips and turns off the light.

Aidan stumbles out a couple of hours later while she's watching TV and procrastinating about writing her article. His button is in the sewing box in the laundry; she should sew it back on for him.

'Good night,' he says.

She nods. Her back is hurting, and there are shimmers of pain in her pelvis.

When the light goes off in the bungalow, she opens a bottle of wine and takes two painkillers.

16

Ida rests on the chair by the lift, her head lolling forward onto her chest. Nobody notices that she looks kind of bluish-grey, like over-boiled egg yolk. Brigitte tells Petula, who waits until all the residents have made their way into the dining room before calling an ambulance to take her away.

Papa's seated near the end of a long table, turning a paper napkin over in his hands. He smiles when he looks up and sees Brigitte squeezing past chairs to get to him. She kisses him and takes the chair in front of her place card. He's wearing his only suit — brown and mothballed.

The staff are wearing Santa hats, and the walls of the dining room are lined with tinsel. Crackers and paper tablecloths bordered with holly and ivy adorn the tables. A balding man plays Christmas songs on a keyboard in the corner: 'White Christmas'. Two carers try to get Rose to take her medication, but she won't sit down. Joyce spits something into her napkin, and Roy complains that the paper hats in the crackers aren't as good as last year's. It's just like the Christmas party at kinder earlier in the week.

When the staff bring around jugs of fruit punch, Brigitte fills two plastic cups with it. 'Merry Christmas, Papa.' They touch their cups together. She takes a big drink.

'Kids at school?' Papa says.

'Kinder.'

'You right?'

She looks into her cup.

Papa pats her arm, 'You'll be right.'

She tops up their drinks.

Petula and the resident podiatrist come over for chats. While the podiatrist is talking bunions with Papa, Petula bends down to Brigitte and rubs her shoulder. 'We have people you can talk to here — counsellors, not just for the residents.'

'Thank you. I'm OK.' She tries to smile.

'Hard time of the year to be without a loved one. Especially with little ones. Just let us know if you need anything.'

Brigitte nods, and tickles the roof of her mouth with her tongue.

'What'd she say to you?' Papa asks when Petula moves away.

'Nothing. Just merry Christmas.'

'None of her bloody business.'

Brigitte takes a big sip of punch.

She's had three cups by the time the staff start relaying plates of lunch to the tables. Ham, roast meat (presumably beef, or maybe pork), potatoes, cauliflower, mushy peas, and tomatoes from a tin, all drowning in a pool of anaemic gravy.

She picks at the food, eating less than Papa does. They both wave away the Christmas pudding and custard, but have more punch.

Her head wobbles as she rests it on her hand and listens to Papa talk about the war. She's had too much to drink. And the Valium wasn't a good idea either. *Stupid.* She has to pick up the twins from kinder in an hour. She refills her cup with water.

The punch wasn't that strong. She should be right to drive — doesn't have far to go. She fumbles with the keys and opens the car. There's a lot of traffic in Church Street. It takes a long time to get a clear run to make a U-turn.

Uniformed cops are stopping cars on Nicholson Street. *Shit.* Random breath-testing. She smiles at the uniform: *Please just let me go past.* But he doesn't — he waves her over. She breaks out in a sweat as she parks and turns off the ignition.

'Have you drunk any alcohol today?' the uniform says.

'Um, might have had a glass of punch. I thought it was non-alcoholic, but maybe it wasn't. At the old people's home. Their Christmas party.'

He tells her to blow into the tube on the device.

'I'm Sam Campbell's wife. Do you think you could just let me go through?' She tries a slow blink, but it doesn't work.

'Sorry, m'am. It doesn't matter whose wife you are, you still have to take the breath test.'

Prick. He has no idea what he's doing. She blows.

He looks at the reading; she inhales deeply, holds it, feels dizzy.

'Unfortunately, your blood-alcohol content reading is over the legal limit, m'am. I'm going to have to ask you to step out of your vehicle and accompany one of the officers to the station for a second breath-test.'

Fuck. She exhales, rubs her forehead, and does as she's told.

'Can I make a phone call? I need to organise somebody to pick up my kids.'

He nods. He's young, too cocky.

She calls Ryan.

'Hey, Brigi. What's up?'

'Nothing. Can you pick up the twins from kinder?'

'What's wrong?'

'Just do it, will you?'

'Tell me what's happened.'

'Nothing.'

'What?'

'I've been pulled over for drink-driving, all right?'

'What!'

She kicks the dirt on the side of the road.

'Did you tell them who you are?'

'They don't care.'

'Call Aidan then.'

'I don't want to call him.'

'Just call him.'

'No.' She hangs up.

***

'Brigitte. What the fuck?' Aidan strides into the colourless room where she's being detained at Richmond police station. 'I don't have time for this.'

She looks up. He seems taller than she remembers. And more attractive. She looks away. Ryan better not have called him. Maybe he just heard — somehow. Fucking cops always know everything. Almost everything.

'Where're the twins?'

'Ryan's getting them.'

'Pretty fucking irresponsible.'

She feels like a naughty teenager.

'Come on.'

'What?'

'Take you home.'

'Aren't you busy working?'

'Yes.'

She's been sitting too long; her back is aching, pain radiating into her legs. It takes two tries to get out of the chair. He reaches for her arm, and it is pity, not lust, she thinks she sees in his eyes. She pushes him away.

'You should go back to the doctor.'

Doctors have never helped anything before. They let Dan die, couldn't save Sam, and made her live when maybe she wasn't meant to. Or was that supposed to be God? Doctors and God — both fucking useless.

On the way out through the automatic doors, Aidan says, 'Sam said you just need another back operation and you'll be right. But you're too stubborn to go back.'

'Is that right? That what you two used to sit around talking about, instead of catching criminals?'

He drives her home in a marked car. It stinks of takeaway food and sweat. She doesn't believe that it was the only vehicle available.

'Will I lose my licence?'

'No.'

'What about my car?'

'Don't worry. I'll bring it home tonight.'

She chews her fingernails.

'Must've been good punch with the oldies.'

She doesn't speak, and has a quick sideways look at him — he's trying not to laugh.

Of course, Kerry has to be out in her front yard when they pull up across the road. Brigitte rushes inside, past Ryan in the hallway. The twins run out to see, and she hears Aidan turn on the siren for them.

***

It's 7.55pm on the microwave clock. The twins are asleep, but Aidan's not home yet. Sober and drug-free for the first time since Sam's funeral, Brigitte stares out the kitchen window at next door's brown brick wall, wondering — not worrying — where he is. Probably out somewhere with his wife.

Some of the tension leaves her shoulders when she hears the click of the padlock and the squeak of the side gate. But she jumps when he taps on the window. She slides it open.

'Can I come in?'

She tilts her head towards the kitchen door and unlocks it. He's holding a pizza in a cardboard takeaway box, and has a bottle of red wine under his arm. 'Car's out the front.' He throws her the keys. 'Air-con wasn't working, so I had it fixed.' She follows him to the lounge room, where he places the pizza and wine on the coffee table. 'Didn't feel like eating alone tonight. Hope you don't mind.'

She's about to say she does mind, stops herself, and says, 'Thank you. For everything today.' The pizza smells good; she feels hungry for the first time in a while.

She gets some glasses and plates from the kitchen, comes back, and sits next to him on the floor, their backs against the couch — too close. She moves away a bit.

They've finished the pizza, and she's on her second glass of wine when she says, 'Was I a suspect?' A guilty person wouldn't ask that.

He swills the wine around in his glass. 'A person of interest at the time.'

'Do you think Sam thought I did it?' Of course Sam thought she did it.

'Who knows what Sam was thinking?' He drinks some wine. 'I bet I know what he was thinking *with*.'

She narrows her eyes.

'And he almost lost his job over the missing evidence.'

Silence. The boom gates ding-ding-ding at the train station.

'Eric Tucker was scum,' Aidan says. 'Used musicians to carry drugs, history of domestic violence, victims all too scared to lay charges. He got what he deserved — doesn't matter who did it.'

'Why was I at his apartment?'

'How do you know this?'

'Ever heard of the internet?'

'Looks like you may have lived there.'

'No.' She shakes her head. 'I lived with Nana and Papa.'

'That's what Eddie and Ryan say.'

'You think they're lying?'

'Dunno.' He pours more wine. 'Tell you the truth — I reckon somebody else was there. A friend, a neighbour, maybe the boyfriend.'

She rubs the scar on her forehead.

'Or the caretaker. Maybe he did more than just find the body.'

'The caretaker!'

'Yeah, Shane McMahon.'

She opens her mouth to speak, but says nothing. He waits a couple of beats before correcting himself, '*Sean* McMahon.'

Good trick, Aidan. But anybody could have learnt that name from the news. Not saying the name makes her look as suspicious as saying it. 'He topped himself with a shotgun up at his parents' farm, not long after Tucker was murdered.'

She doesn't flinch. He plays eyeball chicken with her. He blinks first — a slow blink, with long lashes.

'And the boyfriend?' She has to ask.

He nods. 'Matt Elery. Says you were with him at the time of Tucker's murder.'

She shakes her head. 'He's lying. And if he was my boyfriend, why didn't he come to see me after the accident?'

'This is the funny bit. Reckons Sam told him you'd disappeared, that the police never found you.'

She frowns, and stares into her glass.

'Want me to organise a meeting?'

She shakes her head slowly, and looks at the rug on the floor.

'Have a think about it. But I won't be working on this for much longer,' he says. 'The Cold Case Unit's being scrapped. I'm being shuffled back to Homicide — the Purana gangland taskforce.'

'But, Aid.' Her head snaps up. 'That's really dangerous.'

He turns and looks at her like she's crazy. Somehow they've ended up sitting close together again, their legs almost touching.

'What about this case?' She picks at the fringe on the rug.

'It'll be quietly filed away, so you don't have to worry about it anymore.'

She doesn't believe him. He finishes his wine. She feels sleepy, her head heavy; she would like to rest it on his shoulder.

He stands, and places his empty glass on the table. 'See you in the morning then.'

'And ...'

'Yes?'

'Were you really investigating me the whole time, even at Manny's party?'

'What do you think?'

She shrugs, and watches him walk towards the kitchen. He stops and turns in the doorway. 'I wasn't. Not at Manny's party.' He closes the door softly behind him as he leaves.

17

'Where's Aidan?' Red sauce splatters on Phoebe's cheek as she slurps up a strand of spaghetti.

'Out,' Brigitte says.

'Out where?'

'Having dinner with a friend.'

'His wife?'

'Yes.'

'Will he be home to read us a story?' Finn says.

'No.'

Phoebe pushes her bowl aside, her bottom lip comes out, and she starts crying. Finn joins in.

'Stop it!' Brigitte's back is killing her. Since the drink-driving incident, she's been trying to be responsible, curbing her alcohol intake and taking the meds only when she really needs them.

'Hurry up and finish your dinner. It's bedtime.'

They bawl louder. Brigitte covers her ears and grinds her teeth. Maybe just a Valium — even half of one — wouldn't hurt.

Without Aidan's help it takes longer to get the twins ready for bed. When they're finally asleep, Brigitte sits at the table with a hot-water bottle against her back, and her head in her hands.

Her stomach flutters when she hears the side gate. She wasn't expecting him this early, was even thinking he might not come home at all tonight. But it's not the usual click and squeak — it's a rattle. Brigitte frowns, stands, and walks to the window. Another rattle. She pulls back the curtain. It's raining and dark, but she can tell that the figure on the other side of the gate is not Aidan. The figure tries to climb the gate, falls awkwardly to the ground, and has a couple more failed attempts. Brigitte watches, frozen, as the figure looks around — doesn't notice her at the window — wheels the bin over, and uses it to stand on. She holds her breath, her heart bolting as the figure straddles the top of the gate, pauses for a moment, and then tentatively drops down in the sideway. Gruesome crime-scene images flash through her mind. *All women alone, with young children.* You need to be careful: Aidan's words. She hasn't been careful. She hasn't even locked the back door.

She unfreezes, wrenches her phone off the charger in the kitchen, and calls Aidan as she locks the door. The figure runs down the sideway, past the window.

'What's wrong?' Aidan takes the call, and she can hear restaurant or pub sounds in the background.

'There's somebody in the backyard.' Her hands shake, and she can hardly breathe.

'Sure it's not just a cat?'

'It's a person.'

'Calm down.' The restaurant sounds fade, and a door closes. 'Stay inside with the kids, check the doors and windows are locked, and I'll get a car to come around.'

'Aidan, I'm really scared.'

'Be there as soon as I can.' He hangs up, and she rushes to check on the twins. They're sound asleep.

A squad car comes, with the siren on, within minutes. The police lights flash puddles of runny colour on the wet road.

It appears that the intruder jumped the back fence and ran off down the laneway. After they've looked around and completed an incident report, Brigitte walks out to the car with the officers, and apologises for wasting their time.

'Not at all,' the woman says. 'Lotta crazies around. Can't be too careful.'

Most of the street's residents have come out of their houses to see what's going on. A taxi pulls up, and Aidan steps out. With his wife. Brigitte's heart flips, and she starts shaking again. She hugs herself and rubs her upper arms — pretending to be cold or still scared. This is worse than the intruder. God, she needs a drink.

Aidan strides towards her. 'You OK?'

She nods.

'The twins?'

'Slept through it all.'

He goes over to have a word with the officers, and then he and his wife follow Brigitte down the sideway. He stops to lock the gate, then catches up and introduces them outside the back door. He calls her 'Brig', and she's not sure if she's pleased or annoyed by the familiarity. She feels her neck flush. His wife's name is Megan. She's tall and strong-looking. She looks like a lawyer, wearing a designer suit and polished shoes with high heels and little buckles on the sides. Her glossy, brown hair falls to her shoulders, a line across the middle where it must have been pulled into a ponytail or a bun. Brigitte pictured her as blonde. And smaller.

They look perfect together: a couple on a department-store catalogue cover. Their cheeks are pink from the weather, or maybe the alcohol they had with dinner; a few raindrops glisten on their shoulders. They're standing so close together that Brigitte can't tell who is holding the folded black umbrella between them. She looks down at her tatty slippers, track pants, and faded Nick Cave T-shirt.

'Aidan's told me all about you.' Megan holds out her hand to shake, displaying perfect fingernails.

Brigitte frowns.

'Good things.' She smiles. 'You're still shaking, you poor thing.' She places her other hand on top — no wedding band — and sandwiches Brigitte's hand between her manicured ones. 'Want us to come in with you for a while?'

Brigitte shakes her head and pulls her hand away. 'I'm fine. Might just have a drink to calm down.'

'Good idea,' says Megan. 'Have you got some Valium or something?'

Aidan gives Brigitte a stern look. She gives him a wide-eyed *What?* look.

'Aidan will come over and check on you later.' Megan looks at him. 'Won't you?'

He nods. Tears prickle Brigitte's eyes, and tickling the roof of her mouth with her tongue doesn't stop them. She turns and hurries into the house before Aidan and Megan see. She locks the door as they walk to the bungalow.

She stops in front of the fridge and rests her forehead against it for a few minutes. He's probably kissing Megan out there; she's sucking his soft, full lips. Brigitte opens the fridge door and takes out a bottle of wine. Now he's peeling the clothes off her perfect, strong body — no kids, plenty of time for the gym, flat stomach, no scars. Brigitte puts the wine back and slams the fridge door shut. Now he's fucking her. Brigitte stands on a step stool to reach the bottle of Johnnie Walker in the top cupboard. She pours herself a glass, a big one, and washes down a couple of painkillers with it.

Banging on the back door wakes her from her stupor. She's on the couch with a drink still in her hand, and she spills some on her T-shirt as she gets up.

'Are you OK?' he says when she opens the door.

She looks around him. 'Has she gone?'

'Yes.'

'Did you fuck her?'

He sucks in his breath and shakes his head as he exhales. She can't tell if he's exasperated or amused.

'Did you?' She sounds crazy and jealous, but she can't stop herself.

'None of your business. And why do you even care?'

103

'I don't.'

'Was there really somebody in the backyard, Brigitte? Or did you just want to ruin my night?'

'Go away, Aidan.'

He holds up his hands and walks away. 'Lock the door and go to bed,' he says without turning.

When he's gone, a voice in her head says, *Why don't you just tell him how you really feel?*

She doesn't answer.

18

She dreams of Nana and Papa's old house. The back gate is never locked. It's been raining, and moss grows in scattered patches along the path beside the house. Nana always says, *Be careful, don't slip*. The screen door bangs behind her as she goes into the kitchen. The horse races are on the radio, and Nana is sitting at the red Laminex table studying the form guide. Papa puts pieces of wood into the fireplace; smoke mingles with the aroma of cake baking in the oven.

Kurt Cobain stands in front of the fireplace, wearing the brown sweater. 'I miss you.' He holds out his arms. The safety and comfort in his embrace are even warmer than Nana's baking. The mantel clock chimes. Strange — it hasn't worked for years.

Through the window, she sees a black car with tinted windows double-park across the road. A big man in a leather bomber-jacket stomps into Nana's kitchen. 'Go and pack your stuff. We fly out tonight.' His voice is gravelly. He takes off his hat, and she can see that part of his head is missing; there's blood and smashed brain inside. He's holding a large shard of something that looks like glass. She looks around for Kurt. He's gone. The lights go out.

She runs out the back, and the screen door bangs. She slips on the moss. Crash. Her bones crack. She can't get up, and keeps slipping. It's not moss. It's liquid — dark and sticky, all over her clothes, her hands.

Fuck! Get it off me! She sits bolt upright in bed, and pulls off her nightshirt — it's drenched in the liquid, and her skin is covered with a film of it. *Where's Sam? Oh God, oh God, oh God.* She swipes her hands together and rubs at her face until her eyes adjust to the darkness, and she sees that it's sweat, not blood. And Sam's not here.

On the clock radio, 1:08am glows red. Her heart pounds; pain courses through her body. Drip, drip, drip: rain leaks through the hole in the roof.

She feels for her slippers under the bed, pulls her dressing gown from the back of the door, and tiptoes out, avoiding the squeaky floorboard in the hallway. Clang! *Shit*, she's kicked the saucepan that's been catching the rain. She freezes and waits. There are murmurs from the twins' bedroom, but neither wakes.

She takes a Valium and two painkillers, and wanders through the house. In the lounge room, she flicks through the TV channels: there's nothing on but infomercials. She takes one of Sam's cookbooks from the shelf. He liked to buy them, but never had time to cook. One day, he said. She should bake a cake for the twins. A voice in her head says Sam would like her to do that.

The fluoro tube in the kitchen flickers, threatens to die, and then comes on, assaulting her sand-papery eyes. She finds all the ingredients for the chocolate cake-with-glaze recipe — except for ground almonds. It won't hurt to leave them out. She pulls down the blinds so that Aidan won't be disturbed by the light. She melts chocolate and butter in a saucepan, adds it to eggs, sugar, and flour, and beats by hand so she doesn't wake the kids with the electric mixer. She pours the mixture into a cake tin, and lights the oven. The recipe says: *Light the oven first, then cook at 160 degrees for 45 minutes*. She should have read the instructions properly. Oh well. She licks the wooden spoon. Life's too short to follow instructions, Sam used to say. Sometimes you have to go with your instinct. Sam should have listened to instructions and waited for backup in Chapel Street.

The big man in the leather bomber-jacket with the smashed head walks through the mist of a dream down the path beside Nana and

Papa's house ... Brigitte shakes herself awake; she was nodding off on the couch. The smell of baking — starting to burn — fills the house. She stumbles to the kitchen.

She opens the oven door, reaches for the cake tin with her bare hands, and recoils in pain. The burn across her fingers smarts. She stares at it for a long time, watching it start to blister.

She turns her attention back to the cake, and removes it with a tea towel. It's dark brown and crispy on top, but not cooked in the middle. She runs a knife around the sides of the tin where it's stuck, and shakes it onto a chopping board. It sinks in the middle, deflating like a punctured lung. Maybe the ground almonds and the oven temperature *were* important, after all. *Stupid, can't even make a cake*: Joan's voice in her head as she slides the failure into the bin.

She's too awake, hyper-awake. She needs more Valium.

Back to the cookbooks. She finds — hidden among Sam's beautiful, arty books — a ratty old one with curling yellow pages and a photo of orange pots and pans on the front. She recognises this book from her childhood, but has never noticed it on the shelf before. Folded inside the cover, on transparent airmail paper, is a handwritten recipe for butter cake. Nana's? It couldn't be Joan's. Joan didn't bake. The paper is so brittle, Brigitte is afraid it will crumble in her hands. It smells faintly of vanilla essence — from long ago. She holds it to her nose, closes her eyes, and tries to conjure an image of Nana. She can't see her, but she remembers her smell: vanilla, Joy perfume, licorice chews. Nana must have left that recipe in the book for her to find.

A car's backfire rings like a gunshot in the quiet night. What's that in the window? Not the dark figure again? No, it's her reflection; it startles her. She closes the curtains in case she sees something else — she's not sure what — in the grey emptiness. Nana's recipe trembles in her hands as she heads back to the kitchen.

Her first butter cake breaks when she takes it out of the tin. It goes in the bin with the chocolate cake. But the second one is perfect. Nana would be proud.

As she takes the third cake out of the oven, she hears the first train leave the station: it must be 5.00am. She tidies the kitchen, returns Nana's recipe to the old cookbook, showers, and gets ready for the day.

19

She dreams she's running from the big man with the smashed head. He chases her past a row of empty seats and a fish tank. There's a spray of broken glass. Everything turns red.

Kurt Cobain stands at the top of the stairs, wearing the brown sweater. 'Please don't leave me,' she yells up at him. But it's too late; he's turning away as the tram slows for the stop out on the street.

Then she's lying on the road. Car tyres are going past, slowly. Somebody is screaming. A siren howls.

Sweet voices of little children are singing 'Morningtown Ride'.

She's standing beside the bed, with no memory of how she got here. It's not morning. The sleeping tablets aren't working. She's lost some time. She looks at Sam's side of the bed, and thinks about Aidan out in the bungalow. Maybe she should make another cake.

She walks through the quiet house, and checks on the twins: they're sleeping soundly, with their lips parted and little chests rising and falling in perfect rhythm. She stares down at them for a long time. She's forgotten what she was doing. Then she remembers, and goes to the lounge room.

She finds Nana's butter-cake recipe in the old cookbook, and takes it to the kitchen. She lights the oven, and gathers the ingredients. *Shit* — they're out of eggs. She taps her fingers on the kitchen bench, and checks the fridge again for eggs. Still no eggs, but the cool, frosty bottle of white wine in the door looks inviting. Should she drive to the 7-Eleven for eggs? No, she can't leave the twins alone. *Calm down,* she tells herself, *turn off the oven, take a Valium, and write an article* — or Parenting Today *won't give you any more work.* She leans on the fridge door, traces a line with her index finger through the frost on the wine bottle, and answers the voice in her head: 'Yes, a glass of wine would be lovely, thank you.'

She opens the bottle and pours a glass. She places it next to the recipe on the bench. In the harsh, buzzing light of the flouro tube, she sees it's not handwriting on airmail paper. On closer inspection, it's just a recipe from the internet, printed on copy paper. The floor seems to fall a little beneath her feet, like in a lift. She downs the whole glass of wine, and pours another.

In the lounge room, she turns on the TV with the volume off, and sits on the couch with her laptop, the wine glass balanced on one of its arms, and a cushion behind her lower back. She plugs in her earphones — Nick Cave. She yawns, and checks her email: spam, bills, a kinder notice …

Enough procrastinating. Time to work now. She writes: FUN ACTIVITIES TO SHARE WITH THE KIDS.

HOW TO MAKE BATH BOMBS. Yes. Good idea. The twins love making bath bombs with her. Well, they used to.

Want to make bath time fun for the kids? Or perhaps leave an impression at the next school fete? Then why not make your own bath bombs? They are fun, simple and inexpensive to createeeeeee eeeeeeeeeeeeeeeeeeeeee

Her finger has lingered too long on the key.

Rage is on TV. It must be late. Days and nights are blurring into one. Yesterday is just part of today, and today is part of tomorrow. *Concentrate. Finish the article.*

The best thing about bath bombs is you're only limited by your imagination. Think of fun frothy baths 'bombed' with colours and flavours. Chai aromas (cardamom, nutmeg, ginger and black pepper) are very popular on the craft market scene. If you don't want to use food dye, opt for natural col ...

She can't keep her eyes open — she shouldn't have taken so much Valium. Can't focus, too blurry.

Somebody is in hospital. Nana? No, it's a man. Sam? The curtains are drawn around their sick bed. Death bed? There's a black cross on the floor. She's looking down on all of this, and thinks she's seen it before. An old Jesus-scarecrow man wearing a Santa hat walks through a field of poppies. He climbs onto a crucifix, and crows peck his hands.

Kurt Cobain's here, in a transparent silver jacket. He's out of focus, except for his eyes — they're too blue. And the surreal orange sky behind him is too bright. A little girl in a Ku Klux Klan gown and conical hat jumps up to reach for foetuses hanging from a dead, gnarled tree. Brigitte's eyes keep going in and out of focus. Hallucinating? She knew this would happen. She should never have gone to Dodgy Doctor Rhys. The little girl looks like Phoebe. Her hat blows off — into a pool of water. No, it's blood. Her costume turns black, and now she's standing on the cross in the hospital. Kurt Cobain smiles from a room lined with star-shaped flowers.

Brigitte rubs her eyes, and takes some deep breaths. *It's OK. It's OK.* It's not an hallucination, and not a dream — just an old film clip on *Rage*. 'Go away.' She pulls out the earphones and hisses at the TV screen. 'Leave me alone.'

'Brigitte.' Aidan is standing in the doorway.

She jumps, and drops her laptop on the floor. 'Fuck, you scared me. What are you doing in the house?'

'Heard a noise, saw the light on. You forgot to lock the back door. Anybody could've come in.'

She picks up her laptop.

'What are *you* doing?' he says. He's wearing a pair of grey track pants tied loosely at his hips.

'Nothing. Just working, writing an article.'

'It's 3.30 in the morning.'

'Is it really that late? Early?'

He's still standing there. Why doesn't he go away?

'You all right?'

She nods and smiles sweetly. She can't let him guess that she knows what he's up to. He's bugged the house, tapped her phone, placed plainclothes cops in the houses along the street to watch her, and set up a covert website about her and a dedicated Crime Stoppers line. He knows what happened to Eric Tucker.

'Make sure you lock the door behind me.' The light from the TV reflects on his naked torso. He looks down at her and frowns. 'Sure you're all right?' He's talking in some code now, but he can't outsmart her.

'Get out of my house, Aidan.'

20

Brigitte pushes a supermarket trolley aimlessly around the plaza. The twisting involved in controlling a trolley hurts her back more than anything, but not today — this morning she took enough medication to stop the pain. She can't understand why she didn't think of this before.

Giant gold-and-silver decorations hang from the glass ceiling, and she sings along with 'Winter Wonderland'. She's done the grocery shopping — extra flour, eggs, and butter for more cakes — and bought wine and the last of the twins' presents from Father Christmas. Still, she feels she's forgotten something. If she keeps wandering around, maybe she'll remember what it was. Something from the chemist? The newsagent? The butcher? The crowd of shoppers is reflected on the ceiling — people walking on the roof. It's too bright, and she can see auras. A headache claws at the right side of her head; it's going to turn into a migraine. She always gets migraines at Christmas time. Maybe she should go back to Dodgy Doctor Rhys for some migraine medication.

She gives up trying to remember what she's forgotten. If it was important, it'll come back to her. Things always do. Don't they say that? Sam's not coming back. How can they have Christmas without him? Maybe Aidan will join them? No, he'll spend Christmas with his wife. She thinks about his lips, his deltoid muscles, the tattoo on his arm — whatever it says, his ... *Stop it. Stop it. Stop it.* She shakes her head.

Kurt Cobain walks with her. Sometimes she sees him, but usually he's just a voice in her head.

'You were thinking about Aidan again, weren't you?' Kurt says.

She doesn't answer.

'I know you want to fuck his brains out.'

'I'm too tired. Go away.'

'So cheating on your husband was OK when he was alive—'

'Cheat*ed*,' she says. 'Just one time. And it wasn't my fault. He took advantage of me when I was drunk.'

Kurt knows she's lying. 'But it's not OK now that he's dead and couldn't care less?'

'Leave me alone. I've got a headache.'

'Please don't tell me you think you're in love with Aidan.' Kurt laughs. 'And let me guess, you don't deserve him? Just like—'

'Shut up.'

'You should tell him the truth,' he says quietly, seriously.

She suspects Aidan already knows the truth. About everything. But she keeps that to herself.

'Let's talk about this in the car,' Kurt says.

An old Italian man sitting on the bench seat outside the donut shop, with a salami and a packet of dried apricots on his lap, is watching her. He shakes his head and looks away when she meets his gaze. She's been talking out loud again.

A wave of heat assaults her as she exits the air-conditioned shops. *Fuck.* She can't remember where she parked the car. The migraine's in full swing, and the back pain's creeping up — the medication must be wearing off. The bitumen would be a nice, smooth place to lie down on and cry, but she keeps stumbling with the trolley, her left eyelid twitching, stars swirling in her peripheral vision. Kurt doesn't know where the car is either. He says he'll go have a look and come back if he finds it.

She finally sees it right down the back of the car park. As she struggles with the trolley, it seems to get further and further away, as if she's swimming in deep water, caught in a rip.

The car is open. She mustn't have locked it. The Christmas presents she bought earlier are piled on the seat, right there for the taking. She leans against the door, and takes a few shallow breaths before throwing the groceries in the back.

'Found it.' Kurt climbs into the passenger seat.

She backs out, and slams on the breaks when she hears a metallic crash. *Shit.* She looks in the rear-vision mirror — it's just the trolley where she left it behind the car. She slides the gear into 'Park', and turns to Kurt, but it's not Kurt anymore. It's the serpent, the dream tattoo. It tries to slither away through the passenger-side window, but she grabs it by the tail. Its scales shatter into a million shards of blue-and-green glass. She rests her face on the steering wheel. The horn beeps, and she covers her ears, unable to stand the pain from the noise reverberating in her head. When she looks up, a woman in a white dress embroidered with little sunflowers frowns at her as she opens her car in the parking space opposite.

Brigitte leans her head on the wheel again, careful of the horn this time.

She jumps at the sound of tapping on the window. *God, how did Sunflower Dress Woman get here so quickly?* Brigitte winds down her window.

'Are you alright?' the woman asks.

'Yep. Fine, thanks.' Brigitte forces a tight smile. *Everything's just fine, unless you count Kurt Cobain and a big green sea serpent driving around with you in your car. Oh, and your husband being stabbed when he tried to help somebody, his lungs filling with his own blood, drowning him — because he knew what you did, and he wasn't concentrating.*

'Are you sure?'

'Yes.' She smiles and grits her teeth. *Now please go away.*

At home, she leaves the shopping bags scattered across the kitchen floor. She needs to sit down, lie down, sleep and sleep.

She rings Ryan, and asks him to bring the twins home from kinder.

'Are you all right, Brigi?'

'Yep.'

'You don't sound all right.'

'Just tired.'

'You sure?'

'I just need to rest.'

'Nothing's happened, has it? What time will Aidan be home?'

'How should I know? I have to lie down now, Ryan. I've got a migraine.' She hangs up.

Ryan's looking down at her on the couch. She can't remember letting him in. She's lost some more time. The kids are running around his legs. He seems slightly faded, like a photocopy of himself. She sits up, tries to stand, but it hurts too much. She asks Ryan to pass her handbag — her painkillers are in there.

'How many have you had today?'

She doesn't answer.

He tells the kids to go play outside. When they've gone, he says he knows a good doctor, and he's made an appointment for her tomorrow afternoon. He'll come with her.

'I'm not going to the doctor, Ryan.' She puts her hands on her knees and pushes herself up, taking a while to straighten out.

'I was just saying to Rosie that it might be nice for the twins to come and stay with us for a while.'

'What are you talking about?'

'It's been a tough year, Brigi.'

She shakes her head. 'Don't be stupid. I'm fine. Just a sore back.'

'There are ways to make it not your choice. I don't want to have to do that, but I've been talking to Aidan—'

'I'm scared of him, Ryan.' She grasps handfuls of his shirt, widens her eyes. 'Sometimes he comes into the house and ...' She looks up into his eyes, and sees the truth. Why didn't she realise it before? *Ryan's working with Aidan. A police informant.* She's going to have to be very careful from now on. She lets go of his shirt, and takes a step backwards.

'Would you like a cup of tea?' she says. 'And some cake?'

He raises his eyebrows.

'I made a cake.'

'Yes, Aidan mentioned you'd been doing some baking.'

She smiles, tilts her head, and blinks.

'I'm staying here until we sort something out, Brigi.'

She looks at the floor, bites her top lip, looks back up at him, and says, 'OK, I'll go to the doctor with you tomorrow.' She and Kurt will be far away by then. She turns and heads towards the kitchen to put the kettle on.

21

'Where are we going?' Kurt says from the passenger seat.

'Carlton.'

'I thought we were going on a road trip.'

'We are.' But first she has to renew the car registration, which is about to expire. She doesn't want to be pulled over by the stupid police in an unregistered vehicle.

'Who are you talking to, Mummy?' Phoebe says from the back seat.

They weave their way through the congested traffic in Lygon Street. The wipers struggle with the steamy rain pouring onto the windscreen. Brigitte wipes away the condensation with the back of her hand. She squints and concentrates hard, struggling with cotton-wool vision and another migraine cranking up in her right temple.

'I'll wait in the car,' Kurt says when they get there.

She parks askew, half-in, half-out of a parking space. She rushes — in slow motion, deep-water running — through the rain into the VicRoads office with the twins, their jackets over their heads.

They climb the bureaucracy-brown stairs to the first floor. Lame Christmas decorations are draped around the walls. It smells of sweat and something sweet like old-fashioned carbon paper, plastic, and petrol. She takes a number from the machine.

'Thanks, Marco.' A woman behind a counter collects some paperwork from a man in an *RACV Drive School* shirt.

'Okey-dokey. Have a good Christmas.' Marco, the driving instructor, turns, looks at Brigitte, and tries to hold her gaze, but she averts her eyes. He walks away, scratching his neck.

The room spins. There's not enough air. She can't breathe.

'What's wrong, Mummy?'

She stumbles towards the row of skinny red chairs. She's not going to make it. She's falling. It's lucky Kurt's here to catch her. She thought he was waiting in the car.

She makes Finn and Phoebe promise not to tell Aidan or Uncle Ryan about Mummy 'fainting' at the rego place if she lets them eat potato chips and watch *The Snow Queen* on TV. They eat all the chips, get bored with the movie, and go outside to play.

The pain pulsing through her body verges on unbearable. She runs a shower, and stands under scalding water until the skin on her back is redder than sunburn, but the pain persists. She can't stand it. *Better increase the meds again.*

She looks out the bathroom window as she dries herself. Finn and Phoebe have taken off their clothes, and are rampaging in the warm rain — swinging on the clothesline, and pulling plants out of the garden.

Brigitte dresses, and drags the big suitcase from her bedroom cupboard to the lounge room. She opens a bottle of wine, and starts packing. She's distracted by the blank TV screen. Her reflection seems different: older, thinner. She walks over and stares at it, bends to look closer, and sees it's fading. Disappearing?

'Where's Mummy?' Aidan's deep, soothing voice in the backyard carries through the open window. *Oh, no. Why is he home so early?*

'Resting,' Finn says. 'You want to play with us?'

'Uncle Ryan's coming over soon to take Mummy out for a little while, so we can play then. But first I've gotta get something out of the car for you.'

'When you going back to live with your wife?' Phoebe says.

A pause. 'Did your mum tell you that?'

'When you going back?'

'When hell freezes over.'

Finn giggles.

'What that means, Aidan?' Phoebe says.

'It means never. My wife and I changed our minds.'

'So you can stay!'

'No, I've still gotta go. When your mum's feeling a bit better. Now if you guys get dressed, I'll go get this present.'

The side gate squeaks, the twins giggle, a dog barks.

Inside the house, Kurt beckons to Brigitte. 'Hurry up,' he says. 'It's time to go.' But she hasn't finished packing. She takes the bottle of Johnnie Walker from the kitchen cupboard, follows him to the bedroom, and locks the door behind her.

Kurt sits next to her on the bed. She washes down a sleeping tablet with the whisky.

'We're not going on a road trip, are we?'

Kurt shakes his head. 'Take some more.'

'Don't listen to him.' The man in the top hat and tails on the Johnnie Walker label is talking to her now.

'I'm so tired, I miss Sam, and I can't stand this pain anymore.'

'Go to Ryan's doctor, see a counsellor, get your back fixed,' says Johnnie Walker.

She and Kurt laugh.

'Stop it, Brigitte, you're hallucinating.' Johnnie Walker's getting annoyed.

'No.' She taps the bottle with a chewed-to-the-quick fingernail. 'I know you. I remember you.'

Kurt gestures with his chin towards the pills on the bedside table. She swallows another one. Johnnie Walker's really agitated now. 'How could anybody leave their babies?' he says.

She looks closely at the bottle and says, 'I don't know. Maybe, sometimes, you don't have a choice.' Or is that Kurt speaking?

'You're stronger than this.'

'No, I'm not, Johnnie Walker.' She turns the bottle around so she can't see him anymore. She washes down more pills, lies on the bed, and closes her eyes.

Kurt lies beside her and holds her hand. 'It was an accident, you know. Most suicides are.'

What? This is not suicide. This is just resting.

'Mummy, Mummy,' Finn yells as he stomps down the hallway, looking for his mother. 'Aidan got us a puppy!'

Brigitte barely hears. She's already too far away, free from pain — chasing Kurt down the corridor, past the row of empty seats, the fish tank, and up a flight of stairs. She finds him in a grey room, in front of a cold, empty fireplace. The smell of cinnamon and bergamot fills the air. He's wearing the brown sweater, holding a shotgun. It's too late. The sound of a single shot shatters the silence. But it's not Kurt in the brown sweater. It never was. And it's Brigitte with the shotgun in her mouth.

PART II

1994: About a Girl

22

She opens her dream-heavy eyes, and is confused about where she is for a moment. Light seeps through the timber blind-slats, cutting patterns on the white sheets.

She drags herself out of bed, follows the light stripes to the French windows, and fumbles with the latch. Traffic hums, a lawn mower buzzes in the gardens across the road, the smell of cut grass drifts into the apartment.

Eric has left the TV going in the lounge room. American daytime crap — *Entertainment Tonight*. Why is that even on during the day? She can see the screen from the kitchen, over the breakfast bar, as she makes coffee.

She knocks the plunger and burns her hand when a news flash announces that Kurt Cobain has been found dead, having shot himself. *Get out! No fucking way!* She comes around the breakfast bar and stares at the TV, cup in hand, mouth open. Footage shows a police car parked outside a grey, rain-smudged house in Seattle.

Back in the kitchen, she runs cold water over her burnt hand. What could have been so bad for Cobain to make him do this? She doesn't really care, but for sure today will be one of those days when everybody remembers where they were — like old people talk about JFK and John Lennon.

The phone rings. She turns off the tap and stretches for the receiver on the wall. It's Nana, in tears — that handsome grungy singer has shot himself. *How does she even know who Kurt Cobain is?* There's a knock at the door. *Why isn't the intercom working?* She tells Nana she'll ring her back later.

She steps over a packing box, scrapes her shin on the edge of it, unlocks the door, and opens it a crack.

'Hi. I'm Sean, the caretaker. Just making sure you're settling in OK.'

Eric never mentioned a caretaker. He looks pretty old — not as old as Eric, but late twenties, maybe thirty. He's dressed in black trousers and a white shirt that could do with an iron. His reddish-blond hair sticks up on one side of his head. His green eyes are sad, red-rimmed, as if he's been crying. She opens the door a bit further, and a grin wipes away some of his sadness — probably because it's afternoon and she's still in her Minnie Mouse pyjamas.

'I'm just going down the shop. Can I get you anything?'

She shakes her head.

'I'll get you a coffee.'

'No, I'm just making …' She glances at the spilt coffee on the bench top. 'OK, sure, whatever.' *Just go away and stop looking at my pyjamas.*

She locks the door, showers quickly, and throws on some clothes before he comes back with her coffee. And one for himself. That's unusual, but he seems all right, harmless.

'Got you a flat white. Is that OK?'

'Perfect. Thanks. How much do I owe you?'

'My shout.' He looks at his shoes — the toes are scuffed.

'Is everything OK?' She sips her coffee. It's too hot and burns her lip. She winces, but he doesn't seem to notice.

He sighs. 'Sorry, I don't normally bother tenants, but I'm just so shaken up. Have you heard? About Kurt?'

'Kurt Cobain?'

He nods. 'He was my hero. His songs were, like, my life, my feelings — I dunno. He just knew how to say stuff in his songs. I can't believe he's gone. Did you like him?'

Surely it doesn't look like grunge is her thing. Probably today it does — old jeans and T-shirt, no make-up. 'Actually, I haven't really listened to his music so …'

'You have to. I'll bring you some Nirvana CDs.'

Great. She can't wait.

'Sorry, what was your name?'

'Brigitte.'

'Right-o. Better get back to work then, Brigitte. Let me know if you need anything.'

She nods.

'And, Brigitte.'

'Yes, Sean?'

'Light a candle for Kurt, OK?'

'Sure.' She locks the door behind him.

It's a ten-minute walk to work. The cool darkness of the Gold Bar wraps around her like a security blanket. She pulls back her shoulders, sticks out her breasts, and swings her hips as she leaves stupid, awkward Brigitte at the door, and sexy, confident Pagan takes over.

Downstairs, her pseudo family is busy getting ready for the night shift: waiting for the middle-aged men whose wives don't understand them. Hannah, the housemother — ex-dancer, blonde, expensively groomed — is walking around with a clipboard, checking the roster. Al, the manager — ex-boxer, balding, black Italian suit — is looking over Hannah's shoulder, complaining about something, as usual. Brigitte hands him a shopping bag containing a brick-sized package from Eric, and that cheers him up.

Ember — aka Jennifer, Brigitte's former housemate — is dancing around the pool table next to the bar, singing 'I Believe in Malcolm' to the Hot Chocolate song throbbing through the speakers. How many times does Brigitte have to tell her it's *miracles*?

She asks Ember where Crystal and Angelique are. She thought they were rostered on tonight.

'Gone up to King Street,' Ember says. 'Reckon the girls are earning more money up there.'

'Yeah, but they're doing more than just dancing. Al says they're giving punters blow jobs in the back room at the Platinum Club.'

'Dunno. Probably.' Ember shrugs, and dances off.

Tim, the bartender, pours Brigitte a glass of champagne with a dash of raspberry cordial.

'Thanks. Saw you in the Hungry Jacks ad.'

'It's just a start. My agent's lined up an audition for a film role.' He smiles as he cuts a lemon into slices.

'Good luck.' She nods and sips her drink.

'You're supposed to say break a leg, Pagan.'

'I should know that. My brother's an actor.'

'Really?' He looks up. 'Who's his agent?

'He's at NIDA.'

'Lucky him.' Tim frowns, and goes back to slicing lemons.

She takes her drink to the dressing room. It's always freezing out here. The dancers warm themselves with alcohol and the hand dryer. Scarlett is doing her make-up, and Paris, a new girl, is hiding in the corner shooting up. She won't last long here. Brigitte plops her bag on the bench under the old theatre mirror with light globes around the edges. She undresses, then pulls on a silver-sequined bra and G-string, and squirms into a white dress that barely covers the tops of her thighs.

Scarlett looks up from her lipstick and says that Al says he saw Rita again last night. After closing. Rita is the resident ghost — apparently a dancer who was murdered at the Gold Bar back when it was a cabaret. 'He reckons the cigarette machine started up by itself. A pack of smokes popped out, and then he saw a shadow on the ground.'

'Al drinks too much at closing time.' Brigitte makes a ghost noise, and laughs as she slides her silver stilettos on.

There are only a few punters around when she climbs onto her first podium for the night. 'Raspberry Beret': the DJ knows that Prince is her favourite. Her dress glows under the UV black lights. One guy — business suit — comes over to watch. He takes off his coat and covers his groin with it. His cigarette smoke hangs in a grey cloud, trapped in the dingy air. He waves a five-dollar note at her, but it's going to take a hell of a lot more than that. She swings around the pole, muscles flexing, the beat of the music pulsing through her body. When the punter holds up a fifty, she smiles down at him and blinks a slow blink, her eyelashes a stage-curtain coming down. She's in control up here, powerful, safe, where no one is allowed to touch her. She kneels in front of him, takes the money, folds it neatly, and places it under her garter belt. The beauty queens don't make the most. To do well you have to master the art of tease. Move hypnotically, slowly … slither — until he imagines he is the pole and you are making love to him. It's all done with the eyes. Removal of clothing is secondary. Once you capture him with your eyes, you can make him slip half his week's pay into your garter belt without thinking. Then your ten-minute set finishes, you dress, and you leave him sitting at the podium. Empty. Until the next dancer comes along.

* * *

Eric's colleague Ian is down from Sydney — two wrinkly toads sitting on the new white sofa, playing Nintendo, when Brigitte gets home from work at 4.30am. An expensive bottle of wine, white lines, and rolled-up hundred-dollar bills litter the coffee table. Ian never talks to her, and she ignores him. He jokes about Eric 'playing house' when he thinks she can't hear, and he watches her when he thinks she can't see.

She double-checks that the bathroom door is locked before she showers and gets ready for bed.

Tendonitis has flared up in her arm again — a sickening cord of pain buzzes from her left bicep to her fingertips. She wraps

129

a bandage around it, and swallows some anti-inflammatories, Panadol, and a sleeping tablet. A hot-water bottle makes it all feel better, for a while.

She dreams of Kurt Cobain standing in the apartment doorway, holding a gift box. Behind him, in the foyer, deliverymen struggle with plastic-wrapped furniture on trolleys. She grasps Kurt's arm, and whispers into his ear, 'Please don't leave me here.'

He lifts the lid on the box. Inside is a puppy with a red collar around its neck. She reaches for the puppy, but a huge lizard jumps out. Rainbow patterns reflect off its shiny, silver-brown scales. A syringe sticks out of its back.

Heart palpitations wrench her from the dream, and she instinctively reaches for the Valium on the bedside table. Doctor O'Meara warned her not to mix alcohol with the anti-inflamms. *Rage* is on the portable TV in the bedroom, playing Nirvana all night. She feels around for the remote. *Where the fuck did Eric put it this time?* This film clip with the little girl in the Ku Klux Klan costume creeps her out.

23

The back gate at Nana and Papa's house is never locked. It's 'pie night'. Brigitte can smell baking and wood smoke as she walks down the sideway. It's been raining, and moss is growing in scattered patches along the path beside the house. Nana always says, *Be careful, don't slip*. Brigitte has slipped a few times — on the way out after too many sherries. To fall over with her hands in her pockets would not be a good look, so she takes them out of her white woollen coat. The screen door bangs behind her as she goes into the kitchen.

Papa is setting the red Laminex table. He looks up, 'G'day, Brigi. Where's ya new fella?'

'Working.' She hangs her coat over the back of a chair.

'When are we gunna meet him?'

'Dunno.' *Hopefully never.*

'Fancy a sherry?' He takes one green and one rose-coloured glass, and the bottle, from a bottom cupboard. He pours their drinks, and rolls himself a cigarette.

'Got a house-warming present for ya.' He walks over to the open fireplace and touches the heavy, black iron object beside the mantel clock. 'It was my grandmother's.'

'Is it an iron?' Brigitte sips her drink, enjoying its warmth in her stomach.

'Yeah. She used to heat it on the stove.' He picks at a tobacco thread stuck to his lip. 'But you can use it as a doorstop at ya new place.'

'It looks too heavy to carry home.'

'I'll bring it over for ya in the car.' He throws some pieces of wood into the fire and sits back in the new Chesterfield chair that Brigitte bought for his birthday.

Nana comes in. She brushes flour from her apron and gives Brigitte a hug. Her face is cold, and her hands are red — she's been doing the laundry in the wash house out the back. She smells of vanilla, liquorice chews, and that stinky Joy perfume. Brigitte sneezes.

'Have you buggers been into my cooking sherry again?' Then she frowns. 'Where's Uncle Joe?'

Brigitte didn't call in at The Railway and walk him home. 'I'm sure he can find his own way home from the pub.'

Nana narrows her eyes.

'All right. All right.' Brigitte holds up her hands. 'I'll go back and get him.' She's got her coat half on when the phone rings.

Papa gets up and answers it. He nods and says, 'Right ... Right ... Right ...' He hangs up and looks at his shoes. 'It was Stefan from the pub. Uncle Joe fell off a bar stool.'

Brigitte and Nana stare at him.

'Ambulance just took him away.'

Brigitte asks if he's OK.

'He's dead.'

Shit.

Nana crosses her legs and holds onto the kitchen bench as if to stop herself from falling. Papa rubs Nana's back and asks Brigitte to ring Joan and Auntie Linda. Brigitte does as she's told, while Papa comforts Nana.

Beep beep beep, STD pip tones. 'This is Joan Weaver speaking.'

'Hello, Mum.' It's been a while.

Joan pretends to not recognise her voice.

'It's Brigitte. I'm at Nana and Papa's. You might have to come down.'

'What for?'

'Uncle Joe died.'

132

'Oh, is that all?'

Nana wails.

'Brigitte, what's going on?' Joan says.

Nana collapses, clutching her chest, into Papa's arms. Brigitte drops the phone.

'Brigitte. Brigitte …' Joan's voice from the receiver swings on the cord.

Brigitte asks Papa if Nana's OK.

Papa shakes his head. He kneels on the lino floor, holding onto Nana. Brigitte cuts Joan off and dials triple-O. When an ambulance is on its way she kneels with Papa, stroking Nana's clammy forehead and soft, grey hair.

The pie burns, and Brigitte jumps up to take it out. Smoke billows from the oven.

Nana is conscious when the paramedics arrive, but they think she's had a minor heart attack. They make her comfortable on a stretcher, and joke about her burning the dinner. Papa goes with her in the ambulance. Brigitte wants to go, too, but Papa tells her to wait at home — he'll call with any news.

She checks the letterbox as she walks through the foyer. There's just some junk mail and two Nirvana CDs with a note from Sean, the caretaker: *To Brigitte. Let me know what you think.*

She calls in sick for work. Al says she'll have to do a day shift to make up for it. *Prick.*

She takes a Valium, and stands under a hot shower for a long time, trying to wash away stress with a bar of 'chill out' aromatherapy soap. The phone rings, and she drops the soap. She runs, naked, to answer it, dripping water over the plush cornflower-blue carpet. It's Papa, from the hospital. Nana's doing fine. She should be able to go home in a day or two. *Phew.*

Brigitte dries herself and puts on pyjamas. *Pop*: the happy sound of a champagne cork escaping. Into the bottle goes a big

133

splash of raspberry cordial, and into the CD player, one of Sean's albums. She sits cross-legged on the floor with her drink. When she hears 'Polly' she feels a connection — a shared knowledge of what it's like to be trapped. Cobain couldn't have written those words without understanding. Sean was right: he did know how to say stuff in his songs. No wonder the fans burned their flannelette shirts at his memorial. She should have taken more notice of him when he was alive.

She knocks back her drink, pours another, and thinks about Nana. There's a photo of her on Papa's bedside table; it's been there forever. Nana must be about twenty, maybe younger. She's at a party, smiling — perfect teeth, sparkly eyes, clear skin. She's luminescent, the way some movie stars seem to be — like there's a light shining on her but not on anybody else in that photo. When she was little, Brigitte wished she'd grow up to look like that. Joan looks like that, but without the shine. Nana is always so happy, but growing old and losing those looks must have made her sad. It made Joan sad.

Brigitte thinks she'll end up alone like Uncle Joe: no partner, no children. Eric says nobody else will ever want her. She's too difficult, too much of a mess — and he's right. But Dan wanted Joan, and she was an even bigger mess. Why had nobody wanted Uncle Joe? He was handsome when he was young. Perhaps he inherited the mess gene — probably from Nana's mother, who was an alcoholic depressive. Nana says she was a fragile soul who had bad nerves and liked a drink. Obviously she was the reason Nana never touched a drop. Papa says she was just bloody nuts. He told Brigitte, in sworn secrecy, that the fall down the stairs that killed her was no accident.

Why did Kurt Cobain kill himself? He had everything to live for. Somebody should have loved him enough to save him. Too much of a mess? She finishes her drink, and turns up 'Something in the Way'. She has no idea what the song is about, but imagines it has something to do with the unfairness of life. Or maybe he's just taking the piss out of pescetarians — it sounds like he's singing about eating fish because they haven't got feelings.

When the CD finishes, she upends the bottle over her glass, but it's empty. She goes to the fridge and gets another. *Pop.*

She puts on a Prince CD.

24

Sean brings her coffee every day around noon. She tries to be dressed before he comes in, but today she's still in her pyjamas. Her eyes are puffy from crying, and she's hung-over. *Again. Such a mess.*

Sean's white shirt's been ironed, his hair smoothed with product, his shoes polished. 'What's wrong, Brigitte?' He places the coffees on the breakfast bar next to a Berocca hissing in a glass.

She bites her bottom lip. 'My Uncle Joe died.'

'I'm so sorry.' He looks surprised when she hugs him, a little knocked off balance, then he slowly, tentatively, encircles her in his arms.

'It's all my fault.'

'That's a silly thing to say.'

She blubbers over his shirt.

When she calms down, she apologises and lets go of him. He asks if she'd like something stronger than coffee. She nods, and he heads down to the bottle shop at the corner hotel.

He comes back with a bottle of Johnnie Walker, and takes two tumbler glasses from a cupboard. 'Got any coke?'

'No, but I can ring somebody who can get some for us.' She reaches for the phone.

'Coca-Cola, silly.' He's looking in the fridge. There's not much in there — no champagne left.

'God, no. That crap is so bad for your body.'

'Where's Eric?'

'Working.'

'Where does he work?'

'Everywhere. He's a concert promoter.' She sits at the table, and runs a hand over the shiny walnut finish. 'He's not home very often.'

'You don't work, do you?'

She nods.

'But you're always here during the day.' He places the drinks and the bottle on the table, and sits opposite her.

'I work at night.' She screws up her face — the straight Johnnie Walker tastes disgusting but does the job, faster than champagne.

'Where?'

'At the Gold Bar.' She lets her guard down.

Sean raises his eyebrows.

'Behind the bar,' she says quickly — the same lie she tells everybody. She changes the subject back to poor Uncle Joe, and Sean asks what happened.

'He fell off a chair when I was meant to pick him up from the pub, and hit his head. I forgot about him. Actually,' she takes a big drink, 'I kind of didn't forget. I just didn't want to go in because the publican tried to kiss me last time I was there.'

He puts a hand on hers, comforting.

'Uncle Joe had dementia.'

'Was he in a home?'

She shakes her head. He should have been in a home instead of renting Nana and Papa's spare room. He was always forgetting to pay Nana rent and to turn off the gas on the stove. He couldn't remember where he'd hidden his life savings. But Papa found them — the remains of them, anyway — in an old wooden box hidden inside the disused barbeque, after he decided to cook some sausages to see if it still worked.

'Why didn't I just get him from the pub?'

Sean pats her hand gently.

'And then I had to ring my mother, who hates me.'

'Don't be silly. I'm sure she doesn't hate you.'

'Yes, she does.' She stops talking. He's looking at her the way men look at her at work, the way Stefan the publican looks at her. He wants to kiss her. And if he tried, she'd probably let him. But he doesn't.

'I've heard him shouting at you,' Sean says.

'Who? What are you talking about?' She takes her hand from under his, and crosses her arms.

'Eric.'

'No, he doesn't. Not really. Sometimes he just has a loud voice.' She forces a smile that doesn't reach her eyes.

'You come and get me if you ever need to.'

'Now you're being silly.' She laughs it off. 'The whisky's gone to your head. You better get back to work, or you'll be in trouble.'

'I'm serious. OK?' He looks directly into her eyes, and she looks away.

The intercom buzzes and they both stand. It's Ember/Jennifer. Brigitte opens the door, and Jennifer flounces in wearing a dress too short and heels too high for daytime. She kisses Brigitte on the mouth. 'You OK, sweetie?' She doesn't wait for an answer. 'Brought you some presents to drown your sorrows.' She places two bottles of champagne and a fat joint on the breakfast bar. 'What's your name?' She looks Sean up and down.

'Sean.' He extends a hand, which she takes and kisses. He blushes.

'Hi Sean. I'm Jennifer,' she says, flashing a cheeky smile.

'Just on my way out.'

'Oh. What a shame.'

He kisses Brigitte — politely — on the cheek. 'I'll check on you later.' It's the first time Brigitte has seen a man not turn for a second look at Jennifer.

'Sean's cute.' Jennifer lights the joint with a match. 'You should get with him.'

'Just a friend.'

'Nice place.' Jennifer looks around. 'Eric must really like you.'

25

The intercom buzzes while she's preparing food from *Vogue Entertaining* for the apartment-warming party. It's Papa, too close to the screen. She can see up his nostrils. She giggles, presses the button that unlocks the front security-door, and hears it click out in the foyer.

He whistles when she opens the door. 'Don't ya look a million bucks!'

So she should. She spent almost that much on highlights at the hairdresser, a French polish for her acrylic nails, and a rejuvenating facial at the beauty salon.

Papa tilts his head. 'Ya look like ya mum.'

Brigitte frowns; she hates it when people say that. Papa's brought his grandmother's iron. He props the door open with it, and whistles again as he looks around.

'Bit better than the last place.' He takes out his tobacco pouch and papers.

'Have to go outside to smoke.'

'Why?'

'Don't like the smell in here.'

He rolls his eyes and re-pockets his smoking paraphernalia. 'Where's ya bloke?'

'Away. Working.' She washes some lettuce leaves at the sink. 'How's Nana?'

'Good.'

'Recovered?'

'Miraculously. Tough old bugger.' He shakes his head. 'Got anything to drink?'

'Only champagne.'

'Well, la di da da.' He helps himself to a piece of olive bread.

'Papa, I'm really busy.'

'Too busy for ya old granddad?' He sucks his teeth.

'I've got to get all this food ready for tonight.' She tucks her hair behind her ears.

'All right. All right. I'm going.' He comes around the breakfast bar and kisses the top of her head.

'Thanks for the door stop.'

'See ya at Joe's send-off.'

Sean stands in the doorway with his hands in his pockets until she tells him to come in.

'You look nice,' he says.

'Thanks.' She's too busy to look up. 'Could you please take that stuff to the club lounge for me? I thought we'd have the party in there.' She points at the crate of champagne and the box of hired glasses on the floor. He carries them to the communal lounge across the foyer.

'Ryan!' She sees him getting out of a taxi on the street. She claps her hands, pushes aside the baby beetroot salad with raspberry vinaigrette, runs to the open window, and leans over the black iron grille.

'Hey, Little Sis!' Ryan calls up to her, grinning, squinting in the sunlight.

Brigitte unlocks the security door.

Ryan walks in and drops his bag in the corner. She hugs him, too tight. He smells of the aromatherapy aftershave she sent him. Her eyes moisten.

'Hey, what's wrong?' He holds her face in his hands.

Help. I don't think I want to be here anymore. 'Nothing.' She looks away. 'Just miss you.'

'You're not still dancing at that stupid club?'

140

She shrugs.

Sean comes back with the empty boxes. She introduces him to Ryan, and the three of them go out to smoke a joint down the back of the carpark, the exotic food forgotten on the bench top.

Ryan takes a long drag, and passes the joint to Sean. 'So how long have you and Brigi been going out?' He exhales smoke. Sean turns red.

'Ryan!' Brigitte frowns at him.

'What?'

'Eric,' she says through gritted teeth.

'Oh yeah. Where is the big man anyway?'

'Sydney. I think.'

'With his first family, or his second?'

Sean looks at his shoes, and then excuses himself to check on the food.

'He likes you,' Ryan says.

'Just a friend.'

They pass the joint between them in silence for a few minutes. Ryan looks around at the luxury parked cars, up at the top-floor apartments, and then down into Brigitte's eyes. 'What the fuck are you doing with Eric, Brigi?'

She shrugs.

'He's older than Mum.'

She tries a cute giggle, a blink, but can't pull it off. Ryan shakes his head and crushes out the joint on the concrete with a twist of his sneaker.

She feels so glamorous, swanning around the club lounge in her new, white Chanel sheath dress, pretending she's somebody famous, somebody important. The guests — a group of her neighbours — are mingling. Ryan and Sean are getting along well. It's the perfect party — except for the food. What was she thinking? *Vogue Entertaining!* She can barely make toast. But it doesn't matter, because everybody's too busy drinking to notice. The only things that worked were the rosemary lamb skewers (shame about the onion marmalade that was meant to accompany them) — which she's left in the oven. She runs from the club lounge to the apartment, spilling a trail of champagne and raspberry on the way.

'Can I help with anything, Brigitte?' Sean staggers after her.

She burns her hand on the oven. 'Fuck!' She drops the tray of burnt lamb skewers on the floor. They laugh so hard they don't notice the squeak of the little wheels on Eric's suitcase. Brigitte smells his Juicy Fruit chewing gum, and freezes. She wasn't expecting him home for a couple of days.

'I don't remember agreeing to a party,' he says in his gravelly Benson and Hedges voice. He parks his suitcase against the wall and retracts the handle with a snap. 'You're a fucken mess, Brigitte — you need to go to bed.' His hazel eyes water when he's angry. She hugs her upper arms against her chest.

'And you need to go home.' Eric points a finger at Sean.

'It's OK, mate. Everything's cool.'

'I said *go home*. And you,' he turns to Brigitte, 'go to bed.' He pushes her in the direction of the bedroom. She loses her balance, falls against the breakfast bar, and knocks a bowl of pistachio nuts onto the floor.

'Hey! Get your fucking hands off her.' Ryan strides through the door.

'Don't you tell me what I can and can't do with her.'

'What did you say?'

'You heard.' Eric juts out his chin, and Ryan uses it as a target for his fist. Ryan's not as tall or fat as Eric, but stronger. And less than half his age. Eric wobbles and crashes against the wall, holding his jaw. Brigitte covers her mouth with her hands, and Sean takes a step back.

'You dunno who you're fucking with.' Eric heaves himself off the wall. The bottom button pops off his shirt as it strains against his gut.

'Come on then, old man. Or do you only know how to push young girls around?'

Eric swings a fist at Ryan, but he's too slow. Ryan grabs Eric's arm, twists it, and pushes him down.

'Stop it!' Brigitte screams.

Eric sits on the floor, coughing for a while before hoisting himself up. He points a finger and spits his gum at Ryan, then stumbles towards the bedroom, rubbing his arm. Ryan ignores it, pushes down his anger, and turns to Brigitte. She's still hugging herself, shaking.

'It's OK, Brigi. Let's get out of here.' He holds out his hand. 'We can go to Nana and Papa's. Or a hotel.'

She doesn't take his hand.

'Come on. You don't want to stay with that dickhead.'

She bites her bottom lip.

'Whatever he's got over you, Brigi, doesn't matter. I'm not leaving you here.'

She makes her eyes as hard as she can, and doesn't let her voice falter. 'I think you better go, Ryan.'

'Don't be stupid.'

She takes a couple of steps backwards.

'Please.'

She shakes her head. 'Go.'

He holds up his hands, exasperated, then picks up his bag and leaves. Sean follows him, but looks back over his shoulder mouthing *OK?*'

She nods.

When they've gone, she wipes pointless mascara-black tears from her cheeks as she cleans up the lamb skewers and pistachio nuts.

'Your brother doesn't care about you, Pet.' Eric's behind her,

143

and she stiffens, cold and sober now. 'I'm the only one who does.' He walks over, shoves the iron doorstop out of the way with his foot, and locks the door.

26

The gathering at the chapel for Uncle Joe's funeral is sparse and sad — just a handful of blokes from the pub, and Brigitte and Nana and Papa. Most of the people he knew are now dead. The Australian flag, a few service medals, a faded army photograph in a cheap frame, and budget flowers adorn the budget coffin.

'Stupid old bugger,' Papa says under his breath as the celebrant reads from the standard service, to which few personal touches have been added to reflect the 'loved one's' life. Nana elbows Papa. Brigitte yawns. Stefan from the pub winks at her from a pew on the other side of the down-lit, golden-hued room. Brigitte frowns. Her new 'funeral shoes' are hurting her feet.

She stares at Uncle Joe's coffin, listens to the service, the standard hymns, and remembers Dad's funeral. It was in this same chapel. Or one exactly like it. The smells of diesel and Old Spice emanated from the truckies in bottle-green and indigo shirts with transport logos on the pockets. After they paid their respects, strong shoulders and big calloused hands ingrained with grease carried out the coffin to 'Lights on the Hill'.

Four mourners come back to Nana and Papa's house for sandwiches, and tea or coffee. Brigitte leaves the wake when she gets tired of Stefan panting after her, but not before drinking too much sherry with Papa. It's drizzling, the path is slippery, and she falls on the way out down the sideway, tearing a hole in her stocking. Papa is watching from the kitchen. The window rattles as he jimmies it up; paint chips flake away. He sticks his head out. 'You all right, Brigi?'

She gives him a thumbs-up and stands quickly. Lucky Nana didn't see.

'... No. This is police harassment.' Eric hangs up his mobile phone as she walks into the apartment. He's sitting on the sofa, smoking a cigarette while a plate of sushi and tempura vegetables, and a Nintendo controller, are balanced on his knees. Multi-tasking.

'Who was that?' she asks.

'Nobody, Pet. Why are you all dressed up?'

'Uncle Joe's funeral.' She puts her bag on the breakfast bar, and slips off her shoes; they've given her blisters.

'How was it?'

'Bleak.'

'Good wake?'

She shrugs.

He pauses the game, extinguishes his cigarette, and looks at her. 'What happened to your knee?'

She has a school kid's graze; the edges of her torn stocking are stuck to the dried blood.

'Tripped over.'

He laughs and shakes his head. 'You're a mess. But, God, you look good. A kiss, please.' He puts aside his plate and chopsticks, and waits for her to come over. She bends down and closes her eyes. His tongues worms in her mouth; he tastes of cigarettes and raw fish.

'We're bringing out Death Rowe in December. Would you like to come on the tour?' He holds her hands in his. They're spongy and moist.

Calvin Rowe is pretty cute. But, no, she's over vacuous pretty boys. 'That's a busy time at work. Don't think I could take time off.'

'You rostered on tonight?'

She nods.

'Good. I've got a package for Al.'

She pulls her hands away. 'I have to get ready.'

'So early?'

'We're rehearsing for the jelly wrestling.'

'Jelly wrestling!' He laughs and coughs, and lights another cigarette. 'I'll have to come in to see that.'

She goes to the bathroom, locks the door behind her, cleans up her knee, showers, and gets ready for work.

The Gold Bar has been a bit quiet since the new clubs started opening along King Street, so Al has decided to introduce something different to lure back the punters. The posters are up, and the ads are in the girlie mags, but the bulk order of jelly crystals from the wholesaler hasn't arrived. Al and Big Johnny, the bouncer, have had to drive to Safeway and buy all the packets of jelly off the supermarket shelf.

The dancers look young and tired without the help of make-up and stage lighting. Paris has fallen asleep in a chair, her head lolling to one side, a gob of dribble at the corner of her mouth. Her thin arms — with their track marks on display — rest limply on her thighs. The dancers yawn, and pour jelly crystals and water into a children's inflatable pool on the main stage. This much jelly is going to take a long time to set. Al throws in bags of ice.

There's no time to rehearse, and the jelly doesn't set by opening time, but they have to use it anyway. The dancers complain that it's so cold and sticky they need to shower in between rounds. There are only two shower cubicles in the dressing room; so, while they're queuing for showers, the podiums are empty, and the punters complain as well.

Brigitte watches a few of the other dancers' rounds, and it looks easy. The DJ plays Prince when it's her turn, and she flashes a smile at the crowd as she steps into the pool of runny jelly. She sucks in her breath, shocked by how cold it is.

Al emcees: 'Perfect Pagan versus Tempting Taylor.'

It's ridiculously slippery, her feet slide, and she falls hard. Crunch. Something pops and rips in her left knee as her leg bends sideways beneath her. The pain feels like fire. Taylor doesn't realise Brigitte's hurt, climbs on top, and pins her down in the jelly. Taylor holds up her arms in victory. Her reward: to remove the loser's bikini top. The crowd cheers.

It takes Brigitte a lot of champagne and raspberry to make it through the rest of the night.

Through pain, bleary eyes, and a taxi window, she watches the grey 4.00am city smudge by. One last pack of young men is still out prowling, wearing shirts tucked into jeans, and Blundstones. They're country boys — the worst tippers — let off the farm for a big weekend in the city. A drunk sways, and holds up the corner of a building while he pisses on it. Two women with tanned legs and short dresses sit on a gutter; one lifts her friend's hair out of the way while she vomits on the road. Street sweepers and police officers clean up last night's mess.

At the apartment, Brigitte peels off her opal-sequinned dress, careful not to bend her knee. A missed fifty-dollar note falls from somewhere. She showers, gingerly puts on pyjamas, and makes a mug of Milo.

'Brigitte.'

Fuck. Eric's awake. She was planning to sleep on the sofa.

'Come and cuddle me, Pet.'

'Just a minute.' She limps to the bathroom and washes down some anti-inflamms, Panadol, and a sleeping tablet with her Milo.

She edges into bed against Eric's back. Her arms don't reach all the way around the mountain of cold, white flesh.

'Ooh, Pet, I think I feel something.' He rolls over. The yeast-and-prawn smell of his cock is on his hands; no amount of showering or expensive cologne ever removes that smell. 'Can you touch it for me?'

Too late — she's already falling into dreams, again, of Kurt Cobain and a puppy with a red collar.

27

Brigitte had woken in agony — worse than the pain of tendonitis, worse than the time Eric had accidentally fractured her wrist. She'd guzzled the last of her anti-inflamms, and had made an appointment with Doctor O'Meara.

Now she sits, shaking, in the waiting room.

A poster of a rainforest is stuck on the wall next to one promoting AIDS awareness. A snotty child sits on her mother's lap, coughing germs into the air. Brigitte holds her breath. A grey-faced man comes out of a consulting room and goes up to the reception desk to pay and make another appointment. Brigitte starts to sweat; the anti-inflamms are wearing off. What if something's really wrong with her knee? Maybe it's a cancerous lump — nothing to do with twisting it in the jelly. Her dad thought he only had a cold when he went to the doctor; eleven months later, Dan was dead from cancer.

Her heart yo-yos from her stomach to her throat when Doctor O'Meara calls her name. She struggles to take a deep breath, and follows the doctor to her room.

'Take a seat, and please try to stop that shallow breathing. You'll hyperventilate.'

Brigitte apologises, and explains what happened — sort of, leaving out details about jelly. The doctor examines her swollen knee with a frown on her face.

'What do you think's wrong?' Brigitte says, eyes wide.

'Probably a torn cartilage,' the doctor says matter-of-factly.

'More anti-inflammatories?'

'No. I think you need to see an orthopaedic specialist.' She starts to write a referral.

Brigitte puts her hands over her mouth.

'Calm down. It can easily be fixed with an arthroscopy.'

'What's that?'

'A knee operation.'

Brigitte hyperventilates into her hands.

'Brigitte!' The doctor loses patience with her. 'Stop acting like a child. I've seen a patient with terminal cancer today. Your knee is not that serious.'

She feels stupid for being scared, for the childish tears in her eyes. She looks up at the poster of the muscular-skeletal system, and asks if she can get some painkillers.

'You need rest and an operation, not more medication.'

'Some Valium?'

The doctor furrows her brow, and taps her pen on the prescription pad.

'Please.'

'All right. But try to make it last a bit longer this time.'

28

A brochure arrives along with the junk mail in the letterbox: a short-course guide from the Council of Adult Education. Brigitte throws the junk in the bin, but holds onto the brochure and flicks through the pages. Ceramics looks good. *Why not?* She rings to enrol, but the receptionist tells her that ceramics has been cancelled this term, because the teacher has gone overseas. The next course on the list is creative writing. She enjoyed writing at school — even wanted to be a writer at one time. Her body is exhausted, but her brain could do with a workout. She asks if there are any places left in creative writing. The receptionist says she could do the Thursday two o'clock class, and Brigitte books a place. She doesn't have a credit card, so she organises to pay when she goes in. She arranges for the course information to be sent to Nana and Papa's address, like the rest of her mail. Eric would make fun of her if he found out — tell her she's too stupid to do a writing course.

She opens the windows, leans against the grille, and breathes the first traces of spring air: jasmine, and damp earth starting to dry out. Flower buds are opening in the gardens, and baby ducks are swimming with their mothers on the pond. The wind has lost some of its chill, and she feels herself thawing out, sloughing off the weighty coat of winter. This time of the year always makes her feel like a kid again, as though she could run and run barefoot in the gardens. She closes her eyes and stretches — her knee hurts, her arm hurts — imagining the sensation of running, unburdened by pain, with cool, damp grass beneath her feet. Her mind drifts to thoughts of how clean and peaceful the apartment would be if

Eric never came back. Not through something bad happening to him: just not coming back. She opens her eyes, sighs, and moves away from the window.

She picks up a magazine from the coffee table and slumps on the sofa. A week of vegetable and fruit juices, and peppermint tea, is the key to better skin and a perfect body, according to the latest edition of *Cleo*.

***

The creative-writing class is full of middle-aged women — eight of them — and one older man. Too intimidating. Brigitte walks out, looking down at the CAE letter she's holding, pretending she's in the wrong room. And, smack, she crashes straight into the teacher as he walks in, knocking all the papers out of his hands.

'Hey! Who's trying to escape from my class?'

'God, I'm so sorry.' She helps him pick up his notes and handouts, her embarrassment stronger than the pain stabbing at her knee as she bends down. She feels the gaze of the entire class on her back, and wishes she'd worn a longer skirt. 'I think I'm in the wrong room.'

'What's your name?' the teacher says.

'Brigitte Weaver.'

He checks his list. 'No, your name's here. You're in the right place.'

'Actually, I don't think writing's for me,' she says in a quiet, apologetic voice.

'Well, I think you should stay for the first class and then decide.' He's not so quiet.

She doesn't really have a choice, because they're all looking at her and she doesn't want to make more of a scene. Sheepishly, she takes a seat down the back. The desktop flips up under her elbow, and her notebook and pens fall to the floor. Great — not only does she have to sit through a two-and-a-half-hour class with these scary people, but now they all know she's a clumsy idiot. Her face burns the same shade as her red shirt.

The teacher introduces himself as Matt Elery. He's wearing a brown sweater, jeans with frayed cuffs, and scuffed Converse All Stars. Brigitte guesses his age as late twenties. He's a bit skinny, and his collar-length, dirty-blond hair could do with a trim. There are no designer labels on his clothes. He's had a novel, which Brigitte has never heard of, published. And he writes regularly for food magazines and anybody else who asks him to — including *Mad Monster Trucks Monthly*. The class finds that funny. He doesn't look like a monster-truck kind of guy.

'I think we all know who Brigitte is.' He grins, and they all look at her again. 'But can we go around the class and have everybody else introduce themselves? Just your name and what you're hoping to get from this course will be fine.'

They all wanted to write — loved English lit at school — but never had time because of work or family commitments. One woman's short story was published in an anthology, and now she wants to 'hone her craft', whatever that means. Jack, the older man, has an idea for a Hemingway-inspired novella.

Matt explains the difference between popular and literary fiction. Brigitte thinks she'll write literary fiction, because plotting and following a structure sounds too hard. The marker squeaks as Matt draws a truck on the white board: a cabin with a line connecting it to a rectangle trailer, and wheels. It's not a mad-monster truck, he points out, and they all laugh again. On the cabin part of the truck he writes *subject matter*, and on the trailer he writes *theme*. Then he explains how any truck can pull the trailer.

He talks about stream-of-consciousness writing, and gets them to choose a photograph from a pile on his desk and write whatever it brings to mind. Brigitte takes the photo of a man and a child holding hands, and writes about a day at the zoo with her dad.

He let her look at the lizards and snakes in the reptile house for as long as she liked, he bought her a double scoop of ice-cream, and they took all day to walk around and see the animals twice. She was so tired he had to carry her to the car, and she fell asleep in his arms on the way. Of course, that day never really happened, because he was always away working, and then he died.

Matt encourages them to share their words, but nobody wants to, except for Jack — he's written about the photo of a fishing boat.

At the end of the class, Matt says their homework is to start writing a short story to present. Then he invites them to have coffee at a café on Degraves Street.

They sit outside around two rickety tables. Brigitte feels stupid as she listens to the group's conversation about books and authors she's never heard of. She's been reading Stephen King.

Two of the students finish their coffees, thank Matt for the class, and leave.

'See you next week,' Matt says.

Jack finishes his cigarette, picks up his tobacco pouch and papers, and says he'd better be going, too.

'Would you like another coffee?' Matt says.

Brigitte has things to do at the apartment, and costumes to wash. And Eric's in town; he'll be wondering where she is.

'My shout,' Matt says.

The costumes and Eric can wait a bit longer. She asks for peppermint tea.

'Anybody else?' No, they are all leaving.

Brigitte watches Matt go into the coffee shop to order. The woman behind the counter laughs at whatever he's saying. The light catches in his hair, flickering like sunbeams through leaves. He reminds her of somebody.

He moves his chair around to the other side of the table so he's facing her. 'So, Brig, do you still think the class is not for you?'

'Yes. I mean no. It was good.' He has a small, half-moon-shaped scar under his left eye. The waiter places the coffee and tea on their table.

'Any ideas for your story?'

'Um. Not yet.' She sips her tea.

'Don't worry, you'll come up with something. At the start, it's a good idea to try writing about what you already know.'

She nods.

'But not what you *think* you know. That's where most new writers make a mistake.' He lifts the coffee to his mouth and sips. Steam swirls in front of his eyes — very blue eyes.

★★★

What is that smell in the apartment? It obliterates all her story ideas and happy thoughts about the writing class. Tracy is sitting on the sofa eating a Big Mac and drinking wine cooler from a diamond-cut crystal glass. Kayla is crawling around, dropping French fries on the carpet. Eric didn't mention that his wayward daughter — from his second marriage — and granddaughter were coming down from Sydney for a few days. Tracy's blonde hair is streaked hot pink at the front. She has a black eye. Eric said she has a new boyfriend, and Brigitte is reminded of the theory about women seeking partners who resemble their fathers.

Brigitte snaps on a pair of rubber gloves, and picks up the fries with a paper towel. Kayla pulls herself up on the coffee table and reaches for one of Eric's precious collectable plates. Brigitte snatches it from her reach, just in time. Kayla screams. She stinks. How can Tracy stand it?

'Where's ...' *Your father* would sound weird; Tracy is only a couple of years younger than Brigitte. 'Eric?'

'Gone down the shop to get Kay Kay some nappies.'

Great.

'Want a drink?' Tracy says.

'No, thanks.' Brigitte pulls off the gloves and pours herself a glass of filtered water at the breakfast bar. She lights a candle in the oil burner with a few drops of lemongrass essential oil to diffuse the smell.

Dishes are stacked on the kitchen bench. Why can't Eric just pack the dishwasher? And he won't unpack it, either — he says he doesn't know where things go. Bottles and baby paraphernalia are soaking in milky water in the sink. *Gross.*

'Tracy!' Brigitte points, choking on her water. Kayla is eating from the bowl of potpourri.

'Fuck!' Tracy pulls Kayla across her knee and whacks her on the back. She gurgles and vomits up dried flower petals and spices onto the sofa. Brigitte rushes to the bathroom, dry retches over the toilet, and promises herself she'll never have children.

29

In the second class, Matt teaches them about showing and not telling in writing. Brigitte doesn't understand the difference. *Her eyes were green* is telling, Matt says. *Her eyes were the colour of olives with amber flecks like beer held to the light* is showing. Brigitte thinks that sounds like over-describing. And what if you picture black olives? She doesn't ask. She writes: *His eyes were deep-blue ocean waters in which I would happily drown to soothe my soul from burning.* When she catches Matt looking at her, she looks down at her acrylic fingernails. They're polished the latest shade: *Vamp*, the exact colour of dried blood. Uma Thurman wears it in *Pulp Fiction*, the nail technician told her.

At the end of the class, Matt says to keep working on their short stories for homework. When he doesn't invite them to have coffee again, Brigitte's shoulders slump a little. Maybe he only does coffee as an icebreaker after the first class. He probably has a date with his girlfriend now. Or boyfriend. Maybe he's married. She packs up her things and walks out. But she stops just outside the door, turns, and goes back in.

'Coming down for coffee, Matt?'

'Can't today.' He packs up his notes. He's not wearing a wedding ring.

'Oh.'

He looks up from the papers. 'Don't look so sad.'

Why does she always have to be so transparent?

'A long drive ahead of me. My uncle's funeral tomorrow, in Deniliquin.'

'That's funny. I just went to my uncle's funeral, too.'

'I'm sorry.'

'Great uncle, actually,' she adds, a little too brightly, stupidly.

'Coming for coffee, Brig?' Jack sticks his head in the doorway.

'Not today. I have something on.'

'See you next week then.' He waves a hand.

'Bye, Jack,' Brigitte and Matt say at the same time.

They take the lift together. Outside, Matt walks towards Collins Street, so Brigitte walks with him.

'Do you drive in?' she says.

'Not usually, because I live close.'

That's two things they have in common: dead uncles and inner-city addresses. 'I'll walk with you to your car.'

'Thought you had something on.'

'No. Just didn't feel like listening to more stories about Ernest Hemingway.'

'Fair enough.'

They walk through the dim arcades — most of the shops have closed for the day — turn left into Collins Street, and cross the lights at Elizabeth.

'This is it.' He stops at an old red car parked on the street — a Commodore or Holden or something. He opens the passenger door and throws in his briefcase. She feels like doing something crazy, like saying: *Take me with you, along for the company.* Nobody should go to a funeral alone.

'Want a lift home?' he says.

'My mother told me not to get into cars with strangers.' *Unless, of course, they drive a Porsche.*

'Your mother sounds like a wise woman.'

She laughs.

He walks around to the driver's side and climbs in. He turns on the ignition, reaches across, and winds down the passenger-side window. 'Sure you don't want a lift?'

She shakes her head. 'I need the exercise.'

'No you don't.' He grins.

Who does he remind her of?

'See you next week then.' He does a U-turn, beeps the horn, and waves.

She lingers and watches the tail-lights of Matt's car until it disappears in traffic. As she dawdles towards the apartment, a strange hollowness — an aloneness — aches through her body. A breeze with a touch of warmth blows rubbish along the gutter, and dirt up into her eyes.

30

During breaks at work, when she's not sewing sequins onto costumes, Brigitte starts writing a short story. At first, it's hard to think of something to write. She remembers what Matt said: *Write what you know.* But she doesn't know much about anything. She doesn't have any hobbies or interests — not even the gym, since she buggered her knee — just work, and now this writing course. She hasn't travelled much, and she's seen no further than the inside of hotel rooms and band venues when she used to go on tour with Eric. Nothing interesting.

She jots down in her notebook some ideas about people at work. A story about Rita the Gold Bar ghost would be interesting, but would need a lot of research. A scenario about the disastrous jelly-wrestling night might be funny, in a black-comedy kind of way. Or how about Vince the lawyer? What an idiot. She writes:

Vince the lawyer brought me expensive gifts like lingerie and perfume. I was allergic to perfume, and dancers were not allowed to wear it anyway because wives might have smelt it and guessed that their husbands had been naughty. Body glitter was banned for the same reason. I used Vince's perfume to clean the toilet at my apartment. When Vince got really drunk he would jump up on the podium and try to dance with me. The bouncers told him to settle down but they never kicked him out because he spent too much money at the club. He told me if I went with him, he would leave his wife and take me anywhere I wanted. He was so pathetic I almost believed him. I often thought about going with him — going anywhere with anybody, really.

Forget it — she rips the page out of her notebook and throws it in the bin. Matt's too clever to believe that's fiction.

She tries stream-of-consciousness writing. It uncovers a memory of a holiday at Cradle Mountain in Tasmania with Joan, Auntie Linda, and Brigitte's cousins. It was after Dad died. Brigitte was nine or ten, and Ryan must have been eleven or twelve. It was during the summer, but it snowed. The kids had never seen snow before, and they played in it in their pyjamas, throwing snowballs at each other. Brigitte had imagined snow would feel like cold marshmallow or cotton wool, and she was shocked to find that it was so hard, that it could hurt so much. Joan had some sort of breakdown, and they found her wandering around in the snow wearing a nightdress and only one of her Chanel slippers.

'Watcha doin', Pagan?' Ember jolts her back from the chill of Cradle Mountain with a glass of champagne and raspberry. Champagne is made from grapes, and there must be a trace of fruit in the raspberry cordial; so, technically, she's not breaking the *Cleo* diet.

'Thanks. I'm writing a story for my writing class.'

'You're too smart to be a stripper.' Ember's wrapped in a towel, her hair dripping. She's just come off the main stage after performing her 'wet-n-wild' show. She throws her purple faux-snake skin shoes in the bin, and takes another pair from her bag.

'Don't you think that's wasteful?' Brigitte says.

'The water fucks 'em. Makes the violet colour run.'

'Violet? They look purple to me.'

'They're *violet*. Only cost twenty bucks at the Vic Market anyway. Bought ten pairs.' She dries her hair, reapplies her lipstick, and flitters out of the dressing room to do some lap dances before her next podium set.

Brigitte forgets about doing lap dances as she sips her drink and chews her pen. She writes:

Nobody usually came here at this time of year. The park ranger yawned. Boring routine checks. Hang on a minute — the door to the only occupied cabin was ajar. He'd better have a look. He zipped up his jacket, pulled on the hood and got out of the car. The driver's side of the station wagon parked out front was open. The wind whistled and swung the keys in the ignition. There were no other signs of the family he'd seen arrive a week ago. Down at the old chalet he found one gold ballerina shoe half-buried in the snow.

'Pagan. Podium two in five minutes,' Hannah calls. Brigitte closes her notebook.

31

Matt teaches them about writing dialogue. *Dialogue reveals character and subtext ... avoid adverbs and attributions other than 'said' ... William Faulkner ...* Brigitte can't concentrate. She rubs her knee; it's starting to ache. Matt's eyes are too blue. Focus, focus. He's wearing the brown sweater again, and faded jeans. She still can't work out who he reminds her of. Dad? Maybe a tiny bit; but, no, that's not it.

The pain becomes unbearable, and she excuses herself while Matt finishes up the class. She rushes to the bathroom, takes some Panadol, and tightens the bandage around her knee.

Matt's looking at the notice board in the corridor when she comes out. 'Coming down to the coffee shop, Brig?'

'OK.' She forces a smile through the pain, and tries not to limp.

'Started your story?'

'Yep.'

'What's it about?'

'Not telling.'

He grins. They don't speak in the lift. He puts his hands into his jeans pockets, and she stares at the floor. Then they look sideways at each other and can't help laughing.

They catch up with the rest of the class — the same café, same outside tables. Jack stays longer than the others, smoking, and talking — animatedly, using his arms — about Hemingway. Matt nods slowly, but his eyes are glazing over. He glances at Brigitte, trying to keep a straight face. Jack looks from Matt to Brigitte, back to Matt, then he raises his eyebrows, and Brigitte feels her cheeks blushing pink.

'Ah, well. Better be going,' Jack says, and ambles off towards Flinders Street.

'Are you studying or working, Brig?' Matt rocks back on his chair.

'Working.'

'Where?' It was the question she'd wished he'd never ask.

She twists her hair around a finger, not wanting to lie to him. 'I work at the Gold Bar.'

'No, you don't!' The front legs of his chair hit the ground.

She nods.

'But that's a strip joint, isn't it?'

'I work behind the bar.' Sometimes she does go behind the bar to get a drink for a punter, or for herself.

'I can't imagine you working in a place like that.'

She looks at the table, picking at the edge with a thumbnail as if there is paint peeling.

'You don't seem ...' When she looks up, he catches her out with direct eye-contact — she can't look away. 'You're so quiet and ...'

'Innocent?'

'Yes.'

It was meant to be a joke, and she laughs — not sure if she's flattered or offended.

'What's it like in there?'

'Are you telling me you've never been?'

He shakes his head. Perhaps he's telling the truth. Unlikely, but maybe all men aren't the same.

'It's pretty sleazy.'

'You need to find another job, Brig.'

She runs her thumb-pads across the shiny surface of her fingernails. He looks down at them, too.

'Coffee? Or peppermint tea?'

How did he remember that? She asks for a flat white. She's

off her diet this week.

He goes in to order. The white-and-black tiles are crumbling around the entrance. She looks at the sandwiches and cakes under dome platters in the shop front, and catches her reflection in the window, smiling. There's a crack in the glass. She redirects her gaze to the old building at the Flinders Lane end — it reminds her of Gotham City. She wishes she didn't have to go back to the apartment. She's tired of playing house.

'So what's your story about?' He sits back at the table.

'Told you I'm not telling.'

'I'll get to hear it next week.'

'Next week!'

'Yep. You missed the end of the class when I asked everybody to bring in their pieces to workshop.'

The waiter places their coffees on the table.

'Just remembered I have something on next week.' She laughs again, and sips her coffee.

'No you don't.'

This is the most she's laughed for … ever.

Matt reaches across for the sugar — the back of his hand too close to her, and she flinches.

'Sorry. I …' She doesn't know what to say.

He frowns.

'Sorry. It's OK.' She wants to snuggle up against his sweater. It looks so soft. There's a hole starting to form in the left-shoulder seam; she would like to sew that up for him.

'I have to go.' She stands up, and starts to put on her coat. One of the sleeves is inside out, and when she flicks it the right way she knocks over her coffee. 'Sorry.'

He stands the cup upright, and wipes the spilt coffee with some serviettes. 'Is everything OK?'

She nods.

'You sure?'

166

'Yep.' She rushes off — ignoring the pain in her knee and the stupid tears in her eyes — half-walking, half-running up Degraves Street. She trips on the gutter. *Idiot. He must think I'm crazy.*

32

Ember struts into the dressing room with at least three hundred dollars hanging out of her garter belt. 'R–r–rob's out there asking for you.'

Brigitte puts the costume she's sewing aside and finishes her drink. She slides her feet into a pair of red stilettoes, and sashays out to see him. R-r-rob is a weirdo regular of hers, with a stutter and a fetish for r–r–red shoes — he likes to fill them with money.

He smiles moronically when she sits and puts her feet up on his table.

'Hello, m–m–mistress P–p–pagan.'

'Drink your beer, Rob,' she says. 'And put some money in my shoes. Now!' He likes her to order him around.

R–r–rob's eyes goggle behind his thick round glasses. He's drooling, a bead of saliva shining at the corner of his mouth, and an erection snaking inside his trousers. He drinks his beer, and fills her shoes with twenty- and fifty-dollar notes.

She stifles a yawn, and looks up at the two blue lights above the main stage: Matt's eyes. *Stop it, Brigitte. Stop thinking about him. Especially after the performance at the coffee shop.*

Vince the lawyer saunters in with Doctor Dave, the cosmetic surgeon who brings the dancers cocaine and does their boob jobs for half price. The cash register in her head cha-chings. She tells R–r–rob his time is up. He understands that her other customers will get jealous if she spends too much time with him.

Vince heads for the bar to order a shaker of some lethal concoction, and Dave comes over, waving a fifty-dollar note as Brigitte climbs onto a podium. The DJ plays 'The Most Beautiful

Girl in the World' for her.

'Hi, Pagan. Hear you've hurt your knee,' says Dave. 'Can I have a look at it?'

'It'll cost you.'

He pulls out another fifty, and places them both under her garter belt as she dangles her legs over the edge of the podium.

'Fuck, it's really swollen.' He feels the fluid around her knee, and tells her she needs an arthroscopy.

'I know.'

'You shouldn't be dancing on it.'

Al comes over and jokes about them not being allowed to touch the merchandise.

Vince sits next to Dave, and places a shaker and three shot glasses on the podium ledge. He looks up at Brigitte, 'Hi, beautiful.'

Dave slips his business card into Brigitte's bra and tells her to give him a call. He can get her a job as a medical sales rep, with a company car and everything. She doesn't mention that she can't drive.

'Now, how about taking off some of those clothes?'

Her garters — one on each thigh — are so full of money that they keep falling down. She squashes the cash into her overflowing locker in the dressing room. A few fifties stick out the bottom as she forces it shut and clicks the combination lock. She's managed to get Matt off her mind and kill her knee pain with too many lethal shaker drinks, joints out the back with Ember, and lines of coke with Dave and Vince.

She steadies herself against the wall as she makes her way along the passage back out into the club. A punter sitting in a club chair in the lap-dance area beckons to her with a hundred-dollar note.

The room spins as she drapes herself over him and instructs him to unfasten her bra. She places her hands on his shoulders and sways slowly, softly brushing the insides of his thighs with her gyrating hips. She turns, pauses to remove her G-string, looks over at the door, and sees Sean come in. He looks around and walks towards the bar. He's holding a bunch of white flowers. *What is he doing here?* It's so out of context, it's funny. She laughs, and her laughter — seeming to have substance and colour — reverberates inside her head. He sees her, but she doesn't acknowledge him; she just keeps swaying and laughing. He turns and walks out. *Hey, wait a minute.* She tries to follow him, but doesn't get far — everything is too fuzzy, and the punter pulls her back by the wrist.

Big Johnny cleans up the flowers strewn across the sticky carpet.

33

Tracy and Kayla have gone home, but Ian's back. Eric doesn't look away from the Nintendo game he's playing with Ian when Brigitte, weighed down with shopping bags, walks into the apartment. Ian takes in a quick up-and-down of her, and loses the game.

'Who's Marco?' Eric says.

'My driving instructor.'

'He rang while you were out. He's running an hour late.' He rolls the Juicy Fruit around his tongue, and lights a joint. 'What did you buy, Pet?' He shakes the flame off the match.

'A mobile phone like yours.' And some shoes, cosmetics, books. And lingerie that she had a daydream in the shop about wearing for Matt. *Stop it*, she warns herself.

'Want a smoke?'

She shakes her head.

'Did you say "driving instructor"?'

'Yes. I'm starting a new job I have to drive for.'

'What?'

'Nothing.'

She walks to the bedroom and closes the door behind her. Eric and Ian cough and laugh about something, and then the bip-bip-bip of the game starts again.

Brigitte kicks off her shoes, sits on the bed, and plays with the settings on her new Nokia N100 while she waits for Marco. All the girls at work are swapping their pagers for mobile phones. She works out how to set the ring tone and program phone numbers. She stretches out her legs, and swishes her calves against the gold satin bed linen — it's cool and smooth. Sensual. She thinks of

Matt, and her stomach flutters. She wishes she had his number in her phone. She pretends: types in MATT, and adds a made-up number to the list.

Better do some writing for him. She puts the phone aside, and takes out her notebook. She can't think of what happens after — or rather, before — the park ranger finds the gold ballerina shoe in the snow. But she has an idea, a picture in her head, of the ending:

> Soft snowflakes caught on the protagonist's (Joanne/Joni/Julie?) spun-gold hair. One gold ballerina shoe, one bare foot and droplets of blood left strange pink-tinged prints in the snow. It was a long way to the summit, to find her husband and child. Her dead father took her hand and walked beside her. There was no hurry. Out here, there was no time and nothing mattered.

But what happens in between? Writer's block.

She takes a break and tries to read the paper, but her mind keeps going AWOL. Matt. Matt. Matt. *Stop it! Matt's a nice guy. Nice guys are not interested in dumb strippers with homicidal boyfriends.*

But she won't be a stripper for much longer, she reminds herself. Maybe then … She finds Doctor Dave's card in her purse, and rings the number. She doodles some love hearts on her notebook cover while she waits for him to pick up. No answer. She leaves a message for him to call back about the medical-rep job.

There are plenty of other jobs in the paper's employment section. One of those might be better than the rep job. David Jones is looking for a sales assistant in the cosmetics department. She loves shopping at David Jones. She writes an application letter on the back page of her notebook, and tears it out carefully. She'll post it with a copy of the resume they had to write at school, after her driving lesson.

She puts the notebook aside, lies back in the satiny cloud of big, fluffy pillows, and closes her eyes. After the next writing class they will all sit laughing, crowded around those wobbly little tables in Degraves Street, with not enough room, so Matt will have to move closer to her. Their bodies will touch. She won't freak out this time. He'll accidentally put his hand on her leg. He'll apologise, she'll say it's OK, and he'll leave it there ...

The sound of vacuuming disturbs her fantasy. She opens her eyes; the sheets feel hot, and her pelvis aches. Sean must be out in the foyer. Something happened at work on the weekend. She thinks Sean came in and got angry with her, but she can't remember why.

Eric and Ian don't look up as she walks past them to the door. She opens it, ready to apologise for whatever she did. Sean walks away, and she calls after him.

'Who are you talking to, Brigitte?' Eric shouts from inside.

'Nobody.'

'If it's Shane, tell him to piss off.'

'*Sean.*'

Eric coughs.

'I'm going now.'

'Where?'

'Told you, I have a driving lesson.'

The vacuuming drowns out the sound of Eric's and Ian's stoned laughter. She closes the door behind her, and yells over the vacuuming. 'I'm sorry.'

'I don't want to talk to you.' Sean hits the stop button on the vac and walks towards his office. She follows him.

His office is not much bigger than a broom cupboard, or (having never seen a broom cupboard) the size she imagines one to be. There's a desk with a phone and a computer; a metal shelf holding cleaning products and cloths; and brooms, of course, in the corner. It smells of furniture polish and lemon-scented disinfectant. She sneezes, and looks up into Kurt Cobain's frozen blue eyes in a huge poster above the desk. He's wearing a white

T-shirt with *Captain America* printed across the front in blue letters, and holding a pistol to his mouth. The office is warm and stuffy, but the poster makes her shiver.

Sean stands the vacuum cleaner in the corner with the brooms, and sits at the desk with his back to her. She lingers in the doorway. He rubs his face with his hands. 'Can you please just go?'

'I said I'm sorry.' She studies her fingernails. She remembers what happened at the Gold Bar, while pretending that she didn't — that it was Pagan, not her.

He can't even look at her.

'It's just my job, Sean. That's not who I am.'

'Close the door on your way out, please.'

She climbs into the driver's seat. It feels strange, unnatural. Marco explains how everything in the car works. He has his own brake on the passenger side, just in case, which is reassuring.

'Okey-dokey, Brigitte, turn on the ignition and put the gear into "Drive", please.'

She turns the key, stops angsting about Sean, and smiles proudly as the engine starts. 'Here?' She looks down at the gears, and he guides her hand with his to select 'Drive'.

'That's right. Now check your mirrors, and indicate to pull out into the traffic, please.'

'This?' She glances in the mirrors, and fumbles with the stick next to the steering wheel.

'Yes, that's the indicator — push it down to indicate right. And up for left. Okey-dokey, any time now.'

'But there are cars coming.' She looks to the sides, behind, in the mirrors.

'Those cars are a long way away. It's safe to pull out now.'

'Can we wait just a minute?'

'Okey-dokey. When you're ready.' He folds his hands in his lap. She looks in the mirrors again. 'Now?'

'Now is fine.'

She inhales deeply, puffs out her cheeks, lets it go, and pulls out into the road. 'Ha ha! I'm driving.'

A car beeps at them.

'What?' She glances nervously at Marco. 'What am I doing wrong?'

'You're fine. Watch the road. We can go a little bit faster.'

She touches the accelerator tentatively with her right foot.

'Let's get our speed up to 60.'

God, that's fast.

When she relaxes a bit, Marco tells her about his wife who's in her thirties but still holding onto the dream of being an actor. She was gorgeous when he met her, just 17. A talent scout for a modelling agency discovered her in a shopping centre. The next Elle Mcpherson, they said. Then she started getting acting roles, left school, took drama lessons. Brigitte looks at a dress in a shop window on Lygon Street.

'Watch the red light, Brigitte,' Marco says. 'Slow down.'

She brakes too hard, and the car jolts. 'Sorry.'

'It's all right. You're doing fine.'

The light turns green, and she accelerates. 'Was your wife on TV?'

'She had a small role in a film and a bit-part in *Sons and Daughters*, but never got another break.'

'My brother's an actor.'

'Turn left at the road before the cemetery, please.'

She indicates, and turns the wheel.

'Make sure you get a good education, Brigitte. A good job.' He barely knows her — why is he telling her what to do? 'Left again up here, please.'

She doesn't make the turn. She sits up straighter, in control now. It feels good.

'Okey-dokey, we can go a bit further.' He glances sideways at her, and she lifts her chin. 'You got a boyfriend?' he says.

She shrugs.

'Bet you have at least two.'

She can't help smiling.

'You do!'

It's pie night, so she has Marco drop her at Nana and Papa's house after the lesson. She mails her job application to David Jones in the post box on the corner before she goes in.

34

'Who would like to share their story?' Matt is sitting on the big desk at the front of the room.

Only Jack raises his hand. Brigitte slinks in, late, along the wall, when Matt looks the other way.

'Brig.'

Oh no.

'How about you go first?'

She groans, 'Do I have to?'

'It's your punishment for being late.'

They all laugh, and her neck and face prickle. But if she can dance naked in front of crowds of men, she can do this. *Pagan could do this.*

'OK.' She fumbles around in her bag for the A4 plastic sleeve containing the story hand-written neatly on lined, loose-leaf paper. Jack nods and smiles encouragement. She drops her bag on the floor next to Matt's desk, clears her throat, and takes a deep breath. For a moment, her eyes are unable to focus on the words, and she can't find her voice — she can't do this. She takes another breath and, with the pages shaking in her hands and her face burning, reads her story about the woman who went insane in a cabin at Cradle Mountain after her husband and child disappeared on a bush walk.

When she finishes, the class is silent. *They hated it.* She looks up, Matt is staring at her, and one of the women in the front row has tears in her eyes.

'Wow, Brig.' Matt stands up. 'That was great!'

They all clap, and she feels herself turning even redder.

The class workshops her story. Matt offers suggestions about punctuation, and Jack tells her how Hemingway would have approached it.

It's raining, so they sit inside the coffee shop. Everybody stays longer — congratulating each other on their stories. When they finally leave, Matt tells Brigitte again how much he liked her story. 'That didn't really happen, did it?' he says.

'Of course not.'

The rain stops, the sun comes out, and it's hot behind the window in the shop. They take off their coats, Matt pushes up his shirtsleeves, and Brigitte puts on her sunglasses. Her bag emits a ringtone.

'What's that noise?' he says.

She fishes out her new mobile phone.

'Aren't you going to answer it?'

'Just as soon as I work out how to.' She presses the wrong button and hangs up. 'Oops. It's OK. Just my nana. I'll ring her back later.'

'How do you know it was your nana?'

'It shows up on the screen. See here.' Her chair scrapes on the floor as she pulls it closer to him. She's so excited about her new purchase that she doesn't notice how close he's daring to lean. 'You can program numbers into it. If somebody in your phone list calls, their name will show up on the screen so you know who it is.' She presses some buttons.

'You probably need mine — in case you're running late for class again, or something,' he says.

She looks up and, catches him gazing at her. He looks back at the screen, pretending to be interested in the phone's memory system, and frowns. 'I see you already have a MATT in there.'

'Oh, no, that's a mistake.' She quickly deletes it.

He tells her his number and she keys it in — to be listed

alphabetically between Jennifer and Nana. She places the phone carefully where she can admire it on the table next to her empty coffee cup. He's grinning at her.

'What?'

'You have to give me your number, too, or it won't work.'

She twists her mouth, doesn't get it, but finds a scrap of paper in her bag to write her number on anyway. Their hands touch as he takes it from her. She fiddles with the phone again, and tries to think of something clever to say. She doesn't want to go back to the apartment.

'Feel like going for a drink?' He's read her thoughts.

'Can't. I have to work.'

'You could call in sick.'

She shakes her head.

'One night off won't hurt.'

She hasn't taken a night off since Uncle Joe died.

'Come on. I'll call for you. Show me how to use your phone, and I'll tell them you're too sick to talk.'

Al made her work a day shift after the last time. 'No.'

He makes sad puppy-dog eyes.

'Maybe I'll come for one drink, and then I can still go to work.'

They put on their coats, and he holds the door open for her. At the corner of Degraves and Flinders streets, he takes her hand. She doesn't pull it away. She looks up at him, fighting to hide a smile, but he's looking straight ahead. A rainbow shimmers over Flinders Street Station as they walk into Young and Jackson's brown wood-panelling, mirrors, red-and-gold carpet, and pressed-tin flowers on the ceiling. About a dozen drinkers, mostly men, sit around tables looking at the TV on the wall.

'Beer?'

'Um, I don't normally drink beer.'

'What *do* you drink?'

'Champagne. With raspberry.'

'Champagne and raspberry! How old are you, anyway?'

She doesn't answer.

'Maybe when it's your shout, but I'm on a beer budget. I'm a writer, remember?'

'Beer's fine.'

'I'm joking. You can have whatever you like.' He puts some money on the bar.

'Beer's fine.'

They take their drinks to a window, and sit on bar stools in an alcove. Across the street a red neon sign blinks: *City Hatters*.

'It's not meant to be here,' he says.

She frowns and tilts her head.

'Flinders Street Station. It was meant for India.'

She loses the frown, and studies the arched entrance and the dome: it does look Indian.

'The plans were shipped from England, and got mixed up.'

'Get out of here.'

'It's true. And India got the station meant for Melbourne.'

Young cops are patrolling beneath the station clocks.

'Actually, I think it's just an urban myth.'

After three pots of beer, Matt tells her she drinks like a man.

'Is that meant to be a compliment?'

'Dunno. Cheers.' He clinks his glass to hers. 'I don't think you're going to work tonight.'

'Oh really?'

He smiles and shakes his head. A tram rattles along Flinders Street.

After four pots, she leans on her hand and tells him about her childhood. He's a good listener, and after five pots he knows all about her loving father, her evil mother, her high-school dream of becoming a writer. Their hands are resting on the countertop, almost touching. She's still sober enough — but only just — to realise it's time to go, before she blurts out something stupid about work or Eric.

Matt leans closer. 'Your hair smells amazing, Brig. What do you put in it?'

'Sandalwood and rose oil.'

'Wanna come back to my place?'

Yes, more than anything. 'No.'

'Maybe I should take a hint.' He finishes his beer, and places the empty glass on the counter. 'You're always running off on me.'

She apologises as she stumbles off the bar stool. 'What are you gonna do now?'

'Dunno. Have another drink. Then go get my bike, left it at work.'

'You have a motorbike?' She pictures riding behind him, arms wrapped around his waist, an ocean road, the wind blowing her hair.

'Push bike.'

Oh, not quite as sexy. She stands on tiptoes to kiss his cheek, but he turns his face so it's on his lips. He holds her head gently in his hands. His lips are so soft. She closes her eyes, wants to stay, but pulls away. Eric will be waiting for her at the apartment.

'I'm really sorry.'

'Sure.' And he mumbles something she can't understand.

She shouldn't have come here with him. Maybe he'll pick up somebody after she leaves. A group of pretty office workers are giggling, getting drunk at a table in the corner. One of them would be a much better choice for him.

***

She stumbles up the apartment complex's white marble steps, through the security door, tells herself to 'shh' as she fumbles with the key in the lock. She switches on the light, and smells Juicy Fruit. Eric's been waiting, in the dark.

'Where were you, Pet?' His arm is draped across the back of

the sofa, his fat fingers drumming.

'At work.'

'No, you weren't.' Legs crossed, his trouser seams are stretched to their threshold — sausages about to burst their skins.

'What are you talking about? I'm home early because my knee was hurting.'

'Where's your work bag then? And your money?'

She looks at the carpet. 'Forgot it in my locker.'

'I went into the Gold Bar. They said you didn't come in tonight.'

'Who said?'

'Paris.' He struggles to uncross his legs, hauls himself out of the sofa, and lumbers towards her.

'Paris is a junkie.' She takes a step backwards. 'She doesn't know if she's there half the time. You didn't see me because I was in the lap-dance area all night.' Suddenly sober, her palms are sweaty, and her heart beats like a bird's as she lies to him. 'My knee was too sore to work the podiums,' she adds, unnecessarily, almost in a whisper.

She looks across at the print hanging on the wall behind the sofa: two lovers embrace against a background that looks finger-painted — frosty white smears tinged with aqua. If you could taste it, it would be spearmint. The female figure rests her head against the man's neck. She is veiled in black, her face hidden by a hood. He is shadow-like, grey, his face visible but chiselled, without detail like a sculpture. Against the small of her back he holds a bouquet of flowers: white, perhaps daisies, with centres the colour of fresh blood. Is this their last time together? Is she in his dream? A memory? Or a ghost? Why can't they just be together?

Eric thinks prints are tacky, and when he's away she swaps his original David Boyd for her mass-produced copy of Charles Blackman's *Lovers*. She forgot to change them back this time.

Smack! Eric knocks her off balance with a back-hander. She

falls sideways, and her cheek hits the corner of the breakfast bar.

'Don't lie to me, Brigitte. I talked to Al, too.'

Dizzy with pain, she holds one hand against her cheek, and steadies herself against the breakfast bar with the other. A police car screams past.

'He was expecting a package. I had to take it in myself.' Eric's eyes are watering. She feels herself fainting, leans against the wall, comes back, knows he's going to hit her again, and protects her face with her hands. The dizziness dissipates, and her flesh ices over at the sound of her mobile phone in her bag, but Eric doesn't seem to notice the ringing. Tinnitus.

'Don't fuck me around, Brigitte.'

She nods and struggles to swallow; her throat is too tight, her mouth too dry. He holds her face in his big, doughy hands, and squeezes. Matt's hands were smooth and gentle when he held her head at Young and Jackson's. If she can keep thinking about that, whatever Eric does to her won't hurt so much.

'Do you hear?' he yells.

She starts, and squeezes her eyes shut as tightly as she can.

'You don't want to know what happens to people who fuck me around.'

She nods again without opening her eyes. She won't be going to writing class next week.

35

'Unknown caller' flashes on the little screen. Brigitte blows her nose on a tissue, lies back on the satin sheets, and answers her mobile.

'Hi Brigitte,' says a too-cheery voice. 'How are you?' The cheery voice doesn't wait for her answer. It's Catherine Kerr, the cosmetics-department manager from David Jones. She says that the letter Brigitte sent them was very impressive.

Brigitte had forgotten all about the job application. 'Thanks.' She forces her voice to sound like she hasn't been crying, but there's no way she can match Catherine's tone.

Catherine asks if she could come in for an interview next Thursday, and Brigitte says she needs to check her diary. She sits up and flicks the pages of the magazine on the bedside table. 'Yes, I'm free on Thursday. Anytime would be OK.' She's not going to class, so time doesn't matter.

Catherine makes it one o'clock at the Christian Dior counter on the ground floor. Brigitte thanks her, and hangs up. She folds the tissue, and pushes it inside her sleeve. She's never had a normal, proper job. What would it be like? Normal hours, normal people who keep their clothes on, probably a uniform, lunch in the tea room with her co-workers, drinks — but not too many — on Friday nights after work. Sounds nice. Nice? What is wrong with her? Nice is not her thing.

***

On Thursday, she covers her bruised cheek with lots of concealer, and brushes her hair into a neat ponytail held with a simple black band. What do normal, proper people wear to job interviews? She stands in the walk-in robe, narrowing the choice to her funeral suit or the Chanel dress. She goes with the suit, and digs out her funeral shoes. What colour stockings? Sheer black or natural? Natural is nice. There's that word again.

She applies an extra coat of nude lipstick, and blots it with a tissue. A final check in the mirror: hair, nails, and make-up look good. She fastens her top shirt button, and removes a stray hair from her jacket collar. She wishes she'd bought pantyhose instead of stockings, and hopes nobody will notice the little bumps of suspender-belt clips protruding through her skirt.

Catherine Kerr is wearing a lot of make-up, and she smells of expensive fragrance. Her wheat-blonde hair is swept up into a glass-smooth chignon. She's dressed in a smart black suit, similar to Brigitte's funeral suit. They sit opposite each other at the Christian Dior make-over table, next to a palette of eye-shadow colours too bright for anybody in their right mind to seriously consider wearing. Catherine asks Brigitte questions about her education and work history. Brigitte lies, and feels annoyed at herself for blushing. Strippers shouldn't blush at anything. She won't be a stripper anymore, fingers crossed; she'll be a normal person, going for drinks — but not too many — on Friday nights. *Nice.* She sneezes.

'Where are you working at the moment, Brigitte?'

'Um, I'm a bartender at a nightclub.' Should she tell Catherine she has lipstick on her teeth?

Catherine doesn't ask the name of her work place or why it is not included on her resume. Brigitte rubs a finger subtly across her own front teeth.

'Are you OK?' Catherine says.

Too subtle. Brigitte nods and smiles. Catherine asks why she would like to work at David Jones.

'I'm tired of working hard, long hours, you know.' *Wrong*

answer. She sneezes again, and Catherine hands her a box of tissues. Better add allergy tablets to her shopping list of medication. 'I love make-up. And I always shop at David Jones.' *Better. Shut up now.*

'Great. We have vacancies at the Christian Dior and the general cosmetics counters. The roster for both positions includes Saturday and Sunday shifts. Would you be available to work those hours?'

'Sure.' Why not? She's used to working Saturdays. And Eric's often at the apartment on Sundays, so it would be *nice* not to be there. Her mind meanders to dreamy Sunday mornings in a big bed with Matt — breakfast, reading the papers, sleeping till lunchtime, kissing ... *Very* nice. She wonders where he lives. *Stop it!* That's never going happen — it's over.

'Do you have any questions for me, Brigitte?'

'Huh?' *Come back, focus.*

'Any questions?'

'How much does this job pay?'

'The pay rate for beauty consultants is $10.50 an hour.'

The super-enthusiastic smile falls off her face. She tells Catherine, 'No, thanks.' There's no fucking way she could get by on that wage. Not without Eric.

Her feet and knee hurt as she waits at the tram stop in the mall. She looks at her gold Gucci watch — the circle around the face is interchangeable to match the colour of your outfit, or to suit your mood. It's a black circle today. Almost time for writing class. A busker sings Bob Dylan. Matt would be angry with her for teasing and leaving last week. Or he'd pretend the kiss never happened, which would be worse. He'll be glad she's not there today. Miserable. Pain. No Matt. No job.

Ten minutes, and there's still no tram. And she can't see one coming down the hill. Should she go to class? *No.* She knows what

Eric will do if he catches her. Actually, she doesn't know, and doesn't want to find out. But he's away. And it's just a writing class. No harm in that. *Yes. No.* What if Eric has somebody watching her? She wouldn't put it past him. *No.* The busker sings 'Tangled up in Blue'. *Yes.* She throws ten dollars into his guitar case, and limps across the mall and through the arcades.

Matt's in the classroom, sitting at his desk. She's the first student to arrive. Her heart races. Why did she come? *Stupid.* He hasn't seen her yet; she can still sneak out. Too late — he looks up from his notes with a cheeky grin. Her face burns.

'Wow, you look amazing. Why so dressed up?' He's not angry. She bets he never gets angry.

'Had a job interview.'

'Great. Tell me about it.'

She turns to take a desk down the back.

'Come up the front.'

As she's telling him about David Jones, his grin slips away. 'Brig! What happened to your face?'

She thought she'd covered it well. 'I think I had a bit too much to drink last week.' She laughs it off. 'Tripped and fell against the breakfast bar when I got home.'

'Sorry.'

'It's not your fault.'

'I tried to call you, to apologise for ...'

'It's OK.'

He steps from behind his desk and moves close to her, touches her face, and winces as if the pain is his. She feels the heat from his body. She wants to turn her head and kiss his hand, wants to do more than that — suck his fingers, push her face against his khaki T-shirt. God, what's wrong with her? She feels like she's falling. She looks up into his eyes. So blue. And that's it. The instant. She's gone. Gone, and she'll never be able to get out of it,

187

regardless of the consequences.

'A-hem.' Jack stands in the doorway, clearing his throat before entering the room.

After class, Brigitte feels the warmth from Matt's arm draped along the back of her chair. He crosses a foot over his knee — a Converse All Star almost touches her leg. The other women give her little jealous, disapproving looks, but she's used to those — she's tolerated them from women since she was eleven or twelve. It takes forever for them to leave the coffee shop. Jack, as usual, is the last. 'Ernest once wrote a six-word short story,' he says.

Brigitte and Matt smile and nod.

'For sale: baby shoes, never used.'

They stop smiling.

'Drink?' Matt says.

'No. I have to be going,' Jack says. 'Be good.' Brigitte is sure he winks at Matt as he leaves.

'Brig?'

'OK.' *Gone.* No going back now. Fuck the consequences. Fuck Eric.

'Really?'

She nods.

'Don't you have to work?'

She shakes her head. Fuck work. 'Young and Jackson's?'

'No. Somewhere else.'

They walk hand in hand up the cobbled bluestone street, through the arcades, to Collins Street, where they catch a tram.

Commuters are crammed in, heading home from work, staring at their feet or straight ahead. Brigitte and Matt have to stand, holding onto the hand straps. An old woman with brown-paper skin and dyed red hair gets on, muttering about the lack of seating. She dives for the seat somebody offers her, bumps into Brigitte, and pushes her against Matt. Even when a few passengers get off and there's enough room, she doesn't move away from him. She smiles at the old woman, but she doesn't smile back. As the tram rounds the corner at the start of Brunswick Street, she struggles to keep her balance and is forced harder against Matt.

'Where are you taking me?'

'Next stop.'

The Standard is a nondescript white pub hidden in the back streets of Fitzroy. David Bowie's 'Sorrow' is playing on the sound system as they walk in. It's dingy: brown bricks, wood panelling, maroon carpet, and Brunswick-green doorframes. Big mirrors and pictures of cowboys hang on the walls.

They order at the bar, and take their beers out to the leafy beer garden. It's crowded, but Brigitte and Matt are able to claim a table from a group of people who are just leaving. A breeze blows Matt's hair across his face.

'Cool pub.'

'It's my local.' He pushes the hair out of his eyes. 'Cheers.' He clinks his glass to hers, and they drink. 'Are you going to run off on me again tonight?'

She smiles at him over the rim of her glass. 'Are you writing another book?'

'Trying to. A bit distracted lately.'

'Really?'

'Uh-huh.'

A barmaid collects glasses, and wipes their table.

'What's it about?'

'What?'

'Your book?'

'Told you I was distracted.' He laughs and drinks. 'I've decided to give up on literary fiction and try to write something that sells. A crime thriller.'

'God. That'd be hard.'

'Not really. It's very formulaic. But the police aren't helping much with my research. Told me to watch *Law and Order*, or make it up like everybody else does.'

'How did you get to be such a great writer?' She picks at the edges of a beer coaster.

'I'm not a great writer.'

'Did you do a course?'

He tells her about his journalism degree at uni. He didn't like it, so he did copywriting and editing, and wrote restaurant reviews while he was working on his first novel. Then he got into teaching.

She leans closer to him, resting her chin on her hand. 'You're so clever.'

He shakes his head. 'I've just worked hard. Nothing to stop you from doing something similar. You write very well.'

She scoffs.

'Why don't you do a writing course?'

'I am. Haven't you noticed?'

'There's only a couple more classes to go. And I meant a degree or diploma.'

'Me?' She laughs. 'I didn't even finish high school.'

'How come?'

She takes a big drink. 'I told you about my mother?'

He nods.

'She decided she wanted to move to the country at the start of the year. I didn't want to go with her, so I stayed in the city. A job and somewhere to live were more important than finishing V.C.E.'

'This year?'

She nods.

'That would make you — eighteen or nineteen?'

'Nineteen.'

'No way!' He leans back in his chair. 'I thought you were a bit older.'

Everybody does.

He swishes the last of the beer around in his glass.

'Does that mean you're gonna run off on me this time?' she says.

'Maybe.'

'How old are you?'

'Twenty-eight.'

'God, that's old.'

'Hey, watch it.' He laughs, then says seriously, 'If you studied at night, you could work during the day.'

'But I work at night.'

'You need to find another job. You're better than that. Maybe give David Jones a chance.'

She finishes her drink and looks at the plant growing up the fence, trying to remember the name of it. Matt leans towards her, and she mirrors his body language. He reaches for her hand and holds it gently. His knee brushes against hers under the table, and her leg is on fire. She has never wanted or needed anybody like this. Wanting is an ache through her body, damp stickiness on the tops of her thighs. Needing is something else all together: it fills every part of her — the places that have always been empty and hollow — with an unfamiliar substance, warm and viscous. So close. He's going to kiss her. She closes her eyes.

'Mummy! I can't find my mummy!'

She opens her eyes. A little boy of about five or six is standing beside their table, bawling.

'It's OK, mate.' Matt lets go of Brigitte and takes the boy by the hand. 'We'll help you find your mummy. Probably over there.' He points to a group of what looks like a few families celebrating a birthday or something. Some children are playing around them. Matt leads the boy back to his group, where his mother picks him up and wipes away his tears.

When Matt goes in to order more beers, the boy runs back over to their table with a little girl in a pink fairy dress. Brigitte tries to ignore them; she doesn't know how to talk to kids.

'Is he your boyfriend?' the boy says.

'No. I don't know.' She weaves her fingers together on the table. 'Maybe.'

'He's nice.'

'I know.'

'You're back again?' Matt places the beers on the table. 'And I see you've brought a friend with you. What are your names?'

The children giggle at him.

'Is that your girlfriend?' the boy says.

'She's pretty.' The fairy girl does a ballerina twirl.

'Her name is Brigitte. And yes, she is very pretty.' He looks at Brigitte. 'And also very clever.'

Go away, Brigitte smiles at them. She wants Matt's attention all to herself, but he's playing with the children. Finally, the mother comes over and tells the kids to stop bothering them, and drags them away.

'You're really good with kids, Matt,' Brigitte says.

The boy comes back, throws a tantrum when the mother tries to pick him up, and knocks Matt's beer onto the ground.

Brigitte stands to avoid being splashed. The mother yells, and the child screams louder. She apologises to Brigitte and Matt.

'It's OK. It was an accident. Now be careful of the broken glass.' Matt calmly picks up the pieces, goes in to get a cloth, and cleans up the mess. Brigitte sculls her beer.

When Matt asks if she'd like to order some dinner or have another drink, she grabs his hand and says, 'Let's go.'

Matt lives around the corner above a tattoo shop at the grungy end of Brunswick Street, opposite the high-rise commission flats. Drunks sleep in doorways, and small-time drug dealers do deals in the public phone box across the road. Brigitte kisses Matt hard up against his front door as he fumbles in his pocket for the keys.

Inside, his bike hangs from a hook on the bluestone wall. He tells her to be careful not to trip because the light on the stairs is out. They almost make it up the staircase. Almost, but not quite. They kiss, trip, tear at each other's clothes, and fall together three-quarters of the way up. She kisses his mouth, his face, his neck. His skin tastes salty, and smells faintly of spice and citrus. She slides onto him, forgetting her knee pain, glad now for the stockings and suspenders instead of pantyhose.

A sensation she's never felt before ripples, then swells and surges through her body. She curls up her toes, tenses her muscles, and stifles a cry against his shoulder, but she can't stop the tears streaming down her face. The girls at work talk about orgasm all the time, but she never imagined it would be so ... she has no word for it. Until now, sex has always been somewhat of a chore, mechanical and unsatisfying. But her experience has been limited to a rough schoolboy, an egotistical pop star, and semi-impotent Eric on the rare occasions he's managed to get it up — not for a long time, thank God.

'Are you OK, Brig?'

She shakes her head, unable to speak.

'And I thought you were so innocent.' He laughs and strokes her hair.

She's not sure if she can move, and doesn't want to anyway — wants to stay like this forever. Her hand rests on his chest. Something's wrong — his skin feels strange, bumpy. It's too dark to see what it is. She quickly pulls her hand away, thinking he doesn't notice.

'Still want to come upstairs?'

She finds her voice — it's croaky. 'As long as you're not going to try to take advantage of me.'

He laughs and kisses her. 'You'll have to help me up. I think my back's broken.'

'Knew you were too old.'

Her eyes have adjusted to the darkness, and she sees a flash of a tattoo on his back as he stands, but he pulls his T-shirt on before she can see his chest. Maybe it was her imagination.

Upstairs he leads her past a bedroom, a bathroom with a full-size bath, a tiny kitchen, and up another short flight of stairs to a big living room.

'Feel like a glass of wine?'

'Sure.' She screws up her nose a little.

'Sorry I don't have any champagne. Or raspberry.'

She feels awkward, and can't meet his eyes after what just happened on the stairs. He goes to get a bottle. She slips the funeral shoes off her aching feet, and looks around the room: a scratched antique-looking dining table, brown-leather couch with worn arms, TV, desk with a word processor, and two big windows overlooking the street. Hundreds of books fill the floor-to-ceiling brick-and-board shelves: classics, lots of new-looking books, books on writing and teaching, cookbooks. She pulls her suit jacket tighter around her shoulders and rubs her hands together — she should have brought her coat.

He comes back with a bottle of red and two glasses. He pours their drinks, and crouches to put pages of balled-up newspaper and pieces of wood into the open fireplace. 'Why don't you choose some music, Brig?' He strikes a match and lights the paper.

His CD collection takes up a whole bookshelf — lots of stuff she doesn't know, classical music, Australian music: The Triffids, Died Pretty, Hunters and Collectors, lots of Nick Cave and the Bad Seeds. No Prince. She pulls out *Nevermind* with the baby swimming towards the dollar bill on the cover. How did they take that photo of the baby in the pool?

Matt looks up from the fire, and groans. 'I didn't realise I had that. You don't like them, do you?'

'I think so. But I only really listened when he died.' She returns the CD to the shelf. 'But now I finally know who you remind me of. It's him. You look like him.'

'I do not,' he says indignantly, and stands up.

'You do.'

'No, I don't.'

'He was pretty cute.'

'When — before or after the gunshot to the head?'

'Don't be cruel.'

'Aw, I'm so depressed, I'm so famous, making so much money. I think I'll go kill myself.'

'Stop it.'

'He had a baby, you know? How could anybody leave their baby?'

'I don't know.' She shrugs. 'Maybe he was hurting so much he didn't have a choice.'

Matt shakes his head; he can't understand that. He hands her the new Nick Cave CD, and she puts it on while he rolls a joint.

She walks across to open one of the two windows, leans on the sill, and watches a pair of police officers arrest a shirtless man in front of the commission flats. Matt comes over, stands against her back, and wraps his arms around her. Her body melts into his. Gone. So gone. They blow smoke down over the rooftops of Fitzroy. The noise from the street and the corner pub drifts in: bottles breaking, junkies arguing, dogs barking.

When they finish smoking, she turns to face him, and he tangles his fingers in her hair. 'God, you're so beautiful.'

What happened to very clever? She doesn't complain as he kisses her and leads her to his bedroom. A navy curtain hangs in place of a door, above mustard-coloured carpet. The room is neat: a double bed, made; two wooden side tables; black, bell-shaped lamps; a pine chest of drawers; and a makeshift wardrobe fashioned from a curtain rod, holding his shirts on hangers.

As she lies beside him, the noise from the street disappears, and she is aware only of his breathing. She rests on an elbow, kisses him, and then cautiously pushes up his T-shirt. He's watching her face, with something in his eyes — is it trust?

'Matt!' She recoils, pulls her hand away, and is immediately sorry for her reaction. His chest is covered with small scars — complete versions of the half-moon under his eye.

He starts to pull down his T-shirt, but she stops him. 'What happened?'

'My mother. When I was little.'

'Your mother did this to you?'

He nods. A siren screams over the sound of empty bottles being dumped into a bin.

'You don't have to stay,' he says.

'What?'

'The look on your face.'

'Shh.' She places a finger against his lips, wanting to regain his trust. She kisses the scars, works her way down to his stomach, undoes his jeans. She sucks him until he reaches down for her and slides her up his body. They fuck again, slowly, gently, this time, while Nick Cave sings about letting love in.

Sex was always something to try to avoid, until you ran out of excuses at the end of the night — cold, rough, awkward, often painful, sometimes tainted with fear. This is so different: warm, safe, smooth. Velvet. She wants to do everything to him, with him, and for it to never end. She closes her eyes, holds his hands, and moves her hips faster when she feels that wave rippling, surging through her body again.

Afterwards, she lies back in his pillows. The sheets are pilled, but they smell clean. He massages semen into her thighs. She reaches down for his hand, pulls it to her mouth, and sucks his fingers: the taste of him and the taste of her, combined. He kisses her so he can taste it, too. Salt and earth.

They smoke another joint, and she feels drowsy. Her eyes are heavy as she traces the outline of the serpent tattoo on his shoulder blade: its spiky back and tail.

'The first time you came into my class I couldn't stop looking at your long fingernails. Fantasising about them scratching my back.' His voice sounds like it's coming from far away.

The serpent tattoo seems to breathe as he breathes; blue-and-green scales rise and fall with every inhalation and exhalation. He rolls over, wraps his arms around her, and slides inside her again, but they're both too tired to move anymore. She falls asleep with her face against his chest.

She dreams that Kurt Cobain is sleeping beside her. The puppy with the red dog collar rests its head on the pillow next to him. Tentatively, she pushes the dirty-blond hair off Kurt's face, ready for the horror of his dead eyes. But it's not a dream; she looks into the ocean of Matt's eyes. She reaches for his hand, curls her fingers between his, and falls back to sleep.

The beep-beep-beep of a reversing truck wakes her. Sunlight floods through the window. Maybe she's still dreaming because the dream puppy's here. She rubs her eyes.

Matt places coffee on the bedside table. 'Good morning.'

She stretches and smiles. The dream puppy moves, and she jumps. Matt sits on the edge of the bed and lifts the fat ginger cat onto his lap.

'I thought that was a dog.'

'She's as big as a dog. This is Di.'

She laughs, 'Your cat's name is Di?'

'What's so funny about that?'

'Who calls their cat Di? It's hilarious.' She reaches for her shirt on the floor, pulls it on, and props herself up against the pillows.

'My grandmother named her. She had another one called Charles. But Charles died just after Gran did.'

It's not that funny, but she can't stop laughing, and he hits her over the head with a pillow.

She reaches for her coffee, still laughing, and almost chokes on it. It's in a mug illustrated with three rows of butterflies, their names listed under the illustrations: Dark Green Fritillary, Monarch, Swallowtail, Marbled White, Adonis Blue ...

'Di's going to be a mother soon. Gran said she was spayed. But last month I took her to the vet's, and they said she was pregnant.'

'Poor thing.' Brigitte pats Di's head. 'I thought ginger cats could only be males.'

'That's a myth. The gene for ginger's carried on the X chromosome. A male cat has only one X chromosome, so if he carries the gene he'll be ginger. Females have two X chromosomes, so they need two copies of the ginger variant to be ginger, and that doesn't happen very often.'

What?

Matt lowers Di gently to the floor, lies down next to Brigitte, and she rolls into his arms. She tells him to be careful of her sore knee.

'Old football injury?'

'Something like that.'

Brigitte can't find any bubble bath in Matt's cupboard — only shaving foam, razors, paw paw ointment, a bandage, toothpaste. No prescription medication. No meds at all, not even Panadol. What is wrong with him?

She places her clothes on the washing-machine lid, and pours some of his shower gel under the running bath water. The scent of cinnamon and bergamot fills the room. The scent of Matt. She calls his name.

He's reading the papers in the living room. 'Yes?' he calls back.

'Where do you buy your shower gel?'

'It's not shower gel. It's body wash, from a shop down the other end of the street, near Mario's. It has no sulphates.'

'That's good. Sulphates dry your skin.'

'I know. That's what they told me at the shop.'

'Hey Matt?'

'Ye—es?'

'Coming to join me?'

She smiles and lies back in the water as she hears him push the papers aside.

***

After four nights, she emerges from the cocoon of Matt's place, her thighs and back aching. She feels like one of the butterflies on his coffee mug: metamorphosed, complete. Adonis Blue.

She almost trips over a man sitting on the street.

'Hey love, could ya help me out? I've lost me wallet and just need me tram fare home.'

She smiles, and hands the scarlet-faced drunk a twenty-dollar note, and he thinks it's Christmas.

36

Brigitte walks through the gardens instead of along the footpath so she can see the apartment from a safe distance. She holds her breath as she gets closer. Her heart pounds, her stomach churns, but there are no lights on. The windows are closed, and the blinds are shut. Eric's still away. She lets out her breath. But she doesn't go in. She goes straight to work.

Hannah says Al wants to see her. She can still smell the cinnamon and bergamot of Matt on her skin and in her hair. She thinks of the stairs, and smiles — it's a dumb, teenage-love smile, no doubt, but she can't help it — as she swaggers towards Al's office.

'Where have you been, Pagan?' Al takes his feet, clad in brown crocodile-skin shoes, off the desk. He hasn't extinguished his cigarette properly, and the filter section smells toxic as it smoulders in the ashtray. A poster of the *Penthouse* Pet of the Year is pinned up above his desk — she used to work here. Al taps his knuckles on the desk, his fat gold rings glinting in the fluorescent light. 'I've been calling you for days.'

'Sorry, I —'

'You don't have a job here anymore.'

She loses the dumb smile. 'What?'

'You've fucked me around too many times, not turning up for your shifts. I can't run the business like that.'

'What am I supposed to do now?'

'Dunno. Doesn't Eric look after you?'

'He only pays the rent — nothing else.'

'Not my problem.'

She bites her lip.

He softens. 'Have you heard from Dave?'

She shakes her head.

He takes a business card from a desk drawer and hands it to her. 'My mate Richard's business.'

She turns the card over in her hand: *Lipgloss Promotions*, embossed in gold writing on glossy black.

'Go do some modelling. Better for your knee anyway.'

'But I need this job.'

'Sorry, Pagan. I can only use reliable girls.'

She turns to leave. There's no point arguing with him.

'And another thing,' he says when she's at the door. 'Tell Eric I won't be needing his business anymore.'

She trudges up the hill (still no sign of Eric at the apartment), through the gardens — past the Exhibition Building and the ten-metre-high sculpted fountain of white merpeople — down Gertrude and into Brunswick Street. She knocks on Matt's door. He's not home, so she keeps walking, aimlessly.

A driver in a red car going the other way beeps his horn, does a U-turn, and slows. She ignores it. *Leave me alone, I'm not in the mood.* The car pulls up beside her. Men are so stupid.

The driver reaches across and opens the passenger-side door. 'Hey, beautiful.' It's Matt. He tells her to get in, and they drive back up Brunswick Street. 'What are you doing in this part of town?'

'Nothing. Just going for a walk.'

'What a coincidence.'

He gets a parking spot in front of his place, jumps out, and takes some shopping bags from the boot. She follows him.

'What's wrong?' he says.

She thought her sunglasses were doing a good job of hiding it. 'I lost my job.'

'Good.' He puts the shopping bags on the footpath while he locks the car.

'It's not good.'

'I hated you going to that place.'

'What am I supposed to do now?'

'Don't worry. We'll think of something.'

A black car with tinted windows double-parks across the road in front of the flats. Matt hands her a bag. 'Come and have dinner with me, and we'll talk about it.'

'Where?'

'Here.'

'You can cook?'

'Of course.'

'Too perfect, aren't you?'

While he opens the door, she glances over her shoulder to see the black car driving away. She follows him back into the cocoon, smiling the dumb-teenage smile again as they climb the stairs.

She sits on the bench in his tiny kitchen, sipping white wine and watching him prepare ingredients for paella. He fries some vegetables, adds stock, rice, prawns, and mussels, then leaves it to simmer while he brings out a tray of oysters from the fridge.

'Just happen to have oysters in your fridge?'

'Not usually. But I think I'm psychic, because when I was shopping I thought to myself: *Brig might be coming back, and she will like some seafood.*'

'Really?'

'*And if she doesn't, I'll just have to share it with the cat.*' He places the oysters, a lemon, and sea salt next to her on the bench. 'So, you think I'm psychic?'

'No. But very sexy.' She wraps her legs around his hips and pulls him to her. He reaches over a leg, cuts the lemon into quarters, squeezes juice, and grinds salt onto one of the oysters.

She looks at the slimy grey substance in the dirty shell. 'I don't know if I like oysters.'

'You didn't think you liked wine either. Here.' He lifts the oyster to her mouth, 'Close your eyes.'

She does as he says, chews, and it spurts — explodes — in her mouth. She swallows, it slides down her throat, and she screws up her face. For a second, she thinks she's going to throw up. She washes it down with a gulp of wine. He kisses her softly, slowly, for a long time. She drapes her arms around his shoulders, holding her wine glass aloft.

'Good?'

'Uh-ha.'

'Want another one?'

'Kiss or oyster?'

'Oyster.'

'Maybe in a minute.'

'Kiss?'

'Mmm.' Her body feels limp and warm and tingly.

The rice catches on the bottom of the pan and starts to burn.

Brigitte looks down at the street from the living-room window on the city side. The black car with tinted windows is there again. *It's just your imagination. It couldn't be the same one.*

'So, what are you going to do about work?'

She jumps, and spills wine on her hand when Matt enters the room. 'Can I close the curtains?'

'If you want to.' He places two bowls of slightly burnt paella on the table, lights the two big white candles in the centre, and opens another bottle of wine.

'I've sort of got a job lined up.' She sits opposite him.

He pours the wine.

'As a sales rep. Just have to get my licence, so I've been taking driving lessons.'

'Well done. That sounds great.'

'Can I drive your car sometime?' She tries a slow blink, but her cute little tricks don't seem to work on him. 'To practise.'

He suggests they go away for the Melbourne Cup weekend. Somewhere down the coast. Camping. He might let her drive then.

'Camping! Are you crazy?' She laughs. 'My family has a holiday house on Raymond Island. We could go there.'

He asks where Raymond Island is, and she explains that it's on the Gippsland Lakes. Near Lakes Entrance. The only way across to the island is by ferry.

'Wouldn't your family mind you going there — with a man?' He looks up from his paella.

She shakes her head. 'Nobody uses the house anymore. Not since my brother and I were little, and Nana and Papa used to take us there all the time.'

'Your Mum and Dad didn't go?'

'Dad always had to work. And my mother hates it there. Not sophisticated enough. She wants to sell the house, but Nana and Papa won't let her.'

He tops up their glasses. 'Let's go there — straight after my Friday class.'

'You really want to?' She tries to rein in her smile, but she can't control it.

He nods, then turns his attention to his dinner. She studies the mussels in her bowl, not sure if she can eat them.

'Have you thought anymore about studying?'

She scoops a little of the saffron-coloured rice from the side of her bowl and spills it on her white shirt. He pretends not to notice as she wipes it with a napkin. 'I might do some modelling.'

'Uh-huh. Not sure how secure or reliable that would be.'

And writing is? she thinks, but doesn't say. She sips her wine, and forks the mussels around, not sure how she is supposed to get them out of the shells without totally ruining her shirt.

'What about David Jones?' he says.

'Doesn't pay enough.'

He suggests calling them back; she could say she's changed her mind. It might be OK until she finds something better. He sounds like he's been talking to Marco. Why do men think they know what's best for her?

'Modelling is better.'

'You can't stay young and gorgeous forever.' He looks into her eyes. 'Then what?'

'Dunno. I've still got a few good years left.' She laughs, and pushes away her bowl.

'Eat some more, Brig.'

She shakes her head. 'I'm full.'

When he goes to the bathroom, she calls the apartment. No answer. She peeks out from behind the curtain. The black car has gone.

He comes back, sits next to her, scrapes a mussel and some rice onto the fork, and feeds her like a child.

'Are you trying to fatten me up?'

'Maybe.'

'You're saying I'm too skinny?'

'I didn't say that.'

'You can never be too thin. Or too rich.'

'Too rich or too thin. The Duchess of Windsor said that, didn't she?'

'I thought my mother made it up.'

'You've achieved the thin part. Now how're you going to get rich?'

'My mother also used to say it's just as easy to marry a rich man as it is to marry a poor man.'

'Well, you've come to the wrong place.'

'I never said I was going to marry you.'

'Good, because I didn't ask you.' He laughs.

She looks into those blue eyes, and has the sensation of falling again. He feeds her more paella, and tops up their glasses. 'Did your mother have any other pearls of wisdom?'

'Heaps. Like: Why buy a book when you can join a library?'

'Am I just one of the books in your library?' He puts a hand on her thigh.

'I only like to read one book at a time. Over and over.' She laughs and kisses him.

He asks if her mum and dad are still together, and she tells him about her dad's cancer.

'That's awful. Do you remember much about him?'

'They were singing "Morningtown Ride" on *Play School* when he died.'

She remembers being home from school that day. He was in his old leather lounge chair. An odour like nail-polish remover filled the room, along with the awful, watery sounds of dying. The air felt dead cold. She has no memory of Dad in hospital; maybe she wasn't allowed to visit. It's hard to believe her mother was capable of nursing him at home.

'He loved Johnny Cash,' she says. 'He was kind and gentle. Total opposite of my mother. Don't know how they ever got together.' She thinks of Joan sitting at the Laminex table at the old pink house in Brunswick after Dad died — his scratchy records playing, a cigarette burning down to the filter between two nicotine-stained fingers in one hand, a glass of brandy, lime, and soda in the other. Joan would get so drunk she'd wet herself — indigo rivers running down her tight jeans. Ryan thought it was funny, but her loss of control made Brigitte feel sick. She and Ryan would have to clean her up and drag her to bed, ranting about how she wished she'd never had them, how they'd ruined her acting career.

Brigitte shivers, and covers Matt's hand with hers, curling her fingers between his.

'When he was home, Dad always made pancakes for me and my brother,' she says. 'And he'd always come in and kiss us before he went away on long trips. I'd pretend to be asleep, but I'd always wait for that kiss.' She looks into her glass, and asks if he has any brothers or sisters.

'One child was too many for my mother.'

'Do you ever see her?'

He shakes his head. 'She died when I was ten.'

'What happened?'

'She was allergic to aspirin, and one night she took some instead of Panadol.' He looks away. 'Anaphylactic shock.'

Brigitte frowns. Why would anybody keep medication they were that allergic to in the house? She doesn't ask.

'My mother's not worth talking about,' he says.

'I'll listen if you want to.'

He smiles. 'I don't need therapy, Brig. All that … stuff, was a long time ago. I barely remember. My dad took care of me. He was a good man. A bit like your dad.' He empties the last of the wine into their glasses. 'He was in your Cradle Mountain story, wasn't he?'

'Not sure why, where that came from.'

'You should try writing more about him. Might be cathartic.'

She's not quite sure what that word means — she must look it up. He's made her eat all her paella without noticing. 'I'll have to go to the gym tomorrow to work it off.'

'I had some other kind of exercise in mind for you.'

'Oh really?'

'Uh-huh.' He blows out the candles, picks up their glasses, and she follows him to the bedroom.

'Do you have any condoms?'

'What!' He stops, turns, spills some wine on the carpet, his face contorted with horror. 'But I thought you —'

'Calm down.'

'Brigitte!'

'We'll be careful from now on, OK?'

Sometime during the night or morning, she is jolted from sleep by shouts and banging on the front door. *Oh my God the black car.* She sits straight up.

'Shh, it's OK.' Matt pulls her back and wraps his arms around her. 'Just junkies. They do that all the time.'

The sound of a mug and plate clinking together wakes her, and she opens her eyes. Dust particles shimmer in a sheet of light across the room.

'Hey, beautiful.' Matt places a tray on the bed.

'What are you doing?' Her voice is sleep-croaky.

'Bringing you breakfast.'

Coffee, orange juice. And pancakes! She cries — all of a sudden, tears from nowhere — for her father. Matt holds her and kisses away the tears. She looks over his shoulder at the butterfly mug, knowing the butterfly names by heart now: Dark Green Fritillary, Monarch, Swallowtail, Marbled White, Adonis Blue …

37

The room smells of expensive cologne, flatulence, and Juicy Fruit. Eric's suitcase is open on the bed. He's rolling his clothes into tight cylindrical shapes, and packing them like it's a game of Tetris. Brigitte leans against the doorway and sneezes. 'Tour?'

'Yeah, Bullet Brain. Kicks off in New Zealand.'

'I'm going up to see Ryan for the long weekend.'

'Thought you weren't talking.'

'We are now.'

He turns to face her. 'Which one?' He holds up two ties: one, royal blue; the other, crimson, with small white spots.

'The blue.'

He ties it around his collar, and she straightens it for him.

'Want a lift to the airport?' he says.

'No. My flight's not till later.'

'Have fun.' He zips up his case. 'And tell Ryan he's a dickhead for me.' He grins, and kisses her on the mouth as he leaves. She feels a pang of guilt for thinking he was having her followed. And for lying to him.

★★★

She waits in the corridor until Matt's Friday students have left. She sneaks up behind him while he's cleaning the whiteboard, and wraps her arms around his waist. He turns and smiles; she kisses him, but he pulls back, glancing at the open door.

'I could shut it, and we could do it here on your desk.'

He pushes her away gently and packs up his books.

'You prefer the stairs?'

'Stop it, Lolita. You'll make me lose my job.' He places some pens in the desk drawer. 'Did you bring your stuff?'

She points to the big duffle bag next to the door.

Matt puts his notes and books into his briefcase. 'Let's go, then. Car's parked in Collins Street.' He throws her bag over his shoulder. 'God, what have you got in here?'

'You don't have to carry it for me.'

In the lift, he wraps his free arm around her shoulders and kisses the top of her head. She looks at the emergency *stop* button. Would they have enough time to do it if she pressed it?

Matt lets her drive the Commodore with L plates on when they get out of Melbourne, until she gets scared by the speed and amount of traffic on the freeway. She pulls over, and they swap seats.

He drives with his left hand resting on her thigh. It leaves a warm, invisible imprint whenever he lifts it to hold the steering wheel.

It's getting dark when they reach Paynesville. They drive around the town a couple of times because Brigitte can't remember how to get to the ferry landing. Matt finds it, and they queue at the water's edge.

'Sorry. I haven't been here for a while.'

'That's OK. It was hard to find in the dark.' He unbuckles his seatbelt, and leans across to kiss her. They don't stop kissing, hands all over each other, until the car behind beeps for them to board the ferry. The ferry operator waves them on and collects his fare. Matt squeezes Brigitte's hand and sings, 'Don't Pay the Ferryman'.

She laughs, and reaches into the back seat for her white woollen coat as a cool breeze dances across the lake. Boats bob, and a few lights glimmer on the black wavelets as the ferry chugs across the strait. It wobbles and groans when it juts and aligns with the slip on the island.

Matt follows her directions past the park and community centre, and turns left into Sixth Avenue.

'Sure this is the right street?'

'Yep. That house there.' She points at number six: a white fibro shack, with its sky-blue window-frames and doorframes ghostly-grey in the dark. The Commodore's headlights catch an echidna ambling across the road. There are no other cars around, so Matt stops and lets it pass in front of them before turning into the driveway. Loose gravel crunches under the tyres.

Matt shines a torch around inside the house, and screws up his nose at the stink of mould when he looks in the fridge. 'How long since anybody's been here?' He starts opening windows and doors.

'Ryan and I came down for a weekend just before he moved to Sydney. Nearly two years ago.'

'Who's Ryan?'

'My brother.' She smiles to herself — for a second, he was jealous.

He carries in the Esky from the car while she turns on the power at the main switch and looks for cleaning spray and cloths. The house is full of dusty shells collected by children over the years, paintings of beaches and ships, and old family photographs: lots of black-and-whites of Papa fishing from his little tin boat.

When they've finished cleaning inside the house, they take the covers off the furniture on the back porch and brush away the dust.

'We forgot to bring music,' Brigitte says as she lights a mosquito coil.

'No we didn't.' Matt goes to the car boot and lifts out a portable yellow-and-aqua CD player.

'Cool. Is that new?'

'Yep.' He clears a shelf for it next to the barbeque, where there's a power point to plug it in. 'No Nirvana. OK?'

'OK, Kurt.'

'Stop with that, or I'll start calling you Courtney.'

'OK, Kurt.'

He feigns exasperation, shakes his head, and tests the gas bottle with his foot. 'Empty. I brought some baby octopus I could barbeque. Should we go across to Paynesville for more gas?' He pulls his brown sweater on.

'We could.' She looks at him in the half-light. He's pressing buttons and twisting knobs — trying to work the CD player. He pushes the hair off his face, concentration creasing his brow.

'Or we could ...' She steps towards him, knowing there won't be any baby octopus tonight as she takes his hands and pulls him down onto the black-leather couch. The CD player starts playing. Nick Cave, of course.

They sleep in Nana and Papa's old bed in the middle bedroom. Mosquitoes buzz around Brigitte's ears as she lies awake in Matt's arms. The sleeping tablet she took isn't working. Worries bubble away in her mind: the future, work, Matt. The only thing she used to worry about was which nail-polish shade to choose at the beauty salon. Now she worries about everything. How can she leave Eric without him killing her, or killing Matt? She reckons Eric did kill somebody once, or organised it, or had something to do with it anyway — she over-heard him on the phone talking to somebody about a body dump. She pretended she hadn't heard properly, that she'd imagined it. She's not as dumb as he thinks: the people he associates with, the drugs, are scary stuff, dangerous. She tries to push down her fears, but nothing — not drugs, alcohol, or lying to herself — blocks out the thoughts that froth to the surface during the black, sleepless hours. If only she and Matt could stay here, safe on the island, forever. Her heart races, and sweat beads on her skin. She seeks comfort from Matt's body: she squirms against him, tries to 'accidentally' wake him, and kisses his mouth softly, but he's sound asleep, his lips slightly parted. Streetlight spills under the blind, creating a silver mist on his hair, illuminating the scars on his chest, catching the fragile beauty of his face.

A tightness grips her chest; she's scared that it means she loves him. Or else she's taken too many anti-inflamms, and is having a heart attack. If she loves him, she shouldn't drag him into her fucked-up life. If she really loves him, she should just leave him alone. He won't stay around when he finds out the truth about her anyway. Nothing this sublime could ever be more than fleeting. It will end badly, one way or another. She should push him away before it comes to that, like she did to Ryan. But she can't. She holds one of his hands, listening to him sleep for a long time, with the words *I don't deserve you* repeating over and over in her head. Night thoughts.

She wakes midmorning, and slinks out of the bedroom towards the aroma of coffee. Matt's sitting outside on the couch, writing in an exercise book. He pulls at his hair when he's writing, and it's all messy. She carries out her coffee, and sits next to him. She yawns, and stretches her legs in front of her to soak up some of the delicious sunlight streaming across the porch. 'What are you writing?'

He lifts his gaze from her legs, and kisses her. 'A new chapter.'

'What's happening?'

'Lucy's about to murder her husband so she can be with Henry. They've had it planned for a long time — how they're going to do it, how they're going to cover it up — but something has to go wrong.'

'Ooh, sounds like *The Postman Always Rings Twice*.'

'Have you read that book?'

'No, but I love the movie. Do Lucy and Henry get away with it in the end?'

'Almost.'

'Can I see your notes?'

She snuggles up next to him, and he explains the colour system he uses to write scenes in his exercise book. In blue, he writes what happens. In red, his research. And in green, a summary of his characters.

'There's lots of red,' she says.

'I've finally found a cop who's happy to help me with research.'

She reads through his main points: violence, marks and evidence, cause of death, dental evidence, gunshot residue, fingerprints ...

'What's spatter pattern?'

'Bloodstain spray. It can explain where an attacker stood, how tall they were, how many times they hit the victim with a weapon ...'

'Gross.' She sips her coffee.

'But kind of interesting. I can't believe blood is so aero-dynamic.'

She wrinkles her nose.

'What are you writing?' he says.

'I've got an idea for something non-fiction. Might submit it to magazines.' She feels sorry for the possums in the gardens since the introduction of tree banding. A piece in a magazine about it might help their plight.

'Try the local papers first. Can't wait to read it.'

'Know what I can't wait for?' She takes his exercise book and their coffee cups, places them on the porch, and climbs astride his hips.

'Brig, I'm trying to work.' He laughs.

'Promise I'll leave you alone for the rest of the day.' She pushes the hair off his face, kisses him, and closes her eyes. *I don't deserve you.*

Matt writes for most of the day. She keeps her promise — tries not to distract him. She goes for walks around the island, reads the papers, takes the car across, and refills the gas bottle.

In the afternoon, she has a nap on Nana and Papa's bed. She dreams she's clearing the kitchen table. As she leans forward for the last of the dishes, Matt presses against her back, and the heat of his body is unbearably exquisite. She arches against him. A wave of warmth rises inside her. She turns and pulls him down onto the table, sweeping to the floor the last of the cutlery and plates behind her. She writhes beneath him, then climbs on top. As she comes, Matt presses a shell to her ear. *You can hear forever in here*, he says. She closes her eyes and listens, but she can't hear anything.

The mattress dips and the springs squeak as Matt sits on the edge.

She uncurls her body, and relaxes her hands — they were balled into fists, leaving fingernail marks on her palms. 'What time is it?'

'Nearly five-thirty. You've been asleep for a couple of hours.' He places two glasses of white wine on the bedside table.

'Couldn't sleep last night.'

'We went to bed too early.' He grins. 'And forgot to drink any of the wine.'

She cringes at the unearthly grunt-screech of a koala. 'Why do they have to do that?'

'It's the sound they make when they're mating.' He smirks.

She can't stand him being so close without touching. He reads her thoughts, pushes up her T-shirt, and kisses her stomach, breasts, neck, mouth. She giggles and squirms underneath him as she peels off her pants and undoes his jeans. She reaches back to grip the bedhead, wraps her legs around his hips, and pulls him into her. *I don't deserve you.*

Brigitte sits on the porch couch with a glass of wine in her hand while Matt tosses the baby octopus on the barbeque. He turns down the gas, and goes to the car to get his camera from the glove box.

'Let me take your photo.'

'No. I've got no make-up on.' She covers her face with her free hand.

'Come on. Please.' He points the camera at her. She pulls the tie from her hair, tussles it, and flashes an exaggerated, sexy model-pout.

She places her glass on the table and pulls her hair back into a ponytail. When she looks up, he takes another shot, and captures her forever young, natural, unguarded — as naked as she has ever been, and as free as she ever will be. She frowns, and says she wasn't ready; he'd better tear that one up when he has them printed.

She tries not to screw up her face when he serves the charred, alien-like creatures for dinner. She hides them in the salad, wraps some in a serviette, and puts them in her pocket when Matt's not looking.

After they've drunk their entire alcohol supply, a koala scuttles across the porch, right in front of their feet — its eyes glowing incandescently in the dark. Matt stands to watch it lope across the yard and climb the gum tree at the back. Brigitte and Matt look at each other, for reassurance that they really saw it, and then laugh.

Brigitte is sitting cross-legged on the couch, smoking a joint, when Matt suggests they go for a walk.

'Where?'

'Dunno. Round the island.'

'It's late.'

'So?'

'It's dark.'

'We'll take a torch. Let's see if we can spot some more koalas.'

'OK.' She stands, walks over, passes him the joint, and trips off the porch. He laughs.

'Not funny, Kurt. My knee.'

But it is funny, funnier than the koala running across the porch — they're wasted, and everything is hilarious.

'Come on, Courtney.' He holds out a hand and helps her up. She's got dirt all over her white coat. 'Is that a baby octopus in your pocket, or are you just glad to see me?' He finishes the joint, crushes it out on the gravel, and wraps an arm around her shoulders as they walk up the driveway.

They stumble along the boardwalk, laughing, kissing. She complains about her knee, and he piggy-backs her. The ferry is moored at the landing: still, lifeless in the water until morning.

'How do you get across if you have to?' he says.

'You can't. Unless you swim.'

'Want to?'

'What?'

'Swim.'

'Are you crazy?' She follows him along the jetty beside the ferry landing.

He puts down the torch and strips off — hopping on one leg — down to his boxer shorts. He's singing that R.E.M song, 'Nightswimming'.

'Thought you were sane and now — '

'Come on.' He laughs and jumps into the water. 'It feels great.'

'No way.'

'If you love me, you'll come in.'

She undresses to her lacy, white underwear, sits on the edge of the jetty, and dangles her feet in the water. Matt pulls at her legs.

'Stop it.' She kicks at him, too hard, splits his lip.

'Fuck.' He touches a hand to his mouth and comes away with blood.

'Sorry.'

He grabs her legs again, she slips, and she splashes into his arms. She didn't just say she loved him, did she? No, but her head is spinning, and she can't be sure. She tastes blood in his kiss, leans back, and looks up at the sky: the stars are blurry, and there seems to be two moons. The whole world spins, and she closes her eyes. She pulls at his shorts, wanting him so much, right now. But he pushes her hands away. 'Not yet. First I'll race you to the other side.'

'I'm not a very good swimmer, Matt.'

He swims out a bit and calls to her.

Her stomach tightens. She doesn't like this, but she follows, in a slow breaststroke. Her pulse pounds in her temples. It's too dark: there's just the torch light, the glow of the public phone box on the island, a couple of lights across in Paynesville, and a milky spill of moonlight on the black water.

They swim out further. He dives under, but doesn't come up. This was such a bad idea. She rolls her body around in the water, and suddenly can't tell which is the island and which is the mainland. He still hasn't come up. Where is he? She feels something touch her leg — Matt, being silly, thank God. But it's not Matt. It's a log or something floating in the water. Where the fuck is he? She calls his name, twists to kick the floating thing away, and her head goes under. She comes up coughing, and calls him again. He's gone. This can't be happening. She tries to scream, but salty water rushes into her mouth and down her throat. She thrashes her arms, kicks her legs. The water burns her nose, her lungs. He can't leave her. This *can't* be happening. She knew it would end badly.

She hears a splash, maybe a few metres in front of her, but it's too dark to see. 'Come on,' he calls. 'We're almost halfway across.'

She can't speak, can't breathe. And she can't make her body swim, can't move at all — it's as if her limbs are filled with cement, paralysed.

It sounds like he's swimming back to her. But it's too late — she's drowning. She feels faint, and sinks into blackness and bubbles. He pulls her up, and she paws and clings to him, almost dragging him under as well.

He tells her over and over that she's OK as he swims back slowly to the island with her floundering under his arm.

He lifts her onto the jetty. She stumbles, coughs up water, and lies on the parched wooden boards. Cold air rushes up through the cracks.

He climbs out after her, and covers her with his sweater and her dirty coat.

'I almost drowned,' she splutters as she sits up.

'No, you didn't.' He kneels behind her, and rubs his hands over her back. 'You just panicked. I was right there. I wouldn't let you drown.'

She coughs up more water, and hugs her knees to her chest. 'You weren't there. I told you I wasn't a good swimmer. You left me.' Her voice croaks. 'I hate you.'

'No you don't.' He wraps his arms around her.

'Yes I do.' She tries to push him away.

He holds her tighter. 'No you don't. You love me.'

'No I *don't!*'

'I love you.'

Even after having a hot shower and drinking two glasses of sherry from a dusty bottle that Matt found in a cupboard, Brigitte can't stop shaking. He tells her she should write a short story about what happened — it might be cathartic — and she hits him. He laughs, calls her Courtney, and says it turns him on when she's angry. Hitting him again, harder, is *cathartic*.

'Look what I found on the way back.' He produces a shell from his jeans pocket, and tosses it into the bowl full of other shells on the table. 'Coming to bed?' He puts a hand on her shoulder and sings, 'Night swimming, remember that night ...' She pushes his hand away and doesn't follow him, for a while.

She wants him to know how angry she is with him for leaving

her when she was scared, so she puts up a wall — her back to him in bed. She tries to resist when he moves against her. But she can't.

***

They drive back to the city on Melbourne Cup day, listening to the race on the radio. Duene wins the Cup.

'I thought it was pronounced *Dune* — like the David Lynch film, with Sting,' Matt says.

'I think it's French — *Ju-ane*. My Nana would know. She's crazy about horse racing.'

'Want to come home with me? Or shall I drop you at your place? Wherever that is.'

'Home. With you.'

'You're not still angry with me?'

A bit. But she shakes her head.

'When are you going to invite me over to your place, anyway?'

She looks out the window as they drive through Richmond, pretending she didn't hear.

38

How she came to be naked in the black-marble spa with Jennifer/
Ember, Doctor Dave, and Vince the lawyer is a bit of a blur. It
started when she was getting ready to go to Matt's dinner party
and she heard somebody yelling from the street. She opened a
window to see Jennifer standing up on the back seat of a silver
convertible — a horse emblem on the grille — parked in front of
the apartment complex. Dave was in the driver's seat, and Vince in
the passenger's.

They yelled at her to come down.

'Can't. I'm going out,' Brigitte called back.

'You've gotta check out this car. Just one spin around the
block,' Jennifer said.

Dave revved the engine.

'OK. Just one spin.' It *was* a cool-looking car. And she was still
a bit angry about Raymond Island when she grabbed her phone
and bag.

Just one spin around the block became a drive to the casino,
where she agreed to *just one cocktail*, which became far too many
cocktails, and somehow led to a duet of 'When Doves Cry' with
Vince at a karaoke bar, followed by a failed attempt by him to feed
her sashimi and grilled prawn heads at Tokyo Teppanyaki. She saw
two missed calls from Matt on her phone screen — she'd meant to
call him back and tell him she was on her way, but now it's late,
and she's here. Somehow.

She climbs out of the spa, wraps herself in a fluffy hotel towel,
and takes her glass of champagne with her.

'Hurry back,' says Vince.

In the bathroom, she pours her drink down the sink. She's been doing this since they got here and the vibe changed. She's sitting on the toilet when Jennifer staggers in. She finishes, washes, and dries her hands. Under the down-lighting, she notices the harsh shadows and the fine lines around Jennifer's eyes. She's only 23, but she's already starting to look way older. Men are not going to pay her for much longer. Twenty-five is about the use-by age for a dancer. What's she going to do then? Matt was right, of course: you can't stay young and gorgeous forever. Matt — she was supposed to meet his friends tonight. She's not angry with him anymore. Sober now, she needs to get out of here.

'Come on.' Jennifer wraps an arm around her waist.

'What?'

She guides — pushes — Brigitte into the bedroom. The two men are on the bed. Brigitte looks at Jennifer and frowns. Jennifer giggles, leans forward, holds Brigitte's head, and kisses her fully on the mouth. Brigitte pulls away. 'What are you doing?' She wipes her mouth with the back of her hand.

'Come on, Pagan. Just like at the Gold Bar.'

Their simulated lesbian stage show is always a crowd-pleaser, but it's totally contrived, completely silly. This is not *just like at the Gold Bar*. She senses no hint of humour in the room. And Big Johnny's not here to help if something goes wrong or gets out of hand.

Jennifer holds her wrists; she is much bigger, and stronger, than Brigitte. She pulls her close and whispers in her ear how much they'll be paid — more than their week's combined income. A metallic taste of fear runs down the back of Brigitte's throat, and her pulse accelerates. She glances over her shoulder at her bag and clothes draped on the back of a club chair, and estimates it would take about ten seconds to get to the door if she had to run.

Jennifer tugs at her towel. Brigitte clutches it tighter to her chest.

'What's wrong with you? Just a bit of fun.'

'I want to go now Jen — Ember.' She takes a step towards her clothes. 'Please come with me.'

Jennifer shakes her head and climbs into bed with the men, shimmying under the white sheets down between Vince's legs.

Dave watches Brigitte as she dresses. Annoyance — no, anger — darkens his face. He shoves back the covers, gets up, sways, and walks towards her. He's drunk, slow, and she reaches the door before he catches up, but she doesn't have her shoes. She scans the room for her $500 ruby-coloured sandals. They're on the other side, poking out from under the curtain drawn across the wall-sized window. She decides to leave them, and wrenches the door open.

'You can forget about the sales-rep job,' Dave yells at her as she runs down the quiet, airless corridor towards the lift. 'Cock-teasing slut!'

A fire of jagged pain takes away her breath as she steps from the Hotel Como foyer and onto a piece of broken bottle. She hops, bends, pulls the chunk of glass out of her heel, and limps over to the first taxi on the rank.

'Where to?' the taxi driver says.

She tells him Fitzroy, Brunswick Street. Tendrils of wet hair soak the top of her shirt. Blood drains from her face as it pools on the grey carpet square beneath her feet. She leans her cheek against the cool window. Her breath condenses on the glass as she breathes slowly, deeply, trying to stop herself from fainting. She was going to give the driver a big tip to compensate for the blood — until she sees his disapproving eyes judging her in the rear-vision mirror. *Just another stupid, drunk girl — a dime a dozen on Chapel Street these days.* She wants to tell him he's wrong.

Out front of Matt's place, she looks up: the light's on, and she sees him standing at the window in a blue plaid shirt. Three or four of his friends are still up there with him. A couple lean on the sill, smoking. Matt moves away from the window.

Her phone rings, she presses *cancel*, her shoulders slump, and she tells the taxi driver to take her to the apartment instead.

She sits for a long time on the shower floor, dizzy, watching blood run down the drain.

After the shower, she bandages her foot and makes a mug of Milo. She takes some Panadol and goes to bed. She can't sleep. She calls him — she has to.

He picks up the phone. She hears him breathing, but he doesn't speak.

'Matt?'

It sounds like he drops the receiver and then picks it up.

'Matt, I — '

'You stood me up.'

'I'm sorry, I — '

'Where were you?'

'I — '

'Don't even want to know. Don't want to talk to you right now.'

'I had an accident.' The taxi driver's eyes were right.

'What? Are you all right?'

'Yes, just stupid — I broke a jar in the kitchen, cut my foot open. Must have fainted from the blood. I'm sorry — '

'Is somebody there to help you?'

'No, but I'm OK.'

'I'll come over.'

'No. You've been drinking. You can't drive.'

'What's your address?'

'No. I'll get a taxi to you.'

When she gets there, the door is unlocked and all the lights are on. Matt's asleep, passed out, sprawled across the bed, fully clothed.

Di's sitting on his back, licking her paws.

The cat sat on Matt.

Brigitte turns off the lights, removes his shoes, climbs in beside him, and pulls up the covers. Di hisses at her.

'I know — I don't deserve him.'

39

'Guess where I'm calling from?'

Matt hesitates, sighs. 'Where?'

'Work.'

'What work?'

'David Jones.'

'Really?'

'I called them, and they still had a job vacant. Did a training session, and started straightaway.'

'How's it going?'

'Good.' She sneezes. 'I've already sold two units of Poison.'

'What?'

'Perfume. The manager's coming — gotta go. See you after work.'

Catherine Kerr, lipstick on her teeth again, comes over to check on Brigitte. She tells her she's doing a great job, but needs to go into the aisle and spray perfume on customers when it's quiet. Brigitte can't quite bring herself to do that, so she pretends to be busy straightening products on the shelves.

She has lunch in the tearoom with Gina from Clinique, and Christine from Clarins. It's not as *nice* as she imagined.

'Did you hear Kara was fucking Tim as well as George from the café?' Gina says to Christine.

'*Your* Tim? No way.'

'Yes way. Stupid slut.'

Brigitte glances over her shoulder, hoping nobody from her section is listening. These women remind her of Jennifer: big and loud and brassy. Brigitte feels small and plain next to them.

Christine picks up one of her hot chips, dips it in gravy, and asks Brigitte if she's married.

'Don't be stupid, Chris. Look how young she is.'

'Have a boyfriend?'

Brigitte gazes across at the soggy food in the bain-marie. 'Yes.'

'What's his name?'

'Matt.'

'Cute?' Christine has a couple of gravy spots on the collar of her red blazer.

Brigitte nods, and feels her cheeks turn pink.

'Don't let Christine near him then.' Gina laughs, and slurps her Diet Coke through a straw.

Brigitte forces a smile, and picks at her limp salad.

'Wanna come for a drink with us after work tonight?' Gina says. 'There'll be lots of cute guys from the office there.'

'Come over to my counter just before knock-off time and I'll give you a make-over,' says Christine. 'You need some more colour.'

Brigitte bites into a flaccid cucumber slice. Gina and Christine scoff their chips and Diet Cokes.

'Coming for a smoke before we go back?' Gina fishes a packet of cigarettes and a pink plastic lighter from her gold handbag.

'Sorry, I don't smoke.' Brigitte shrugs, and they leave her to finish her lunch in peace.

When she gets back to the counter, she rings Matt again. 'Just letting you know I'm having drinks with some of the girls after work.' That sounds like such a grown-up thing to say. 'I won't stay long.' Grown-up, sensible, *nice*.

'Brig, you don't have to tell me everything you do.' More grown-up.

'What's that supposed to mean?'

'Nothing. Just that's it's OK to have our own lives.'

'Fine.' Maybe she will stay long. A child again.

'Don't be silly. I'm just saying — '

'There's a customer at the counter — gotta go.'

She hangs up and smiles at the customer. 'Hi. How can I help you?'

'Can I get one of these eye pencils, please?' The customer points to a tester on the stand.

'Nice colour.' *Black.* Brigitte takes a new pencil from the make-up drawer. 'Can I help you with anything else?'

The customer shakes her head.

The transaction goes smoothly. Brigitte bags it and sticky tapes it. 'Thank you. Have a nice day.'

She hums as she tidies the drawers under the counter. When she looks up, a man is waiting patiently at the perfume section. 'Hi there,' he says. Young, tall, nice suit. 'I'm after a gift.' He tilts his head to one side and smiles. 'For my fiancé,' he adds, somewhat reluctantly.

'Perfume?'

He nods.

'Do you know what she likes?'

He shrugs and holds up the palms of his hands.

'I like this.' She places a bottle on the counter. 'It's a floral-oriental fragrance.' She strokes her index finger down the side of the bottle. 'With amber-scented flowers, very sensual.' She looks directly into his eyes, capturing him. 'Want to try some?'

'Sure.'

She sprays some on to a card and hands it to him. 'What do you think?'

'Nice.'

'I like to use it straight after a shower. Before I get dressed I spray it into the air and stand under it to *clothe* my skin.' She demonstrates, does a little spin under the perfume mist, holding her breath so she doesn't sneeze. He gets out his wallet.

'Want to make it last longer?' She widens her eyes and blinks a couple of times.

He nods, swallows, and puts his wallet back for now as she places two more products on the counter. She takes his hand and massages some body moisturiser onto the back of it. 'Does that feel nice? This is called layering. When you spray perfume on top of the moisturiser, it will last all day. Or all night. And this,' she touches the other product, 'is hair mist. To intensify your fragrance experience. Want one of those, too?'

He nods.

'Need a tissue?'

'That's OK, you could just rub it in a bit more.'

'The eau de parfum is more expensive than the eau de toilette,' she says as she undoes his cuff button, pushes up his sleeve, and continues to massage his arm. 'But it's much better. And there's also a soap.'

He purchases the entire range with his credit card, which means Brigitte has already doubled her daily sales target. Too easy. He leaves his real-estate business card — in case she ever needs help buying or selling a house.

Another customer: a large woman with ruddy skin and jowls like a bulldog is tapping on the counter with her purple fingernails.

'Hi. Can I help you?' Brigitte says in a sing-song voice.

'I want to return this.' The red-faced woman produces a bottle of anti-ageing emulsion from her handbag. Brigitte hasn't been shown how to process returns; she looks around for help, but her counter manager is on a tea break.

'I said I want to return this,' the red woman says.

Brigitte takes the product from her and looks at it. It's almost empty. 'Was there a problem with it?'

'Gave me an allergic reaction.'

'But you've used most of it.'

'No, I only opened it last week.'

Another customer, in a floral dress, is waving Brigitte over, wanting her help at the make-up stand. 'Won't be a moment,' she calls cheerfully.

'Listen, I don't have all day,' says Red Woman.

'Do you have any other shopping to do?'

'What?'

'Excuse me.' The floral-dress customer is calling to her. 'There are no tissues left. I need to wipe off this lotion.'

'Won't be a moment. Sorry.' Back to Red Woman. 'I haven't been trained how to do returns, so if you could come back when my counter manager is here — '

'How rude. I'd like my money back, please.'

The phone starts ringing.

'If you could just wait — '

'I want to speak to the manager.'

'Excuse me!' It's Floral Dress again.

Brigitte bends down and takes a bottle of moisturiser from a drawer. 'Here!' She slams it down on the counter-top in front of Red Woman. 'Just take another one. This will suit your *sensitive* skin.' She blows the hair, which has escaped from its ponytail, off her face.

She smoothes her uniform and crosses to Floral Dress.

'I'm sorry, but I do need a tissue.'

'I'm not sure where we keep the tissues, but I'll have a look for you.' Brigitte forces a smile; her mouth is dry, she needs a drink of water.

'While I'm here, I want to try some of your new body oil.' Red Woman is still hanging around. 'Do you have any free samples?'

'No. But feel free to try the tester.' Brigitte hands her a glass tester-bottle of body oil, and sneezes.

Red Woman frowns, reaches for the bottle, and misses it. Brigitte sucks in her breath as it rolls across the counter top, teeters on the edge for a moment, and then goes over and smashes on the tiled floor. 'Stupid girl,' Red Woman shrieks. 'Look what you've done!' There's oil and broken glass on the floor; oil has splashed on the woman's shoes and all up her legs.

'I'm so sorry.' Brigitte starts shaking, and feels herself turn the same colour as the woman.

'Do you know how much these shoes cost? You've ruined them!'

Brigitte knows exactly how much those *violet* faux-snake skin shoes cost.

Heat prickles her eyes as she opens and slams shut drawers, looking for tissues, a cloth, anything, to clean up the mess.

'Oh my God!' Floral Dress yells.

What the fuck now? Brigitte looks over the counter to see that Red Woman has slipped in the oil slick, and is moaning and flailing about on the ground like a fish on land.

'What on earth is going on here?' Finally, the counter manager is back.

'Where the fuck are the tissues?' Brigitte rushes off to the bathroom.

When she composes herself and returns to the sales floor, the area around her counter has been cordoned off with rolled-up towels. A cleaner is mopping the floor. The counter manager tells her Red Woman was taken away in an ambulance, and Catherine Kerr is in her office writing an incident report.

***

'Hi there.' Matt opens the door. He takes something from his pocket, and presses it into her hand.

'What's this?'

'Spare key,' he says — like it's no big deal. 'So you don't have to knock.'

She looks at the key, and tries not to smile — like it's no big

231

deal. It's on a key ring attached to a silver letter J, with diamantes across the top.

'What's the J stand for?'

'Don't know. Last tenant left it on the key.'

She puts it in the inside pocket of her handbag.

'Thought you were going for drinks.'

'Changed my mind.'

'How was it?'

She holds onto the banister and drags herself melodramatically up the stairs. 'It was fucked.' Her feet are sore, she has a headache, itchy eyes, a sore throat, and her face aches from smiling. And all for $73.50. No shift at the Gold Bar ever felt so long.

'I thought you said it was good.' He follows her to the bedroom, where she throws herself backwards onto the bed.

'Kill me. Kill me now.'

'Can't have been that bad.'

She groans.

'You smell nice.'

'No I don't. I stink of perfume. I'm never going back.'

'Yes you are. You're stronger than that.'

'No I'm not.'

'Let's get a course application for you then.' He pulls off her shoes, and rubs her feet.

'Ouch, watch my heel.'

'Sorry.'

'Ooh, that feels good … Higher … Higher … Higher.' She bends her good knee and giggles, suddenly not so tired anymore.

40

She catches a train to Carnegie, and walks up Koornang Road
— following the map on a page torn from the Melways — to the
number on the *Lipgloss Promotions* business card that Al gave her.
There's no signage. In the shop-front window, a black-and-white
poster of a child holding a cat is displayed on an easel. It looks like
a photographic studio. Is this the right place? Brigitte checks the
number on the card again.

A bell tingles when she enters. A man calls for her to please
take a seat — he'll be with her in a minute. An orange curtain
separates the front of the shop from the back, so she can't see
him.

On Brigitte's side of the curtain, there are two black kitchen
chairs next to a small wooden table piled with fashion magazines.
She sucks in her stomach, smoothes her dress, sits down, and
flicks through a magazine without noticing what's on the pages.

What is she doing here? She doesn't want to be a model; she
wants to do one of the courses Matt was talking about. She could
model part-time — fit it in around study, and it would have to be
better than David Jones. Or is that a stupid idea? She's too short,
too fat, has bad skin, isn't pretty enough — all the things Joan has
told her. There's no way this agent is going to want her on his
books. She tosses the magazine back on the table, picks up her
bag, and stands up, ready to sneak out.

'Good afternoon.' A middle-aged man with floppy grey hair
and thick-rimmed glasses appears from behind the curtain. He
seems flustered, and pushes his glasses higher up on his nose as
he stares openly at her. 'I'm Richard Headley.' She tries not to

smirk at his name. 'And you must be Brigitte Weaver?' He shakes her hand. His is smooth and white. 'Is Brigitte spelt the same as Brigitte Bardot?'

'Yes. My mother was a big fan of hers.'

He holds the curtain aside and tells her to come through. She follows him to a desk stacked with folders. He gestures for her to take the seat next to his. Photographs of glamorous models in evening gowns and lingerie are displayed on the wall above his desk, next to a few wedding shots.

Richard offers her tea or coffee, and she asks for coffee with no sugar and a tiny bit of skim milk, if he has it.

'Good girl. Sounds like you know how to watch your figure — so many girls come to see me with no idea about diet.' He's funny. Old fashioned. She feels safe with him.

He goes to make the coffee. A black-lacquered screen, featuring a painting of a geisha girl, conceals the far side of the room. She hears a kettle boiling. There must be a kitchen out there. She looks around. Along the wall, next to Richard's desk, there's a filing cabinet, and a bookshelf filled with photography books, magazines, and boxes of film rolls. A peacock chair stands in the corner. A camera on a tripod points at a white dropsheet against the opposite wall.

Richard comes back with weak instant coffee in a *Playboy* mug.

'Brigitte, let me tell you about what I do, so you can decide if you're interested in joining Lipgloss Promotions' books.'

She sips her dishwater coffee.

He glances at the framed photo next to his phone of a plump woman and two smiling children, and tells Brigitte he runs the agency with his wife. She does all the bookwork. Photography is part of the business — he waves a hand at the photos on the wall — weddings as well as fashion and glamour. Some of 'his girls' have been in *Vogue*, as well as *Penthouse*. The work's usually for *People*, *Picture*, magazines like that. His girls also do promotional and hostessing work. And he supplies lingerie and topless barmaids to hotels.

Brigitte nods.

'The rules?' he says. 'I forbid any alcohol or drug-taking during jobs.'

Uh-oh.

'And no sleeping with clients.' He looks over his glasses with fatherly eyes, and tells her the agency takes 10 per cent of modelling, promotional, and bar work. And 20 per cent of anything that goes to television.

'Television?' She sits up straighter.

'Yes, occasionally we get a commercial. One of my girls even went on to a bit part in *Neighbours*.'

'Do you think I could get work?'

'I think you could do very well. You have a fresh face, and, from what I can see, a great figure. Have any marks — scars or tattoos?'

'No.'

He notes that on her details form, and asks what kinds of modelling she's interested in.

She looks at the photos on the wall. 'Lingerie, swimwear, I guess.'

'Fashion?'

'Aren't I too short for that?'

'I've got a couple of girls on my books who are only five-foot-six, and they do fashion. How tall are you, Brigitte?'

She shrugs. 'Five-six, maybe.'

He points to the height chart stuck to the wall, and instructs her to slip off her shoes and stand against it. She stretches up as tall as she can while he measures her. His armpits smell of Old Spice.

'Five foot four. Just. Never mind,' he says. 'You have great boobs. You'll get lots of glamour work.' He crosses fashion off the form. 'Can I take some photos of you?'

'What, now?'

'We need to get your portfolio started so I can put you forward for jobs.'

She smiles — he must really think she's good.

He walks across the room. 'How about a black backdrop? It will look nice behind your hair.' He pulls a cord that changes the white sheet to a black one. 'There's a rack of costumes behind the screen for you to try on.'

'Should I leave my underwear on underneath?'

'No. The costumes are clean. I get them dry-cleaned after every shoot.'

Behind the screen, she chooses a red bustier and G-string — a costume she saw on one of the models in a photo on the wall. She picks up a hand mirror from the little dressing table to check her make-up. There's a crack down the middle, so that her reflection is distorted unless she looks to one side. A piece falls out.

Richard calls to be careful of the broken mirror. Too late — she's sliced her right index finger on the sharp edge of it. Blood trickles down her hand, and she reaches for a cloth to wipe it before it drips onto her costume. The cloth is a white silk negligee.

'Nearly ready?' Richard says.

'Nearly.' She'll have to leave him some money for extra dry-cleaning. 'Do you have a Band-Aid?'

He tells her to look in the first-aid box in the kitchen.

Richard stops what he's doing — light checks, or something with a contraption the size of a mobile phone — when she comes out. He shakes his head, and tells her she has an amazing body. He directs her to stand in the middle of the dropsheet while he does more light checks and snaps a couple of Polaroids.

He talks her through some 'glamour model poses', and takes photos with the camera on the tripod. She keeps her bandaged finger hidden discreetly behind her back.

She changes into a fluro-green bikini, and he takes some 'casual beach girl' shots. He says she's a natural, and suggests some topless photos.

It's just skin — no big deal. She undoes the ties, and pulls off the bikini top unselfconsciously. Her body has been merely a tool of her trade, but she feels a twinge that maybe what she's doing is wrong. What would Matt say if he knew? But it's just work. She doesn't answer to him, anyway. And he did say she doesn't have to tell him everything — it's OK for them to have their own lives.

'Wow. That's fantastic, Brigitte. You're making my glasses fog up.'

He gets her to tussle her hair and do some 'Brigitte Bardot pouts'. It's kind of fun — when she lets go of her Matt-guilt. She drapes herself over the peacock chair for some nude shots, but refuses to do open-leg poses. Richard says she could try for *Playboy*, but not *Penthouse*. '*Penthouse* has to see everything, inside and out, so to speak,' he says.

It feels a bit sordid, but at the same time very business-like. The session ends abruptly, with Richard packing up his camera and saying it's time for him to pick up his kids from school. He keeps talking to Brigitte as she dresses behind the screen.

'It was lovely to meet you, Brigitte. You did really well today. I can't believe it was your first time in front of the camera. I'll choose some prints, and send them to you when they're ready.'

She asks how much it's all going to cost, and he says not to worry — he'll deduct it from her first modelling job. He walks her back through the orange curtain, and says to say hello to Al.

'Don't think I'll be seeing Al. I'm not working at the Gold Bar anymore.'

'Where are you working?'

'I'm not.'

'Oh, well, you'll need something straight away then. I can get you some bar work to start with. And I'm looking for a couple of girls to hostess at the car races. Would you like me to put you up for that?'

She nods, sure that hostessing won't be too difficult — whatever it is.

She thanks him, and they shake hands. What a strange man. She blinks in the sunlight as she steps back into the real world with the feeling that she's leaving Oz or Narnia or somewhere.

She catches a train back into the city. Eric's still touring Bullet Brain, so she walks to Matt's place — her knee feels stronger since she stopped dancing. She buys a bottle of good white wine on the way. Christmas decorations are already in the shops.

She takes out her key and hesitates, uncomfortable with just letting herself in. She knocks.

She kisses Matt as soon as he opens the door. Her heart skips; it feels like she hasn't seen him for a long time.

'Wow, you're chirpy today.' He wipes her cherry-red lipstick off his face. 'And you've got a lot of make-up on.'

He has a dazed, faraway look in his eyes, and his hair is all messy. He must have been working — on his novel, or on an article for *Mad Monster Trucks*.

'I have a new job,' she says as she climbs the stairs.

He follows her to the kitchen, rubbing his eyes. 'Really. What about David Jones?'

'I'm going to be a model.' She puts the wine in the fridge. 'Today I got an agent, and had some photos taken for my portfolio.'

She thought he'd be happy for her, but he's not smiling when she turns to face him. 'Where'd you find this agent?'

'Carnegie.'

'What kind of modelling?' he asks suspiciously.

'Clothes, swimwear, you know — a bit of everything.'

'What the fuck are you doing, Brigitte? Go do some study. I'll help you with your application.'

'I need to earn money, Matt.'

He sighs, shakes his head, and goes up to the living room. She follows him.

'Why so serious?' She sits next to him on the couch. 'Where's my funny Matt?'

He is silent. She kisses his neck.

'Stop it. You can't get away with that with me.' He pulls away from her.

'What are you talking about?'

'I know you're smart. I don't want to watch you waste it. I won't accept that.'

Why is he talking to her like this? He's not her teacher anymore. And he's not her father. She tries to kiss him again, but he pushes her away.

'I said *stop it.*'

She sits back, and sticks out her bottom lip like a naughty child. Matt ignores it. He reaches for the remote on the coffee table, and turns on the TV. In the news: the Gold Bar has been closed down because of a shooting out the front. A blonde reporter in a pearl-blue suit is standing in front of the club, saying that alleged drug baron Alphonse La Rocca has been shot dead in front of the strip club he managed and allegedly laundered money through … Footage shows a sheet-covered body lying on the footpath behind police tape. The tip of a brown crocodile-skin shoe pokes out from underneath the sheet.

Matt walks out of the room.

41

Brigitte throws the heavy duffle bag, containing her belongings, over her shoulder, and looks around the apartment one last time. Her 'Dear Eric' letter stands against a crystal vase on the breakfast bar. Her *Lovers* print hangs above the couch; it's too big to take with her. It's for the best — it would just be a reminder of this place, this time.

In the quiet foyer, the sound of the door closing echoes behind her. There's nobody around to say goodbye to. Sean's office door is shut. Maybe she'll call him when things have settled down. Her heels click on the marble steps as she walks down towards the glass front door.

As she steps into the street, she looks up and sees a sky-writing plane overhead. She tries to make out the word it's forming, and almost crashes into a couple with a baby in a pram and a pre-school-aged boy in hand. The mother is blonde, pretty, young. Brigitte apologises, and they smile at her. They look so happy, so *nice*. She freezes.

Back inside, she tears Eric's goodbye letter into a million pieces and throws it in the bin. She unpacks her bag and puts her things away.

When Eric gets home, she's sitting on the sofa, beneath the David Boyd, sewing sequins onto a costume. He looks fatter, and he's jubilant after the Bullet Brain tour, ready to play house again. He shrugs out of his grey-leather bomber jacket and throws it over the back of a chair. He smiles, produces a little black box from his suitcase, walks across, and hands it to her. She hesitates, he nods, and she opens it. Inside is a gold link bracelet. He helps her fasten it around her wrist.

'Let's go for a drive, Pet,' he says.

The phrase *body dump* flashes through her head. 'I'm a bit tired, Eric.'

He pulls her by the hand, not taking no for an answer. His driver is waiting out front in a limo.

Eric tells his driver to take them to St Kilda.

They drive along the beach road. Eric has dark sunglasses and an inane grin stuck to his face. He runs his window down, and a salty breeze tussles their hair — Brigitte's hair, anyway. Eric has little hair to speak of. He twists, leans back, and groans as he reaches into his pocket for a pack of squashed Juicy Fruit.

'Chewy?' He takes a piece, and offers one to Brigitte.

She shakes her head.

He turns on the radio. It's Nirvana — all you hear anywhere these days.

'We were in negotiations to tour them next year. Would've made a mint. Fucken Cobain.' He changes the station.

She thinks about Matt sitting at his desk typing, pulling at his hair. Is he wondering where she is? Is he still annoyed with her? Still judging, still not accepting? She deserves more than that. She touches the bracelet.

Eric asks if she feels like stopping for lunch soon.

She's looking at a boat on the ocean. Torn. What does she deserve? What does she *want*?

'A bit longer, then we'll head back to the city,' he says as he lights a cigarette.

The waiter knows their names and finds them a table, even though they don't have a reservation. Eric orders a bottle of Bollinger.

'What have you been up to while I've been away, Pet?'

She twists the bracelet around her wrist. 'I got a new job.'

'King Street?'

'No. David Jones.'

'David Jones!' He chokes on his champagne.

She frowns.

'Can't imagine you working there.' He takes out a cigarette, and the waiter glides across the red-carpeted room to light it for him. 'There are plenty of new clubs you could try.'

She nods, and scans the menu.

'Should we order a banquet to share?' Down-lighting glints on the bald part of his head. It's as shiny as the polished-wood pillar behind him.

'I'm not really hungry.'

'I'm starving.' Eric waves the waiter over, and orders a three-course banquet.

She looks at her fingernails. They need refilling; she hasn't been to the beauty salon for a while.

'What's wrong, Pet?'

'Nothing.'

After a couple of glasses of champagne, she tells him about her day at David Jones. He laughs loudly, and coughs. The birthday party at the next table turn their heads to look.

'You weren't cut out to be a shopgirl, Pet.'

He's right.

He pours more champagne. 'Seriously, if your knee is that bad and you need time off, I could give you some extra cash to get by. You don't have to work at David Jones.'

The waiter covers their laps with crisp napkins, and serves the banquet, starting with plates of lamb dumplings, quail, and Peking duck, followed by red emperor fillets, a chicken dish, and grain-fed eye fillet. Brigitte picks at the food, and Eric eats most of her share.

'Another bottle of champagne, Pet?'

She nods.

She sways and leans against the wall as Eric opens the apartment door. A sick, acidic taste rises in her throat, and fills her mouth; she swallows it, and wants to lie down.

'How about a thank you for your present, Pet?' he says when they're inside. The bracelet swings as he kisses her hand, her wrist, along her arm. He grabs one of her breasts and pushes her up against the wall. His teeth grind against hers in a rough kiss — Juicy Fruit, alcohol, and cigarette taste in his mouth. She turns her face away. She can't do this. He pushes his other hand up under her skirt. She struggles and squirms out of his hold.

'What's wrong?' He forces her face up so she has to meet his eyes. A sliver of Peking duck is lodged between his front teeth. The lift dings in the foyer.

'I …' She thought she could.

'What?'

'Can't.' She looks at the door.

A blast of loud music from a car driving past fills the silence.

'Can't?' He holds her wrists above her head, against the wall. 'Maybe I can't pay the rent then.'

There's no way out of this. The best thing to do would be to get it over with, to close her eyes and shut her mouth, but she keeps talking. 'I'm sorry. I — '

He slams her hands, balled into fists, against the wall.

'Eric, I think I'm going to be sick.'

'I know who he is, Brigitte.'

Fear flickers in her eyes, and the nausea subsides for a moment.

'Or should I say *was*.' Eric smashes her hands, her knuckles, against the wall again. One of her fingernails snaps. 'Haven't you heard what happened to your boyfriend?'

What the fuck is he talking about?

'Al.' Eric nods, his eyes watering. He lets go of her wrists, puts two fingers to his temple, and pulls the trigger with his thumb. 'Now you know what happens to people who fuck me around.'

Whack! He smacks her across the face, and she gets an instant blood nose; the tinny taste of it runs down the back of her throat.

She wipes her nose with the back of her hand, and steadies herself against the wall. 'Eric, I'm really going to be sick.' He lets her go to the bathroom.

She vomits in the toilet, reaches up to flush, and rests her head on the seat. She watches a glob of blood swirl and flower in the bowl. She feels for a towel, drags one down, holds it against her nose, and pulls herself up on the rail.

'What's the matter, Pet?' Eric's reflection looms above hers in the mirror as she turns on the tap and splashes cold water over her face.

'How long had you been fucking Al?'

She leans forward; the basin is cool against her cheek.

He pulls her up by the hair. 'How long!'

'I hate you,' she whispers, between clenched teeth, and immediately regrets it.

A police siren wails somewhere far away. He balls his right hand into a fist. She cowers against the basin and says over and over that she's sorry, that she didn't mean to say it. But it doesn't help.

42

By the heavy-traffic sounds, it must be morning when she wakes up on the bathroom floor with the taste of rust in her mouth. She lies still for a long time — listening to the rain spattering against the windows, swooshing down the gutters — scared to move in case she can't. When her thirst and the pressure in her bladder become unbearable, she reaches for the cupboard top. Her hands knock over a stack of aromatherapy soaps, and they fall like dominoes as she hauls herself up. An essential-oil bottle smashes on the tiles; the aroma of *Bliss* mingles with that of the rain in the air. She pulls her skirt on as she sits on the toilet.

She stumbles to the kitchen, and gulps down two big glasses of water at the sink. There's a bloody handprint on the wall near the door. A condom lies in the corner like a dead jellyfish, holding about half a bottle-top of semen. She rips off and throws the bracelet at it on the way past.

She walks through the foyer, down the marble steps, and out of the building. And then she runs along the street, across the rain-slicked road, without looking. A car beeps at her. She hears brakes screech and tyres slide, and she tenses for a bang, but there is none. She keeps running — doesn't look back — through the gardens, across to the tennis courts, where her torn knee collapses under her. She lies on the wet grass, thankful for the pain that has taken the edge off the fear. *Now you know what happens to people who fuck me around.* She punches the ground, rolls onto her back, pulls up handfuls of grass and throws them away, breaking more fingernails. The gunmetal sky rains and rains.

Every fibre of her cries for Matt, but she drags herself up, and goes to Nana and Papa's house.

The sideway is slippery: the garden beds are flooding, the geranium pots over-flowing. When Nana sees Brigitte stagger through the back door, she doesn't yell or carry on. Doesn't judge. In silence, she helps her undress, wraps her in blankets on a chair in front of the fire, and puts her clothes in the tumble dryer. She cleans the blood from her face, gives her an icepack to hold against her cheek, and wraps a fresh bandage around her foot. Nana doesn't speak for a long time. When she does, she says, 'Bloody Melbourne weather.' Then she towel-dries Brigitte's hair gently, like she used to when Brigitte was little.

Papa has assembled the plastic Christmas tree in the corner of the room, and trimmed and trapped it with mismatched balls, tinsel, and dusty paper-chains from Brigitte's childhood. She and Ryan used to help him with the tree when they were kids, and it would stay up until Easter. She sniffs. 'Please don't tell Papa.' Her voice is barely a whisper.

Nana turns on the TV — a soap opera. She puts on a floral apron, and heats some soup on the stove, but Brigitte feels too sick to eat. She dozes in the chair, and when she wakes there's a game show on, and Nana is folding her clothes.

'Don't go back, Brigi,' Nana says.

Brigitte looks at the tacky Christmas tree, and bites her lip. The mantel clock chimes.

'You could stay here. Papa's fixing up the room out the back. It's as big as a flat.'

Brigitte wobbles as she stands up and puts on her clothes. Nana follows her down the passageway. 'Please, Brigi.' She clutches her shoulder.

Brigitte pushes her away, too hard; Nana loses her balance, and bumps against the wall.

As Brigitte walks away, she glances over her shoulder at Nana standing on the front step, wringing the corner of her apron. The doorway is in shadow behind her like a dark aura. For a moment, Brigitte almost runs back to her.

The storm is over. The sky looks finger-painted, like the background of her *Lovers* print, long cloud smears tinged with blue: peppermint instead of spearmint. She slides her sunglasses on, over her puffy eyes; they hurt her face. She reaches into her handbag, the side pocket, for Matt's spare key on the J keyring. She holds it in her hand as she limps back to the apartment, her heart hammering.

Eric's not there.

She rings Matt, and hangs up when he answers. Her mobile rings, and she turns it off. Nausea swells inside her, and she rushes to the toilet to vomit. She smells bad — even the aromatherapy scents can't cover it — like sour milk and off meat. Standing makes her woozy, so she sits on the shower floor while she washes her body gently and thoroughly with rose soap. It stings between her legs.

She dries herself, slips her bathrobe on, and peeks out under a blind slat in the lounge room. A black car parks across the road in front of the gardens. She checks the window latches, takes out Matt's key, and curls into a ball under a blanket on the sofa. Despite a Valium and a sleeping tablet, sleep drags its heels in coming, but when it does it stops her shivering. The blast of a car's backfire drags her back. She pulls up the blanket, shuts her eyes tight, and clutches the key in her hands. Through shallow sleep and restless dreams, she runs and runs.

She wakes with the letter J imprinted on her palm. She puts the key back into her bag. The room spins, and she steadies herself against the wall as she hurries to the toilet to vomit again. A headache throbs in her right temple. Something's wrong. Maybe Eric hit her too hard this time. She pulls on jeans and a T-shirt, and goes outside for some fresh air.

43

Breathe, breathe ... God, she's going to vomit in the waiting room. She leans forward, resting her head on her knees; perspiration trickles down inside her T-shirt. The person sitting next to her moves away. There's no air. If the doctor doesn't call her within one minute, she's out of here. Sixty cat and dog, fifty-nine cat and dog, fifty-eight cat and dog, fifty-seven cat and ...

'Brigitte.'

When Doctor O'Meara asks what happened to her face, Brigitte says she fell down the steps. She bursts into tears, and the doctor passes her a box of tissues. She takes a couple, and describes her symptoms — in between sobs — convinced that it's a brain haemorrhage and that she hasn't long to live.

'Have you missed a period?'

She stops wiping her eyes with the tissues, and looks up. The doctor is wearing Christmas tree earrings with little red lights. 'I'm not pregnant.'

'You're not sexually active?'

'Um yes, but — '

'What contraception are you using, Brigitte?'

She shakes her head. 'I'm not pregnant.'

'How do you know?'

'I just — it was only a couple times without ...'

'All right. How about we do a urine test? Just to be sure.' The doctor swivels around on her chair, and takes a specimen jar from the cupboard. 'All you have to do is go to the toilet and wee into this jar for me.'

Brigitte takes the jar to the bathroom. She's shaking so much, she gets urine all over her hands. A poster about foods to avoid during pregnancy is Blu-tacked to the toilet door.

Back in the consulting room, the stick Doctor O'Meara places in the jar of urine turns blue. 'It's positive.'

What? No! Brigitte stops rocking on her chair.

'This is not good for you, is it, Brigitte?'

She shakes her head, and pinches the bridge of her nose.

'We'll need to do a blood test to be sure.' The doctor's conservative little heels click as she walks across the room, opens another cupboard, and takes out a syringe.

'So this might be a false alarm?'

'Urine tests are not 100 per cent accurate, but they're more likely to show false negatives,' Doctor O'Meara says matter-of-factly. The lights on the Christmas tree earrings flash every time she moves her head.

'So I might be OK?'

'I think the test is right.' She tells Brigitte to make a fist, and wraps a band around her arm, pulling it tight. Her deodorant is jasmine-scented. As she draws Brigitte's blood, she says, 'If somebody is hurting you, we could contact the local domestic-violence service.'

'I told you, I fell down the ...' The room fades to a fuzzy, sepia-tinged outline.

'Brigitte? Brigitte!'

She's sliding down the chair. Doctor O'Meara catches her under the arms as she faints.

***

The doctor's receptionist phones at quarter to five with the blood-test results. Brigitte's heart thumps as she hears the word 'positive'. *Fuck, fuck, fuck.*

God, she needs a drink. Where's the bottle of Johnnie Walker that Sean bought? On top of the fridge. There's a little bit left. She looks at the striding man in top hat and tails on the label, and hears a stupid nagging voice in her head — she tries to shut it out — telling her it's bad for the baby. *Shut up, Johnnie Walker.*

God, what has she done this time? She remembers Matt's horrified face when she told him she wasn't on the pill. *Stupid, Brigitte, so stupid.*

Hang on — Matt never has to know about this. Nobody has to know. She'll just get rid of it, and everything will be as it was. She pours a drink.

Johnnie Walker nags: maybe now is the right time. Leave Eric, make a new start. Everything happens for a reason, doesn't it?

It's not the right time! It would be too hard. I'm a stupid stripper, for God's sake. The child would grow up to hate me. Having it is not an option, so I'll never know, will I? I never want to have a baby. So shut up, Johnnie Walker!

But how can she destroy this natural, innocent life growing inside her? *Stupid, stupid, stupid, Brigitte.* She takes a big drink. *Sorry, baby. No, you're not a baby. Just a bunch of cells — too small to be anything yet.* But still, she can't finish her drink. She goes to the bathroom, rubs some arnica cream on her bruises, and lies on the floor. The cold of the tiles eases the pain in her head. Doctor O'Meara said migraines were common during pregnancy.

She dreams of her high school boyfriend's old house. He's been hitting her again, calling her 'frigid Brigitte' because she won't have sex with him. She rings Joan from the phone on the little green table in his hallway; there's blood on the receiver. Joan says she's too busy to come get her: it's your problem; sort it out yourself, Brigitte.

But he's hurting me, Mum, Mummy … Please don't leave me here. The phone turns into a child's toy.

She wakes on the bathroom floor again. It's dark. The light hurts her eyes when she turns it on. She opens the cupboard under the basin where she keeps her anti-inflammatories, sleeping tablets, sedatives, and other assorted prescription and non-prescription medication. But she listens to Johnnie Walker and closes the cupboard door, leaving them untouched.

She starts when her mobile rings on the bedside table. It's Ryan.

'What's going on, Brigi?'

'Nothing.' She gets up from the bed and walks through to the lounge room. 'I thought you were angry with me.'

'More worried than angry. You OK?'

She peers through a blind slat. It's raining again, and car and streetlights spill like a Monet painting across the road. She can't see any black cars.

'Nana's worried about you.'

'Did she tell you to call?' The gardens are deserted. A possum, illuminated by a streetlight, lopes along the path and tries to scuttle up an elm tree, but is thwarted by a tree-band.

'Do you want some help getting out of there?'

She shakes her head, and doesn't answer.

'Is Sean there?'

'Sean's not talking to me.'

'Go to Nana and Papa's.'

A pause.

'Brigi, I'm coming down.'

She takes out Matt's key, turns it over in her hand. 'No. I'm fine. I've met somebody.' She balances the phone against her ear as she wraps a blanket from the couch awkwardly around her shoulders with one hand, still holding the key in the other.

'Can you go to their place?'

A dark figure in a bomber jacket walks along the path though the gardens. It looks like Eric. 'I have to go, Ryan.'

'Brigitte — '
'I love you.'
'Don't you hang up on me, Brigi—'

44

The Fertility Clinic. Stupid name — it should be called The Knocked-up and Desperate Clinic. Sparse Christmas decorations are draped around the reception desk. Brigitte has a referral and an information brochure from Doctor O'Meara in her bag, but she's too scared to read it, doesn't want to know about the procedure. *Fuck. Fuck. Fuck.* What is she doing here? She wants to run out, call it off. But she does as she's told: she sits on a hard plastic chair, fills in the forms, and stares, without seeing, at the fish swimming aimlessly through bubbles in the tank while she waits for the counsellor. The smells of disinfectant and air freshener make her sneeze.

The counsellor doesn't really counsel — just asks questions about Brigitte's health and medical history. And why she wants to have an abortion. She says she's lost her job, she can't afford to take care of a baby, she's too young, it was unplanned: excuses as empty as the fish's eyes. Her voice sounds like somebody else's — tinny, far away, as if through one of those string-and-can phones that she and Ryan used to make when they were kids.

Next, a gynaecologist examines her internally. He treats her with as much compassion and dignity as a farmer might treat one of his calving cows. His gloved hands are big and cold and rough. He hurts her, and she bites her lip so hard it bleeds.

Finally, the receptionist makes an appointment for the operation. They have times available on Thursday and Friday next week; after that, they'll be closed for Christmas. Brigitte's driving test is on Thursday, so she books in for Friday morning.

She walks, drifts, without noticing where she's going, from

East Melbourne to the city. Families with young children are lined up to look at the Myer Christmas windows. She pictures Matt standing in line, holding a child's hand. She blinks away the image, and goes into the store. Carried along by the crowd and a wave of Christmas music — 'Winter Wonderland' — she finds herself in the baby section. She smiles at the little grow-suits and booties and hats. How could anything ever be so tiny? She reaches out to touch a bunny rug on the shelf: a yellow one, with a little blue dinosaur embroidered on one side. She holds it up to her cheek. She has never felt anything so soft, and wonders what it's made of.

'When are you due, love?' A sales assistant startles her, and she drops the bunny rug. 'Your baby — when's it due?' She picks up the rug and hands it back to Brigitte. 'You're not showing yet — so, June, July?'

Go away stupid woman, leave me alone.

'A winter baby. Lovely. You'll be needing that bunny rug.'

Brigitte almost smiles.

At the apartment, she lies on the bed, cuddling her yellow bunny rug. She's sick, with a migraine and waves of nausea rolling over her. Soon it will all be over. On Friday, the baby will be gone. If that's what you want: Johnnie Walker again. *Shut up! It's not a baby yet. It's* nothing. *Stop fucking up my head.* In fact, it's such an early pregnancy — only six weeks — the doctor at the Fertility Clinic said they'll need to do a test on the tissue afterwards to make sure they get rid of it. It will be that hard to tell. There'll be no little arms and legs being torn apart out of her womb. No telling if it's a boy or a girl.

She hears the shower stop running, then the sounds of towelling and grooming, and of jars and bottles clinking. The toilet flushes. Steam and a waft of expensive cologne follow Eric out of the bathroom. He looms in the doorway in his white underpants, a drip mark on the front. She wants to scream at him to leave her alone, go away, go play Nintendo or something. But she's scared that if she makes him angry he'll hurt her again, and hurt the baby.

'Get up and pack your stuff,' Eric says.

'What?'

'The Death Rowe tour. We fly out tonight.'

'I'm not coming.'

'Yes you are. Booked you a ticket. Can't trust you to stay on your own anymore.'

She buries her face in a pillow.

'I said *Get up and pack now!*'

She doesn't deserve this.

Johnnie Walker says: Get Doctor O'Meara to refer you to the domestic-violence service. Or go to the police, tell them about Eric, make sure he never hurts you again. Matt even knows a cop, remember? You'll be OK.

Brigitte gets up and packs her duffle bag.

'What are you doing, Brigitte?' Eric says as she walks through the lounge room, her bag over her shoulder. 'Flight's not for hours.'

'I'm leaving.'

'No you're not.' Eric lunges, but she moves too quickly for him.

'And I'm not coming back.' She slams the door behind her.

From the street, she looks back once and sees Eric standing at the open window, his gut wobbling like the half-set jelly at the Gold Bar, swearing at her. People on the street look up at him. He coughs, and yells that she's really going to get it when she comes back. She runs like a frightened rabbit.

She doesn't stop to catch her breath until she reaches Gertrude Street. Halfway between Nicholson and Brunswick, a black limousine crawls along the curb, then stops beside her. This is it. The instant where it ends badly. Lucky she didn't make it to

Matt's. *I never deserved him.* She shouldn't have listened to Johnnie Walker. She freezes, holding her breath, bracing herself for *what happens to people who fuck me around*. The window slides down, and she sees his slick, brown hair, dark eyes, black suit. Her stomach liquefies, and she closes her eyes. *Blood spatter. Body dump.*

'Show us ya tits!' he yells. She opens her eyes. It's just a drunk kid, in a limo load of private-school boys on an end-of-year celebration. She exhales, and leans against a shop front as the limo drives off. She almost laughs as a line from one of Sean's Nirvana songs, about being paranoid, comes back to her.

Matt is at his desk writing, pulling at his hair, listening to Nick Cave, when she appears — out of breath — at the top of the stairs. He looks up. She can't read his expression — no wry smile, no raised eyebrows, just a kind of knowing, the way a parent looks at a naughty child when they've come back to apologise. She drops her bag in the corner of the room. He pushes the hair out of his eyes, leaves his work, walks across to stand in front of the cold, empty fireplace, and waits for her to come to him.

She shoves her face against his chest. His faded flannelette shirt feels almost as soft as the bunny rug, and it smells of cinnamon and bergamot and a little bit of sweat. Her knees buckle, he sits on the floor, holding her with him so she doesn't fall. Nick Cave starts singing the song about sailing ships and burning bridges and losing doubts.

45

Brigitte lies on the bed, gently stroking Di's swollen belly. It's warm, and she can feel things moving around in there. 'Don't worry, it'll all be over soon,' she whispers.

Matt comes out of the shower, a royal-blue towel around his waist, steam rising from his skin. He pulls on jeans and a T-shirt. 'Would you like to keep one of her kittens?'

'We're not allowed to have pets in my apartment complex.' Still pretending. 'Will they all be ginger?'

Di meow-screams. Brigitte pulls her hand away and sits up. 'God, are the kittens coming now? What do we do?'

'Calm down. I'll ring the vet.'

Di has settled and fallen asleep by the time Matt comes back from the phone.

'False alarm,' Brigitte says.

'Phew. I was just about to start boiling water.'

'What's the boiled water for anyway?'

'Don't know.'

'Thought you knew everything.'

'Not everything.' He lies next to her on the bed and pushes the damp hair off his face. He creases his brow to look up at her. *No, not everything.*

If I tell you now, she thinks, *right at this very moment in time, you'll be happy. Johnnie Walker says you'll be such a great dad. I love you.*

'Are you OK?'

'Yep.'

'You sure?'

She nods; if she speaks, she'll cry.

He pushes up his faded Bad Seeds T-shirt that she's been sleeping in, and kisses her stomach. Can he tell it's not quite as flat? When will it start kicking? Will it have blue eyes?

She drifts, with a migraine, in and out of sleep all day. She dreams of her childhood safe place: the sleeper compartment of her father's semitrailer. It's warm, the rocking of the motor lulls her, and Johnny Cash sings on the eight-track tape player about strange things like falling into a ring of fire.

But then Dan pulls over into a parking bay. It's a hot night, so they lay a blanket on the ground to sleep. The exhaust pipe ticks as it cools. Joan says the night sky is a beautiful infinite space, and she knows the names of all the stars. But the blackness closes in, presses down.

Joan and Dan smoke, drink beer from long-neck bottles, and fall asleep under the stars. Dan is young and handsome, his muscular arms tattooed with snakes and mermaids. Joan is small and perfect — she looks exactly like Brigitte Bardot. *Too good to be a truckie's wife,* the trees whisper.

Brigitte curls herself into a corner of the blanket beside her parents. The silence rings, and hair itches her face, but she can't take her hands from under the blanket, or something will get her: a robber, a murderer, a yowie.

Dan gets up and walks around the side of the truck, kicking the tyres. Digger is tied to the trailer, his lead attached to his new red collar.

'Whatya doing?' Brigitte says.

'Just havin' a leak.'

'Are there yowies out here, Dad?'

'Nup. Too hot for 'em tonight.'

She looks out at the deserted highway and sees Eric wandering along the white line in the middle. From nowhere, a truck carrying chickens swerves into him; the impact cuts off his head. For a moment, his decapitated body is stuck to the windscreen, and then it's thrown into the air as the chicken truck rolls and slides sideways along the highway. Brigitte stands and walks through the chickens and blood. It's not Eric's body on the road. It's Digger's. His collar is missing.

'Get back in the truck,' Dan says. 'We have to make the Brisbane market.'

She turns, and Dan is dying in his old leather lounge chair at the pink house. Colourful TV presenters sing 'Morningtown Ride' on *Play School*. An oxygen tank breathes for him. His arms are emaciated, the tattoos shrivelled and faded. 'We're not gonna make the market. I've run out of time.'

'There's still time to make it, Dad.'

'No.'

Dad, don't leave!

Then she registers the comforting sound of the tumble dryer and the fresh smell of clean washing. It was just a bad dream, Dad's alive, and he's doing the laundry — he always does it when he's home.

She wakes in Matt's bed. She can hear him working — typing on the word-processor keyboard at his desk in the living room.

The vibration from the dryer in the bathroom becomes the lullaby of the Kenworth's motor again.

More strange dreams. Matt's holding two babies on his lap, twins — wrapped in the yellow bunny rug, in front of the fireplace. He's leaning down talking to them softly, hair falling forward over his face. He looks up. It's not Matt. Golden flames reflected in dark eyes. *No!*

'It's OK. It's OK.' Matt's stroking her hair, the way her dad used to. 'Just a bad dream. Shh.'

Sleep drives her away again.

Matt brings the papers and a bottle of wine up to the bedroom in the late afternoon. The smell of the wine nauseates her, and she can't finish one glass.

'Maybe you should see a doctor,' he says.

'Just the flu.' She smiles weakly.

'Want to see a movie?' He reads the film guide. 'When you're feeling better?'

She nods.

'*Pulp Fiction*'s supposed to be good.'

'*The Lion King*.'

'*The Lion King*!'

'It's not just for kids.'

'I forgot — you are a kid.'

'No, I'm not. I'll be twenty next week.'

'Next week?'

'Boxing Day.'

'Really?' He looks back at the paper and says, '*The Lion King* starts on Boxing Day. We could see it and then go somewhere for a special birthday dinner.'

'Can I drive?' She sits up, feeling a bit better.

'Maybe. Still getting your licence in the morning?'

'If I pass the test.'

'Of course you will.' He puts a hand on her thigh. 'Would you like to spend Christmas with me?'

She wrinkles her brow and looks up at the ceiling, pretending to think about it. 'Yes.' *And every other day of the rest of my life.* 'What will you be cooking?'

'Promise no seafood.' He folds the paper and places it on the bed. The pages fan out, and Brigitte sees the start of a story about Death Rowe: Tour cancelled, Calvin Rowe arrested at the airport for drug possession. She lies back, feeling sick again.

46

She gets up early on the Thursday before Christmas, showers, and puts on her Chanel dress. It feels tight. She forces herself to eat half a piece of toast, and makes a pot of weak tea. The poster at the doctor's said coffee was bad for the baby. She sits on the top step, and drinks her tea from the butterfly mug.

Matt's still asleep when she goes into the bedroom to say goodbye. Di sleeps beside him, her kittens due any day now. Brigitte smiles. Is that flutter in her stomach a kick? No, it couldn't be. It's something else; something has shifted, changed — but not just in her body. 'I'll be back later.' She kisses Matt's lips softly. 'I love you.'

'Love you too, Brig,' he mumbles in his half-sleep.

She scores 100 per cent on her driving test. At the VicRoads office in Carlton, Marco gives her a Christmas present. She can tell it's a box of chocolates. He hugs her — tighter, longer than he should, then realises what he's doing is inappropriate, and reluctantly lets her go. He tells her to call any time — with questions about driving, or road rules, or just to talk. Or maybe go out for dinner some time.

She looks happy, even though you're not supposed to smile, in the photograph on her probationary licence. Her body is heavier, but she feels light.

She has the taxi driver pull into a bottle shop on the way to Matt's. As she weighs a good bottle of champagne in her hands, she makes the decision to tell him about the baby today. And about

Eric, about everything, and then they'll go to the police, and it will all be OK. She'll cancel her appointment at the Fertility Clinic. She pays at the counter, and rushes back to the taxi.

Heat haze shimmers on the roads as they drive through Fitzroy. The hot weather has brought out all the junkies and drunks. They're wandering around like zombies in singlets and shorts, white flesh mushrooming and turning pink over waistbands. Brigitte's dress is stretched uncomfortably tight across her stomach. There's a Paul Kelly song on the radio, her theme song: 'Dumb Things'. But today, for once, she is going to do what has clearly become — thanks to Johnnie Walker — the smart thing. The right thing.

She *is* going to tell Matt. About the baby. Eric and the police can wait until later. And they'll celebrate with the champagne — he can drink it anyway, and she might have just a tiny sip. He's going to be happy, and everything *is* going to be OK.

She asks the taxi driver to pull up across the road from Matt's place. She's searching in her handbag for her wallet to pay when she looks up and sees the postman, holding an A4 size envelope, in Matt's doorway. Matt opens the door. He's wearing a white T-shirt and long denim shorts, and his feet are bare. He should be more careful, with syringes always in the street. He looks out of place in this part of town: fresh and shiny against the grunge. She can see the flash of his eyes from here — Adonis blue. He chats with the postie, takes the envelope and the rest of his mail, smiles and waves, and goes inside.

Brigitte looks at her change from a fifty in the taxi-driver's hand. He's not handing it over; he's still talking to her — about Fitzroy in the old days, Squizzy Taylor or something. She nods her head vigorously, not listening. Yack, yack, yack. *Come on.* Her whole body tingles. She's afraid she won't go through with this if she has to wait much longer. She's ready to tell the driver to keep the change as a tip. He writes something on a piece of paper and gives it to her — his phone number. *What?* He finally hands over the change, tells her she's beautiful and to call if she wants to go out for a drink with him on the weekend.

She lets herself in with her key. Her heart flutters. She leans against the cool wall for a moment. The bluestone needs a few consecutive days of hot weather before it absorbs and holds the heat. Her hand sweaty, she climbs the stairs, holding tight to the banister for courage. The comforting smell of clean washing steadies her; she inhales a deep breath of it. Matt's brown sweater hangs in the doorway at the top of the stairs, drying on a coat hanger. The butterfly mug is where she left it this morning on the top step. She smiles and relaxes when she sees him through the bedroom doorway, folding laundry and placing it neatly in piles on the bed. The outline of the serpent tattoo shows through his T-shirt. The bottle of champagne clinks against something in her bag. He hears her come in, but doesn't turn around.

'I saw the photos, Brigitte.'

'What?'

'The photos,' he says, deadpan.

She doesn't understand what he's talking about until she sees on the bed the A4 envelope with 8" by 10" prints poking out the top — the ones Richard Headley took: her in the red bustier and G-string, the fluro green bikini, topless, nude.

'How could you do that?'

She stands in the doorway, looking down at her swollen feet in new, backless Versace sandals.

'What were you thinking?' A vein pulses in his temple.

She grasps the door frame, dizzy. 'Why were you going through my mail?'

'You didn't tell me you had it redirected here. I didn't even look, just thought it was for me — a manuscript coming back or something.'

She sees underneath the ripped envelope some other letters

263

with redirection stickers addressed to her, a couple of university logos, the course-enrolment information she had posted out. Why couldn't he have opened those first?

'How could you let yourself be exploited like that?'

'I wasn't being exploited. I agreed to do it.' She sticks out her chin. 'And they're only shots for my portfolio. I haven't done any jobs yet.' How is she going to get around to telling him about the baby now?

He keeps folding the clothes, faster, less neatly.

'It's not exploitation. Just a way to make money. No big deal.'

He shakes his head, and sucks in his breath.

'All those men's magazines ...' She should stop now and acknowledge how upset he is, but she goes on, her voice taking on a screechy edge, like Joan's. 'It's the women who are getting paid for the photos, and the stupid men who are paying to look. So who's really being exploited?' Her face is hot.

'You seriously believe that?' His voice sounds deeper, still calm, but only just.

She shrugs, wanting to dismiss it now, to say she's sorry, it was a mistake — make it go away so she can tell him what she desperately needs to. But he's not letting it go.

'And I know you didn't really work behind the bar at that club.'

Her eyelids flicker as she looks into the corner of the room. Three gift boxes are stacked on the bedside table: one wrapped in Christmas paper, one in birthday wrapping, and the third is a little blue Tiffany box tied with white ribbon.

She looks back to Matt. 'You came into work to check up on me?'

He shakes his head. 'I'd never go to a place like that. But I know you couldn't afford all your designer clothes, your beauty salon appointments, on a bar tender's wage.'

She looks at her sandals again.

'Come on, Brig, you're better than that. Put it behind you.

Don't you want to start again?' He softens, and this could be her out, but she doesn't take it; she feels the need to defend herself. He's not her father.

'How do you know what I want?' She glances at the Tiffany box again, and unconsciously rests a hand on her abdomen.

'I don't. But surely it's not this.' He picks up the envelope, throws it back onto the bed so that the photos spill out further. She meets her own gaze in a photo: a young Joan, tussled hair, the provocative Bardot pout that Richard had her do for the camera.

'What the fuck were you thinking, Brigitte?'

She starts — she has never heard him raise his voice before. She reaches down to pick up the photos, but he holds her wrist. 'Leave them.'

'Don't do that to me.' She wrenches her arm away — over-dramatic, as he was barely holding it — and backs out of the room. She trips on the stairs, clings to the banister, and falls to her knees on the third top step.

He rushes towards her, reaches out a hand to help her up, but she pushes him away as she stands.

'Don't touch me!' Something has snapped. 'You can't tell me what I can and can't do. You don't know anything about me.' She's yelling at her mother, at Eric, at her dad for leaving her, at everybody who has hurt her. 'Why don't you just leave me the fuck alone?' She screams in Matt's face, hears Joan's voice, remembers how Joan's eyes shined when she yelled. He backs away from her.

She picks up the butterfly mug and throws it at him. He protects his face with his hands. It misses his head, but smashes to pieces against the bedroom doorframe.

He opens his mouth to say something, but, shocked by her violence, nothing comes out. He holds up his hands. A red line buds with blood along his little finger where a shard of mug must have sliced it. He doesn't seem to notice.

She takes a few tentative steps down the stairs, uncertain now, and sorry, but it's too late. She looks up at him.

'Just go, Brigitte. Go back to him.'

'What?' No more screaming — she's speaking in a whisper now.

'You always tell me how clever I am, but you've treated me like I'm stupid.'

'What are you talking about?'

'Just go.'

'No, Matt. I swear — '

'Go!' Now he's yelling.

'There's nobody else.'

'*Go!*' He stands at the top of the stairs — he needs a haircut — looking more like Kurt Cobain than ever. He knocks the brown sweater onto the floor as he turns away.

She slinks out, stops at the door, takes his key from its pocket in her bag, turns, and leaves it on the bottom step — the letter J facing up so that the diamantes are showing.

A French window is open at the apartment; the light is on. Her mobile rings as she walks through the foyer. It's Matt. She turns it off, goes out the back, and throws it in a rubbish bin. It's over. She could never be good enough for Matt. But Eric accepts her as she is; he doesn't judge her. He'll be angry for a while, and maybe hit her. Then everything will go back to normal. She'll get rid of the baby, have her knee fixed, take a job in King Street. Pagan could do that.

The apartment stinks: Juicy Fruit, a mountain of dishes piled up on the sink, the ashtray overflowing with cigarette butts, empty wine bottles on the table. Eric is sitting on the sofa, beneath his David Boyd, gazing at the cricket match on TV. The glow from the screen casts an unearthly sheen on his face.

'Where've you been, Pet?' His voice is strangely placid, with an edge of something else. She hasn't heard this tone before, and the sound of it prickles her skin. She can't find her voice to answer.

She forgot her duffle bag at Matt's — all her stuff is still there. He said he loves her. It's not too late. She glances at the door.

'Asked you a question.' Eric flicks off the TV with the remote control, and heaves himself off the sofa. He pulls the window shut, and latches it. He turns and sways a little as he lumbers towards her. Drunk? Stoned? Both? His eyes are red and watery.

Her heart rebounds from her stomach to her throat, and her palms are sweaty ice — the fight-or-flight response. Before apes evolved into humans, sweaty palms helped them to grip the ground as they 'flew' from danger. Brigitte doesn't 'fly' — she just stands there, nodding slowly, halfway between the door and the breakfast bar.

'For me?' Eric takes the champagne from her handbag, peels off the brown paper bag, reads the label. 'Moet et Chandon. You shouldn't have.' With the fastest action she's ever seen him make, he smashes the bottle against the breakfast bar. A spray of champagne and glass fragments glitters in the air. She closes her eyes and winces as a shard grazes her cheek. When she opens her eyes, Eric lunges at her, gashing her forehead with the broken bottle. She closes her eyes again, and feels warmth but not pain. Not yet. Another fight-or-flight effect is a decrease in pain response, kind of like an emergency anaesthetic. Was it Doctor O'Meara who told her all this?

'Not so beautiful now,' Eric says. 'He won't want you anymore. Nobody will.'

He backs her into the corner near the door. The moment seems to freeze in time: a photograph, a snap shot in her head. And then a movie trailer: all the fun at the start when Eric picked her out at the Gold Bar, so glamorous. She pretended to be somebody special, swanning around in her designer outfits, imagining how proud Joan would be. Even when he hit her it wasn't that bad. Not fun now. Not so glamorous as blood runs down her face, stinging her eyes, tasting salty in her mouth. It's going to drip, and stain her dress. The apartment is all red.

Every muscle in her body tenses — steeled for what is to come. Her foot, in its backless sandal, scrapes against the iron doorstop. It feels cold and smooth, and suddenly comforting.

Eric lifts a handful of blood-soaked hair off her face, tenderly pushes it behind her ear, and says, 'When I'm finished with you I'm gunna go visit your boyfriend in Brunswick Street.' He unzips his jeans and puts his hands on her shoulders.

No, he's not going to finish with her, and he's not going to visit Matt — she's never been more certain of anything in her life. The fight-or-flight response also produces extra strength. She summons all she's got to smash her good knee into Eric's groin.

'Fuck!' He recoils, doubling over. 'Bitch!'

Everything starts to fade to a sepia haze, but Brigitte has just enough time, before she loses consciousness, to reach behind her, lift up the doorstop, and bring it down. It makes surprisingly little noise — a pulpy squelch, a smashed melon sound — against the bald patch on top of Eric's head.

***

The sound of the phone rings through the fog in her head. Matt? No, he doesn't have the landline number. She tries to stand, can't, falls to her hands and knees, and crawls to the phone. The pain in her head makes her want to scream, but she can't make a sound — her mouth is too dry, and tastes of metal. Oh God, the baby? She can't be sure, but it feels OK — still there. It's only her head that hurts. The smell of cigarettes and stale alcohol makes her dry retch.

It's 7.30pm on the VCR clock. She reaches up, fumbles with the phone receiver, and pulls it to the floor so she can lie down. It takes her two attempts to speak. 'Hello.' That rasp can't be her voice.

It's some detective calling for Eric.

'Eric's not here.'

'Tell him I'm very sorry to hear about the cancelled concert tour. And I'll see him in the morning.'

As soon as she hangs up, the phone rings again.

'Ms Bardot?'

'Who?'

'Brigitte, it's Richard Headley from Lipgloss Promotions.'

'Richard?'

'Just wondering about your availability for some barmaid training at a hotel in Collingwood this evening.'

The room spins.

'It's paid training.'

She closes her eyes, but it's still spinning.

'You can keep your underwear on, but at the end of the shift the punters usually pass around a hat for new girls if they take off their bra.'

'Sorry, Richard.' Her voice sounds as if it's coming from far away. 'I'm not feeling very well.'

'Never mind. I'll give you another call next week.'

She coughs.

'Hope you feel better. Take care.'

There's blood all over the receiver. Hers? She leaves the phone bleeping off the hook, and passes out on the floor.

47

It's dark when she wakes — barely morning, so there are no traffic noises from the street. A big lump lies on the floor near the door; she sees it out of the corner of her eye, and avoids looking directly at it.

In the bathroom, Eric's Clarins For Men range is lined up neatly against the mirror. Brigitte vomits in the sink when she sees her reflection.

Ignoring the mirror, she slips off her blood-soaked dress, takes a Valium, and runs the shower. She stands under the water for a long time, scrubs her hands, her nails, her body, and brushes her teeth. Foam runs pink down the drain as she shampoos her hair. She works conditioner through the ends, and dabs gingerly at the gash on her forehead. Strange little sobs rise from her abdomen and shake her whole body as she combs and rinses.

The fluffiness of a big, white towel against her skin is comforting. The normality of it steadies her, and she buries her face in it for a moment; it comes away red.

She ties her hair back in a ponytail. The wound on her forehead looks serious, deep; it won't stop bleeding. She covers it with a big sticking plaster, and pulls on a shirt long enough to cover the button on her jeans that she can no longer fasten.

She puts on rubber gloves, and wipes away all her blood and fingerprints from surfaces. When she's finished cleaning, she fills a couple of garbage bags with the gloves, cleaning cloths, her dancing costumes, the last of her clothes, and her Chanel dress. She throws a blanket over the lump on the floor and walks around it. Her fingers fumble for the snib on the door, and she recoils as if it's charged with electricity. She hadn't locked it — anybody could have walked in.

She has a quick look around as she carries the bags out to the bins. Sean's not in yet. None of her neighbours are up. And so what if they were? It's rubbish day; she's just taking out the rubbish.

Back inside, she shakes so much it's hard to turn on the kitchen tap to wash her hands. Her fingers are numb.

She walks through the apartment. All her stuff is gone. It's as if she was never here, except for the *Lovers* leaning against the wall in the walk-in robe. She slides Eric's shirts along the rack so she can see it clearly. A dream? A memory? A ghost? The little sobs start again. It's just today, one day to get through, she tells herself. Tomorrow will be better, and the day after that, and the day after that. And there'll come a moment in a day, in a year, sometime far away, when she won't remember this. She'll make herself forget, somehow. Pagan could do that. The floor rocks under her like a boat. She rushes to the bathroom and throws up again.

The sour and meaty smell in the apartment churns her stomach as she throws blood- and vomit-stained towels into the washing machine. She adds an extra scoop of laundry powder before the fabric softener.

On the way out, she wipes the door handle and leaves it unlocked, the door slightly ajar: *anybody could have come in during the night*. In her imagination, she hears a low, nightmare moan from the lump under the blanket. She turns and rushes away.

On the street, a garbage truck — tinsel on the mirrors — rounds the corner. It's going to be another hot day; the sun already has a sting to it.

★★★

Brigitte walks halfway to East Melbourne before she feels wobbly again and hails a taxi. In the back seat, she rests her cheek against the window. The taxi driver asks if she's all right — does she need to go to the hospital? He frowns, probably worried about having to clean his car if she throws up.

The doorstop? She shivers. She should have thrown it in the bin. *Oh well, never mind. It doesn't matter. Nothing matters anymore.* Nirvana on the radio.

She's early for her 8.00am appointment. She waits on a bench seat around the corner, and picks at the remnants of nail polish, chewing her fingernails so far down the fingertips bleed. Her senses alternate between dead numbness and hyper-reality, where everything looks brighter, every sensation feels more intense. With each throb of pain in her head, the streetscape expands and contracts in her peripheral vision.

There's a crack across the face of her Gucci watch: 7.55am. Time to go in.

Two men in grey suits stand in front of the Fertility Clinic, handing out anti-abortion literature. They ask if she needs help. She shakes her head, but takes their flyer. It's still not too late, Johnnie Walker says. *What the fuck is he doing here?*

Christmas carols are playing in the waiting room: 'Silent Night'. Beneath the fish tank, a row of five young women, about Brigitte's age, sit waiting on hard plastic chairs. One woman looks younger — just a girl. She's here with her mother. How awful. And sitting next to Brigitte, an older woman sniffs; it's probably her last chance for a baby, so why is she here? Two of the women chat; they laugh about something. One reads a magazine. How can they? On this day? How can they laugh, or read, or do anything? Brigitte reaches into her bag, then remembers she no longer has Matt's key, but her fingers find the yellow bunny rug. The woman next to her — she must be pushing forty — asks what happened to Brigitte's head. She hasn't changed the plaster, so blood must be seeping through by now. She's going to have a scar — she'll never be a model for Richard now. She shakes her head;

she can't speak, and starts shivering.

'You'll be OK, sweetie.' The older woman touches Brigitte's arm as if they're members of some secret club. Underneath a lot of make-up, her right eye is black. She smells of cigarettes and chewing gum — Juicy Fruit. Brigitte pushes away a grizzly image to a very deep place she never plans to access again. The fish swim pointlessly from one side of the tank to the other. Brigitte wishes Matt was here to hold her hand. She clutches the bunny rug, and Jack's six-word Hemingway story about the baby shoes comes into her head.

One of the women starts shaking; her pain begins as a quiet whimper, and turns into weeping. Nobody pays any attention — this is a place for crying.

The mother pats her daughter's hand. Brigitte suddenly wants her mother. Why didn't Joan ever love her? Why was Brigitte never good enough? She was a quiet, obedient child, got good grades at school, and never complained about those stupid designer clothes that Joan thought were important when all Brigitte wanted was to wear jeans and T-shirts like the other kids. She dieted when Joan said she was getting fat. She spent a lot of time on looking good because, for Joan, it was always about appearances. But nothing was ever good enough. Lucky Joan can't see what she looks like now.

Nana. She needs Nana, not her mother. Nana doesn't judge, doesn't care about appearances. She would tell her not to go through with this, to come home to her and Papa's house. Home? To the warm smells of wood smoke, and soup, and cakes baking. She'd call Nana now if she had her mobile phone.

One of the women stands up and goes into the reception area. Brigitte can see she's making a call on a pay phone out there. The woman has brittle, over-bleached hair. The hint of a baby bump rises from underneath her white tank top. She has a tattoo on her arm; it's a serpent, a bit like Matt's. She would have had to cover it with a lot of Dermacolor make-up if she'd been dancing at the Gold Bar. Brigitte looks at the ceiling. What the fuck is she doing here with these people? *Hypocrite.* She chides herself for judging, for being like Joan. She's a beaten-up stripper, for fuck's sake. These women probably all have respectable jobs. Or go to school. And they've surely never killed anybody. *Oh God, oh God, oh God.* She puts her head in her hands, and they come away covered in blood. Lady Macbeth. Hilarious. *Yet who would have thought the old man to have had so much blood in him?* But it's real blood on her hands. The nurse comes over, wearing disposable gloves, and cleans her up, changing the dressing on her head.

'Why haven't you had this stitched?' The nurse shakes her head, and speaks as though Brigitte is a naughty child.

When the over-bleached blonde gets off the phone, Brigitte goes out to call Nana, not sure of what she's going to say or if she wants to hear what Nana will say back. Maybe she won't tell Nana anything — just say that she loves her. Yes, she'll at least do that. She puts the coins in the slot. And dials Matt's number. So stupid.

'Hello. Matt Elery.' His voice sounds different, tired, with no hint of humour.

She can't speak.

'Hello?'

'Matt.'

'Brig, where are you? I've been so worried, calling and calling your mobile. I got really scared because I don't have any other way of finding you. I don't even know your address, and I'm sorry I — '

'It's OK. I'm OK.' Her tone is so flat and dead she's surprised he recognises her voice.

'You sound funny. Are you all right?'

A pause.

'Brig, are you still there?'

'Matt?'

'Yes?'

Silence.

'Matt, if anybody asks, can you say I was with you last night?' Words she regrets as soon as they're out.

'Tell me what's wrong.'

She grips the receiver tighter.

'Brigitte, it doesn't matter what's happened. Just please come home.'

Home?

'Tell me where you are, and I'll come and get you.'

'It's OK. I just have something to do, and then I'll come.'

'Brig?'

'Yes?'

'Di had her kittens this morning. I wish you could have been here.'

Cars drive by out on the road, just like every other day.

'I don't think Lucy and Henry should go through with it,' she says.

'What are you talking about?' he says, panic back in his voice.

'The characters in your book — they should just run away together.'

A courier, with a package for reception, walks through the door, and a warm breeze blows the Christmas cards off the desk. She opens her mouth to tell Matt she's sorry, but it hurts to speak; her throat is too tight, and the words get stuck.

'I'm coming to get you right now. Where are you?'

She doesn't want to hang up on him. But she does.

Now Nana. She clears her throat as she dials. Papa answers. 'Where are ya, Brigi? Ya phone's not working. Been trying to find ya. Nana had another heart attack. She's in hospital. Not too good. Askin' for ya.' He sounds frantic.

The nurse is calling her.

'OK, Papa. I've gotta go now, but I'll be there as soon as I can.' She hangs up.

The nurse pushes a box of tissues at her, and she takes one. It feels soft against her fingertips. The tissue box is covered with blue butterflies. *Sorry, Matt. Sorry, Nana.* The nurse ushers her into a cubicle area with a bench seat, and leaves her to change into a shapeless, disposable gown. A poster about safe sex is Blu-tacked to the wall. She folds up her clothes and places them in a neat pile on the seat. Still not too late. *Yes it is, Johnnie Walker. Yes it is.* Of all the women there for 8.00am, she's the last in line to be operated on. From her little cubicle, she can hear the sounds of surgical implements clashing around.

The nurse comes back to escort her to the operating theatre. Brigitte takes off the disposable gown and starts getting dressed.

'What are you doing?' the nurse says.

'I'm sorry. I've changed my mind.'

The nurse frowns.

Brigitte runs out through the waiting room, past the row of empty seats, the fish tank, and the reception desk, still buttoning her shirt.

She glances at her watch: 9.30. A tram slows for the stop out on the street. If she's quick, she'll make it. One of her heels gets caught in the tram track as she runs across the road. She bends to pick up her sandal, and doesn't see the blue, out-of-control Camry swerving into Wellington Parade.

Black.

Nana stands at the end of the operating table under the bright, cold theatre lights.

'God, you scared me. I thought you were meant to be in hospital,' Brigitte says. 'Is it over yet?'

'Nearly.' Nana comes around and kisses her. Brigitte hears a monitor stop beeping. Hers? No, it's Nana's. How can that be?

Sweet voices of little children sing about the train whistle making a sleepy noise, the sunshine, and the day. There must be a kindergarten or school nearby.

Brigitte opens her eyes. Car tyres are going past slowly. Somebody is screaming. A siren howls. The nurse said the anaesthetic might cause hallucinations. The nurse? But she changed her mind.

The long, lonely wail of an air horn. The hiss of air brakes. A red-and-white Kenworth pulls up across the road, with 'Dan Weaver' painted in swirly script on the door. Dan jumps onto the running board, young and strong and handsome. He crosses the road, his hand held out to help Brigitte up. Watch the traffic, Dad. He bends to pick up the yellow bunny rug from a pool of blood.

Warm blood flows down the insides of her legs. Where's her baby? Where's Matt? He said he would come and get her. Matt …

In her safe place, Brigitte feels the warmth, the rocking of the truck's motor.

Red.

Black.

Not going to make it to Morningtown, Dad. It's too far away.

Blank: everything broken, everything gone.

PART III

2008: Come as You Are (cont)

48

Dull electronic sounds ripple through the amniotic greyness in which she swims. It's warm and comfortable here, floating.

Blip, blip, blip.

She opens her eyes. The curtains are drawn around the bed. Kurt Cobain sits beside her.

'What's going on?'

'You tried to kill yourself.' *He's lying. She loves her children; she would never do that. He's standing up and leaving.*

'Come back. Don't you leave me here!' *she screams and tries to follow him, but she's hooked up to drips and monitors.*

'Shh. It's alright. I won't leave you,' says a deep, soothing voice from the greyness.

But she swims back down to Kurt. She hands him the red dog-collar and the key on the letter-J key ring. 'I kept them safe like you said. I didn't lose them.'

Kurt puts the key into his pocket, but tells her to keep the collar.

'Where's Matt?'

'Not here.'

'Can I stay and wait for him?'

'Don't know. Might be a long time.'

'I don't care. I have to tell him I'm sorry.'

'We all have things we're sorry for. It's just life.'

Kurt fades away, turns into Sam, and Sam turns into Dan. Dan takes the red dog collar. 'Here, boy.' Digger comes running, and Dan clips his collar back on. He takes Brigitte's hand and she walks with him, out of the hospital and along Degraves Street. Nana's a bit further up, holding a tiny baby swaddled in a yellow bunny rug. Brigitte wants to hold that baby, but Nana doesn't offer it to her.

'You should let go, Brigi,' Nana says.

'But Matt ...'

'No,' says Dan.

'I can wait.'

'Let go now. You can't leave your babies. They need you, and that's more important than something that never was.'

'You left me!'

'Let go now.'

A long bleep sounds in the greyness. And an alarm, the sharp scrape of a chair, footsteps running.

She lets go of her father's hand, forgives him.

***

Blip, blip, blip.

The sounds of muffled voices and echoes disturb the surface tension of the greyness.

Footsteps. Paper rustles. A scrape. 'It's OK, mate. She's gunna pull through.' The deep, soothing voice is here again. Or still here?

'Fuck.' Another voice, louder. 'What happened? What'd she take?' Keys jangle.

A third voice, in a foreign accent, says, 'Zoldipem, dextropropoxyphene, diazepam, and —'

'What?'

'Sleeping tablets, painkillers, Valium. And alcohol. Large quantities. Lucky Detective Serra got there so quickly.'

'Fuck,' says the one with the loud voice. There's another scrape, a thud.

'We've pumped her stomach, had her on dialysis, and now she's getting fluids through the I.V.' It's the one with the foreign accent.

'Fuck. God.'

'She'll feel terrible when she wakes up.'

'How long till she wakes up?'

'Should be sitting up by this time tomorrow. Be home for Christmas,' says Foreign Accent.

An electronic alarm. Squeaky footsteps.

'Where'd she get all that shit from?' Loud Voice says.

'Had scripts for it all,' says Deep Soothing Voice. 'From a dodgy bloke in Richmond who'd have had a visit from one of my mates by now. Reckon the AMA'll be having a chat with him soon.'

'Fuck.' A sigh. More scraping. 'Where're the twins?'

'Campbells'.'

49

Motion. Not swimming. Flying? No, rolling. Wheels, echoes, bursts of light, grey amorphous shadows around, above. An alarm sounds, a telephone rings, a conversation is whispered.

Then the rolling stops, with a click, a jerk.

Crack: a blind furls up. Different shadows move around, attached to the two familiar voices — she recognises them now.

'How come you've got no kids?' Ryan asks. He's here a lot.

'Wife didn't want them,' Aidan says. He's always here. 'Career more important.'

'I hear you.'

'Fair enough, though. Can't all want the same things.'

'You wanted kids?'

'Of course. That's why she fucked me off in the end.'

'What?'

'Nagging, I think she called it.'

'You do come across as a persistent sort of bloke.'

Aidan's unfitting squeaky laugh. 'One of the reasons.'

'What else?'

'Preferred architects to cops. And builders, electricians …'

'How'd you find out?'

Another squeaky laugh, no answer.

A scrape. 'I reckon Rosie's having an affair.'

'Really?'

'With a woman.'

'Fuck.'

'Wish we'd had more kids. Lucky Brigi's got two.' A sigh. 'She *will* be OK, won't she?' Ryan says.

'Yeah.'

'Not like — '

'It was just the drugs. Doc says she'll be fine.'

'Thank God you were there.'

'Nothing to do with God, mate.'

'Wish she'd hurry and wake up.'

'Soon. Just thought of something might help.'

'What?'

'Be back later.' Footsteps.

50

Wheels rattle past. A toilet flushes, water runs, a door opens and closes.

'Back again? I thought cops didn't get time off.' Ryan. A scrape.

'Been working. Finally closed that case.' Aidan.

'Eric Tucker?'

'Yeah. She didn't do it.'

A long pause, and then Ryan speaks softly, 'Are you sure that's true?'

'What it says on the file, mate. Has to be true.'

Shuffling.

'Somebody came in after she left,' Aidan says.

'The caretaker?'

'After the caretaker.'

A bird twitters, traffic rumbles, a plane flies overhead.

'But Sam …'

'At first I reckoned Sam covered up for her because he had a thing about domestic violence,' Aidan says.

'I knew it had to be more than just because she was a cute twenty-year-old.'

'Because of his father.'

'Doug?'

'Doug's the stepfather.'

'I never knew that.'

'Biological father was violent. Hit him. And his mother and sister. Put him in hospital one time when he was a kid. Almost killed him.'

'God. Poor bastard.' Another long pause. 'But how could he

have got it wrong?'

'He didn't. He wasn't covering up for *her*.'

'What?'

'Found some old stuff wasn't meant to be found. Personal documents, that kind of thing. And had a chat with the caretaker's mum.'

A pause.

'Tucker was still alive when the caretaker found him, but not when the uniformed officers got there. In his statement, Sam said he was first on the scene, after having received a call from D24 — half an hour before the uniforms arrived. He just happened to be driving past? I don't think so. Reckon he was paying a visit, and came across an opportunity too good to resist.'

'But ... I don't understand.'

'The family took Doug's name. But Sam's original birth certificate says Tucker.'

'What the fuck! He was Eric's son?'

A shuffle.

'Tucker had made harassment complaints. Sam was obsessed with him — he'd been stalking him.'

'Jesus,' says Ryan, a hand-over-mouth muffled sound. 'Lucky Brigi doesn't remember any of it.'

Aidan clears his throat. 'Are you OK?'

No answer.

Minutes pass in silence. A clock ticks.

A mobile phone rings.

'I thought you weren't allowed to have those on in here.'

'Those rules don't apply to police.' He takes the call. 'Detective Sergeant Serra ... Yep, she's out of the ICU ... OK, mate. Meet you at the front desk downstairs, escort you up.' A rustle, a creak, a long shadow. 'Got somebody here to see Brigitte. Might help.'

'Campbells are bringing the twins in, too,' Ryan says.

'Good. Why don't you go for a walk? Get some fresh air and a coffee.'

'I need a drink.'

'Join you for one later.' Footsteps.

'Hey, what's it say on your arm?'

The footsteps stop. 'Huh?'

'The tattoo.'

'Come as You Are.'

'The Nirvana song!'

'Unconditional acceptance.'

'Really? I love that song, but I thought it was about drugs and guns.'

'No. It's about people and how they're supposed to act. Accept things as they are, and not as you wish them to be. And then look ahead, not behind.'

'I had you pegged as a dumb cop, mate. Not a philosopher.'

'Had you pegged as a classical-music geek. Not a Nirvana fan.'

Almost a laugh.

'And you can tell your grandfather I caught the bastard in the blue Camry.'

A pause.

'She likes you, you know,' Ryan says.

'Bullshit. Hates my guts.'

The footsteps fade.

***

A cart rattles by, and cutlery clangs. The smells of roast meat and vegetables and disinfectant fill the air. She tastes metal in her mouth. It's so dry — she's never been so thirsty. The unbearable thirst drags her up through the greyness and into the light. Absolved. Free.

Her head throbs, with the worst hangover ever. Her eyes feel glued together. She forces them open, squints at the light, blinks away the fuzzy edges, and looks up. Into Adonis blue. Time has not faded the colour of his eyes, but life has made lines around them, and around his mouth — from laughter more than from pain. Sunlight glints on the wedding band around his finger. He closes the book he was reading, and saves his page with a handmade bookmark — stick-figure people and hearts lovingly drawn by a child's hand. He puts the book into his satchel bag and holds it open on his lap.

She struggles to swallow, and looks at the jug of water on the bedside table. He reaches for it, pours a cup, and helps her sit up to drink.

She looks at the tube in the back of her hand; her eyes follow the IV line to the clear plastic bag hanging on the stand beside the bed. 'Why didn't you ever look for me?' Her voice is a whisper, hoarse.

He hesitates and then doesn't really answer the question. He doesn't need to — it was in the hesitation. 'Detective Campbell made it *very* clear that you couldn't be found.'

Their fingers touch as he takes the cup and places it back on the table.

'I kept that photo I took of you at Raymond Island for a long time,' he says. 'On the dashboard of my car. It made me sad, but I couldn't throw it away. I turned it to face the windscreen so I didn't have to see it and miss you every day. But at night when I drove past lights, your image would flash backwards.' He closes the flap on his bag, sits on the edge of the chair, uncomfortable. He's not planning to stay long. 'In the end, it faded so much you couldn't tell what it was. I left it in the old Commodore when I traded it in.'

Now is the chance she's pined for, to tell him she's sorry. She doesn't say it.

He's looking at the scar on her forehead, not at her eyes. Ryan once taught her an acting trick to calm nerves: look just above the brows of your audience members, instead of into their eyes. Most people can't tell the difference, but she can.

'It was a long time ago.' He smiles, but the smile doesn't reach his eyes. 'I met your children downstairs. They're beautiful. You should be with them now. Not me.'

She nods. She has nothing more to say to him.

He puts his bag over his shoulder, looks at his hands, brushes things from his jeans that aren't there. 'I'll go tell them you're awake.' He stands up and walks to the door.

'Matt?'

'Yes?' He looks back.

'Is Aidan here?'

Acknowledgements

I would like to thank my family: Greg, Reece, Paige, Jaime (for their love and patience) and my mother Pam; Henry Rosenbloom and everybody at Scribe; Graeme Simsion (coach, mentor, inspiration); Fran Willcox (for Johnnie Walker, cuffs with buttons, and all the other great advice, and for the encouragement when the chips were down); Anne Buist; Felicity Clissold; Nancy Sugarman; Danny Rosner Blay; Amy Jasper; Allison Browning; Michelle Aung Thin; Jim Brandi; Mark Brandi; Edwina Vance; Meg Dunley; Liz Steele; Baia Tsakouridou; Krysia Birman; Zoe Naughten; Jo Stubbings; and all my RMIT Professional Writing and Editing teachers and fellow students.